"Hood's caustic wit, brightly detailed prose, and thoughtful delineations of two women struggling with private, powerful regrets supply *Ruby* with rich and surprising emotional depths."

—Megan Harlan, *The New York Times Book Review*

"Ann Hood has a wonderful ear for conversation and is terrific at delineating the small bits of intimacy that make up a close friendship."

—Joanne Kaufman, *People*

"A solid tale...genuinely affecting." —*Kirkus Reviews*

"Ann Hood's *Ruby* shines!" —*Vermont Times*

"A luminous, memorable novel that will resonate long after the covers are closed." —Sam Coale, *The Providence Sunday Journal*

"As always, the rich, complex emotional texture of Hood's writing inspires admiration and catharsis in the reader. She is, quite simply, an emotional genius." —*The Whitehorse Review*

"You'll chuckle; you'll sniffle; you won't want it to end so soon. And for a while you'll remember not to be so cavalier with the people you love." —Jan Williams Banker, *Tampa Tribune*

"Hood is one of those quietly wonderful, straight-ahead novelists...she leaves us entertained, touched, and reassured."

—Donna Seaman, *Booklist*

"Ann Hood's clever touch will make you feel as though it's all happening to you." —Samantha Harrison, *New Woman Magazine*

"Packed with convincing detail and effortless description, Hood's tale of romance and loss mixes the venerable with the vulgar and brings the adult world into vibrant contact with adolescence."

—*Publishers Weekly* (starred review)

"An intimately scaled novel." —Amanda Heller, *The Boston Globe*

Also by Ann Hood

Somewhere Off the Coast of Maine

Waiting to Vanish

Three-Legged Horse

Something Blue

Places to Stay the Night

The Properties of Water

Ruby

a novel by

Ann Hood

PICADOR USA
NEW YORK

For information on Picador USA Reading Group Guides, as well as ordering, please contact the Trade Marketing department at St. Martin's Press.
Phone: 1-800-221-7945 extension 763
Fax: 212-677-7456
E-mail: trademarketing@stmartins.com

Library of Congress Cataloging-in-Publication Data

Hood, Ann.
Ruby / Ann Hood.
p. cm.
ISBN 0-312-19553-2 (hc)
ISBN 0-312-20430-2 (pbk)
I. Title.
PS3558.O537R8 1998
813'.54—dc21

98-23451
CIP

First Picador USA Paperback Edition: October 1999

10 9 8 7 6 5 4 3 2 1

For Lorne

Acknowledgments

For the time and space to write this book, I would like to thank The Vermont Studio Center, Jessica Hempel, and Hillary Day; for legal advice, Bruce Sondler; for their love, support, and understanding, I give my heartfelt thanks to my parents, Melissa Hood, my husband and our children, Ariane, Sam and Grace; for her wise counsel and good faith, many thanks to Diane Higgins; and to Gail Hochman—agent and friend extraordinaire—my deepest thanks for her patience, advice, loyalty, and wisdom.

Ruby

chapter one

Dear Amanda

Olivia had so many things that she wanted to tell the girl who killed her husband that she wasn't even sure where to begin.

For example, she wanted the girl to know that she, Olivia, had once been someone who used to hum in public places, in an absent way that made people scowl at her. Still, she found herself doing it as she waited in line at the post office or for a spot at an ATM. She had been a hummer all her life, even humming in appreciation when she ate something she found especially delicious. During the trailers at movies, someone always shushed her, or turned to glare. "Sorry," she'd whisper. But before she knew it, she was humming again. Maybe if she hummed an actual tune, she'd often thought, people would not mind so much. But she hummed randomly, absently, without direction.

She wrote:

> *Dear Amanda, since you killed my husband, I don't hum anymore. My mother used to say that I hummed before I even talked. I hummed one way for yes and another way for no. I hummed something that meant good night and something that meant bye-bye. In my baby book—and my mother kept scrupulous records of everything from bowel movements to ounces gained each month—under the column that says "First Words," my mother wrote that I didn't talk; I hummed. So for thirty-seven years, I've hummed my way through life. And now I feel like I can't even remember how to do it. If I press my lips together and try, I sound like I'm strangling.*

But humming wasn't what Olivia really wanted to talk about with the girl, Amanda. So she tore up each new letter and threw it away.

Olivia was a milliner. She made hats and sold them in a small shop on St. Mark's Place in the East Village. Long before Amanda killed her husband by running him down while he was jogging, long before Olivia even had a husband, she had this shop. It was sandwiched between an occult store and a store that over the years changed from one that sold used clothing to one that sold used books, until finally it was once again a store that sold used clothing.

Olivia's shop was called the Rose Tattoo because she was unable to remove those words from its one front window. The old Rose Tattoo sold memorabilia of famous gay men—like James Dean and Tennessee Williams. People still came in and asked for a James Dean calendar or postcards of Liberace's piano-shaped pool without even noticing the antique hat forms Olivia had bought at a flea market, or the hats that sat on top of those forms. Other times, people came in to get tattooed, thrusting pictures of Yosemite Sam or floral arrangements at Olivia and asking how much. They pointed to shoulders, hips, ankles. "How much for one here? Or here?" She always apologized and opened her arms to point at her hats. "I make hats," she would explain.

To reach the Rose Tattoo, one had to walk down five steps and then turn right. The steps led to the occult shop, with its magical candles and books and tarot-card readers. Olivia always paused and waved to whoever was at the cash register. Over the years, she'd come to know them all. While she unlocked the grate over her shop's door, the guy who ran the used-clothing shop would open his own door and say, "Oh, it's you. You scared the shit out of me." Then he'd go back inside his shop.

This trio of stores was hidden from view at street level. But there were signs with big arrows pointing the way. Often, Olivia had to rouse someone sleeping off a binge of some kind in the little walkway in front of the stores, or ask the young teenagers who liked to congregate there and smoke pot and read out loud books they'd bought at the occult store to please leave. But once she stepped inside, she did nothing but make, trim, design, and sell women's hats. The shop smelled vaguely of falafels from the restaurant above it and of wet wool and incense and mothballs. To Olivia, it was the most wonderful combination of smells anywhere. She was certain that if someone blindfolded her and led her here, she would recognize it instantly by its unique aroma.

It was here, in the Rose Tattoo, that Olivia had met her husband. That was another thing she would like Amanda to know, the story of how David and Olivia met. She would like to tell Amanda about her life before David, too, because somehow that made finding him—and losing him—even more important.

Sometimes when Olivia tried to write a letter to Amanda, these were the things she thought of. "Dear Amanda," she'd write, "I was a woman who liked to dance alone. In my apartment, in my hat shop, I would put on music and close my eyes and dance. What I liked to play most was the tape of Louis Armstrong and Ella Fitzgerald singing together. Their rendition of 'They Can't Take That Away from Me' always sent me twirling across the floor."

On the winter night that David walked into the Rose Tattoo, that's exactly what Olivia was doing: dancing alone while Louis and Ella crooned "They Can't Take That Away from Me." It was Valentine's Day. For Olivia, it was the first Valentine's Day without her long-term live-in boyfriend, Josh, and she was planning on celebrating. At home, she had a bottle of champagne in the refrigerator, which she planned to drink with a take-out Indian dinner, alone. She had a new apartment, so small that she cleaned the floor with a Dustbuster instead of a vacuum cleaner. For a thousand dollars a month, she got one room on Avenue A, a galley kitchen with a bathtub in it, and a tiny balcony where she stood every morning and drank her coffee—it was too small for chairs to fit.

When she glided, eyes closed, right into David, she stopped and gasped. Olivia thought she had put up the CLOSED sign, but she saw the window signless except for the curlicue writing of the store's name.

"I'm here for a hat," he said, grinning.

Olivia frowned at him. Unlike her humming, her dancing was a private thing. In her years with Josh, he'd never caught her at it.

"We're closed," she said.

She saw that he was clutching a wrinkled clipping from *New York* magazine's "Best Bets" column about her hats.

Still grinning, he took a step toward her. Behind them, Louis and Ella were reaching a crescendo in their singing.

"It's Valentine's Day," he said.

Then he did the most unexpected thing. He took her hand in his, placed his other one around her waist, and danced a perfect waltz. She heard him humming softly to himself as he spun her away from him, then into him. The humming made her nervous.

The song ended, and he released her as easily as he had taken her.

Olivia stepped back to look at him. He had curly brown hair and eyes too close to his nose. But it was a lovely nose, straight and Roman, slightly too large for his face. His teeth were also a bit too large, and very white. He had on a beat-up leather bomber jacket, faded jeans, and sneakers, despite the winter slush in the streets. Olivia liked the face she was studying. Josh had been shorter, blonder, with broad Scandinavian features. He had always worn black: boots, pants, jacket. A bit of bright blue poked out from the collar of this guy's jacket and made Olivia smile. But he was moving past her, toward the hats.

She stayed in the middle of the floor and watched him.

"What's with the name of this place?" he said as he rubbed the felt brim of a hat between his thumb and forefinger.

"Well, *The Rose Tattoo* was a play—"

"I know that," he said, without turning toward her. "Tennessee Williams." He picked up another hat, a buttercup yellow felt one with black trim, and looked at Olivia. "I saw his house once," he said. "In Key West. So tiny, like a miniature house, a doll's house. With these tomato-colored shutters. I don't know why, but I stood in front of it for a very long time and it made me so sad."

He's probably a frustrated writer, she thought, almost satisfied. Nothing was worse than a wannabe writer or actor or artist.

"I thought budding writers went to Key West to see Hemingway's house," she said.

"That was a bit of a letdown," he said. He handed the hat to her. "Would you mind trying this on? To give me an idea, that's all."

Olivia put it on her head and pulled it low, the way a person was supposed to wear hats.

"Of course, she's much taller than you," he said absently. "And she doesn't have those wonderful ripples of hair."

He traced the air on both sides of her head, drawing curly lines with his fingers. Olivia reminded herself how much she was enjoying her still-new independence. She had hung every painting in her apartment exactly where she wanted, had bought sheets in a girlie pink, had arranged the silverware and glasses in the order she preferred. At night, she ate in bed, let her cat, Arthur, eat out of her dish, watched whatever she pleased, sometimes sleeping with the television on all night. Plus, she didn't have to trip over Josh's ridiculous bass every time she walked through the dark to the bathroom. It was so large, it had been like a third roommate.

He sighed. "She does look good in yellow."

Olivia took off the hat and tried to smooth her uncontrollable hair. It had been damp all day and now rain splattered the shop's windows. Her hair frizzed and curled, had a mind of its own.

"It's a great hat," she offered. "Your wife will love it. Women are always extremely satisfied with my hats."

He held up the wrinkled clipping. "So it says."

No wedding ring, Olivia noticed as he reached for his wallet. But also no correction on the word *wife*. She reminded herself how she'd sworn off dating until summer. After six years with someone, she thought six months alone was more than necessary.

"What's that?" he said.

"What?"

"I thought you were humming something."

Olivia cleared her throat and busied herself wrapping the hat, writing up the sale.

"Check okay?" he asked.

She pointed to the sign taped to the counter. "Make it out to me. Here's how you spell it."

He let out a low whistle. "Bertolucci," he said. "That's a mouthful."

"We're Americanized, though. TV dinners. Lots of lime green and raspberry clothing. The works."

"Well," he said, handing her his check, "I'm from California. No ethnicity at all. Just Californian. Third generation, which is really something."

"Pioneers," she said. She held out the hat in its hat box to him.

His name was David Henderson and he lived across town, in the West Village.

She didn't expect him to walk out the door just like that, but he did. He turned and said, "Thanks for the dance." But before she could answer, he was gone.

At home, there was a bouquet of roses from Josh, sitting on the landing in front of her door. She supposed they should make her miss him, but they didn't. That was how ready she had been to move on. For the occasion, she'd strung lights shaped like red hearts around her rubber tree, and she turned them on now, refusing to think about David Henderson, the wannabe writer who used words like *tomato-colored* and was one hell of a good dancer. Her best friend, Winnie, had a date, or else Olivia would have called her to ask why, just when a person got her life the way she wanted it, another person popped in and turned everything upside down. Not that David Henderson had done that exactly. But Olivia recognized that he easily could. He with the brown curls and smooth steps. He with the wife, she reminded herself. A wife who looked good in yellow.

Olivia ate her tandoori chicken, her saag paneer, her samosas.

She let Arthur lick her plate clean and then kiss her on the lips with his curry breath.

"Arthur," she said, digging her fingers into the cat's fur, just the way he liked it, "we're headed for something."

She didn't know what that something was, but she felt it coming, as strong and reckless as a hurricane running its unpredictable course.

Olivia wasn't exactly surprised to see him the next day. In fact, when he walked in the door of her shop ten minutes after she opened, she felt her bones and muscles and organs shift and settle. And, even deeper, her *cells.* Her goddamn DNA. It was what she had kept waiting for all the years with Josh and his bass. She had waited and waited and it had never happened.

"She didn't like it?" Olivia said.

In his hands, David held the hat. He twirled it around and Olivia thought that if she stared at it long enough, it might turn into butter. There was, she noticed, a dent in the crown.

"You should never break up with someone on Valentine's Day," he said. "Especially someone you've been with almost forever, who knew you when it was cool to have an Afro and wear bell-bottoms."

Olivia was listening and frowning, but she couldn't stop watching his hands twirling that dented hat.

"She threw it at me," he said.

"'Break up' means you're not married," Olivia said.

"Right. If I was married, I'd have to divorce her."

Olivia nodded.

"Your hair," he said, and this time he didn't trace the air in front of her. Instead, he put down the hat and touched her face, and then her hair. "It's even curlier."

"I was blocking the wool for some hats." She pointed behind

her to the spot where a big pot of water boiled on a hot plate. "It makes my hair do this."

"Do you want to dance?" he asked her.

"Yes," she said. "I do."

Months later, after she had moved in with him and married him and lost him to Amanda driving her blue Honda Civic around a curve one bright sunny September morning, Olivia thought, Dear Amanda, I am not the kind of person who does something like move to the West Village to live with a guy I've known for something like six weeks. I mean, Amanda, it took me almost four years to move in with my last boyfriend, Josh, and even when I did, I kept my real apartment, subletting it to one of the witches from the occult store next to my hat shop. I am not the kind of person to marry someone I've known for four months. What I'm telling you, Amanda, you stupid, careless little shit, is this was love. The *big one.* And you took it away from me.

"Dear Amanda," Olivia wrote. "I hate you."

They had moved in together and fought.

"Who are you?" she'd scream at him.

She threw things, too: Arthur's dish, old hats, the flowers he brought her to make up for their last fight.

The witch who sublet her apartment told Olivia that fire signs and air signs were good for each other. "Trust me," she said. "Your Libra and his Leo are perfect. And both of your moons are in Cancer. Perfect."

"Oh, shut up," Olivia said.

Sometimes she longed for those few months alone in her tiny studio on Avenue A. Sometimes she missed her twinkling red heart lights, her nights sleeping with Arthur purring beside her.

How could she have left her freedom behind so quickly? She and Josh had finally broken up and stayed broken up, and what did she do? She had gone and fallen for a guy because he made her body feel like it all fit together right. Like it fit together right with his body, she reminded herself.

"My mother always told me to marry at the height of your love," David said after one of their fights. "Then you have that to keep you going in all the hard years ahead."

"Your mother has been married three times," Olivia said. "I don't know if I would trust her."

"Because she never married at the height!" He took Olivia's hands in his and looked straight in her eyes. Whenever he did that, she felt as if he were somehow boring through her skull and reading her brain waves.

"Don't be creepy," she said.

"Listen. She went through the dating period, the get-to-know-you period, the living-together period, the engagement period. By the time she got married, she was already disappointed."

"Uh-huh."

"So just because you tend to be bossy and domineering—"

"Excuse me?" Olivia said.

"And also fly off the handle over the stupidest things—"

"Like being called bossy and domineering, Mr. Disorganized? Mister Can't Make Up His Mind? 'I don't know if I want the Bay Burrito or the Enchilada Embarcadero? I can't decide. They're both good, but I've been eating a lot of poultry lately—' "

"My point is, we should just get married now."

Had that been in my brain waves? Olivia thought. She blinked hard and shook her head from side to side.

"This," David said, satisfied, "is our height."

. . .

"And to think all you wanted was a hat," Olivia said as they waited in line at City Hall to get married.

"What ever happened to her?" Winnie asked. She was one of the witnesses.

Olivia felt very cranky. She and David had had an argument in the cab on the way down here and Winnie was wearing brown. "It's the new black," Winnie had explained. Being an editor at the women's magazine *You!* made her say things like that all the time. "No," Olivia had told her, "it's brown." Some wedding day, Olivia kept saying to herself.

"What was her name?" Winnie was saying. "The doctor."

"Rachel," David said.

"Yes. Rachel. What ever happened to her?"

This was what the fight had been about. After so many years together—seventeen gross, nine net, David liked to say—he thought he should track her down in goddamn Central America to tell her that he was getting married. Rachel, for an ex-girlfriend, was a pain in the ass. Josh, who only lived across town, stayed out of their lives. But Rachel sent them a clever computer-made change-of-address card with her head back in San Francisco and her feet lifting up and out of New York, the whole country in between strewn with clever images of her things: a stethoscope, a Jack Russell terrier, various plants. Even a Stickley chair.

"What do you want to know?" Olivia said, hearing the snap in her voice. "She keeps us posted, constantly."

David looked pained, and Olivia found herself wondering if they were going to call the wedding off, right here in the line. Imagining it, she realized how much she wanted to go through with it. She was meant to marry David. It was that simple. The thought of packing up Arthur and moving him back to that little apartment, of living out the rest of her life without David, was so terrible that she actually gasped.

"What?" David said.

"God," Olivia said. "I want to marry you."

"I want to marry you, too," he said, laughing.

"I hope so," Winnie said. "I went all the way to midtown to borrow this dress from *You!* Brown is this year's black, you know," Winnie said, for what seemed like the hundredth time.

"So I've heard," Olivia said.

Winnie could always be counted on for information like that. Of course, she could be counted on for scores of other things, too: sample shoes in exactly Olivia's size (ten) and give-away moisturizer and shampoo and books in galley form. She could be counted on to come with you in the middle of the night to the twenty-four-hour emergency vet all the way on the Upper East Side when your cat got mysteriously sick. She could be counted on to move your stuff across town when you moved in with your boyfriend, whom you hardly knew. She could be counted on to tell you that you were crazy to move in with him so soon; that clearly the two of you were crazy for each other; that you should, every now and then, throw caution to the wind. She could be counted on to show up at a moment's notice with a bouquet from the deli, a love poem, and even something blue—lapis earrings that had been her grandmother's. Which made them old, borrowed, *and* blue, Winnie had pointed out.

She could be counted on for everything, Olivia knew.

"I don't care what you say," Olivia said, softening. "Brown is brown. Besides which, I brought you a black hat to wear and you can't wear black and brown together."

"You can now," Winnie said. "It's okay. You can even wear navy and black together."

"Oh, sure," Olivia said. "What are you going to tell me next? That you can wear white shoes after Labor Day?"

She shifted Arthur's case to her other arm. Inside, he meowed at her, angry. Arthur hated his case and would hate to put on his little cat top hat that she forced him into on every holiday and special occasion.

"Oh, good," David said. "There's Rex."

Rex, his best friend and today's best man, loped toward them, unshaven and still with bed hair.

"Couldn't you at least comb your hair?" Olivia said. She spit on her fingertips and reached for Rex, who backed away from her. Now that she knew she was doing exactly the right thing, Olivia wanted everything to be perfect.

"No way," Rex said. "I don't even let my mother do that."

David slapped him on the back, all male and happy. "Hey, man."

"Hey, man," Rex said.

Olivia and Winnie rolled their eyes at each other.

Three years earlier, Rex and David had both moved to New York from California. Olivia loved the way they said they were from "the Bay Area," the way they called beer "suds," the way they searched the city for a good burrito. Thinking of all these things made her remember to be happy: she was marrying David. She put down Arthur's case and moved into David's arms.

Rex was talking about the new play he was working on. He did the lights for theater and, once, for Barney's Christmas windows.

"Don't talk about work on our wedding day," Olivia told him.

"No, no, no," Rex said. "I'm talking about love."

"Who's the lucky one this time?" Olivia said. She had wanted Rex to fall in love with Winnie, but now she knew better. Rex fell in and out of love with each new show.

"Get this," Rex said. "Her name is Magnolia. For real. Her mother loved magnolia trees."

Olivia tried to count the people in front of them in line. Since everyone brought witnesses and even entire families with them, it was difficult to tell how many people were actually ahead of them. A group of bikers. A very pregnant woman with a sullen guy. Two women dressed in extravagant wedding gowns. A Chinese family. A Spanish family. Then them. She smiled. They would be married in no time.

David's voice drifted above her. He was talking about work. He was an industrial designer, and right now he was talking about stainless steel. Olivia tilted her head back and watched his chin move. She hadn't really studied him from this angle and she kind of liked it. She was short enough and he was tall enough that when she looked at him like this, he looked oddly elongated, like someone in a fun-house mirror. She could see a small spot on his chin that he had missed when he'd shaved. His curly hair reminded her of a topiary and his nose looked bigger than it really was. Although he did have a good-sized nose, a Roman nose, even though he wasn't Italian at all.

She was Italian. Exactly half. But except for her hair—also brown and curly, although she used an eggplant rinse on it—she did not look at all Italian. Her eyes were blue and she had such fair skin that she always wore a hat in the sun, which, of course, she enjoyed doing, large straw ones with wide brims and fake fruit or flowers on them.

"We really should buy that house at the beach," she said. On their last excursion up to Rhode Island, they had fallen in love with a run-down purple house. For weeks, they'd been debating whether or not to buy it. It needed work. It needed furniture. Whole sets of things: dishes, utensils, towels, pans. All of it felt so big and grown-up to Olivia.

"I would love to buy it," David said.

He'd been saying that all along. Like getting married, Olivia realized, they would probably end up doing what he said.

"I would love to be able just to walk down to the ocean early in the morning and stick my toes in," David said.

Olivia turned to face him. "Should we do it? It would be so romantic."

Rex raised a hand. "Not in the Hamptons, okay? I hate that scene."

"No," Olivia said. "We would buy this house in Rhode Island that we saw."

"Even though your whole family still lives there?" Winnie said. "That sister?"

"We would let them visit us only once a year. On the Fourth of July."

David said, "Are you sure about this? You said you were scared of owning two sets of everything."

Olivia nodded.

"We could drive up and show them," she suggested.

"I thought we were going for dim sum," Rex said.

"Dim sum, then we'll go look at the beach house," David said.

"Goody," Winnie said. "A road trip."

"She even has to come on our honeymoon?" David said.

"Magnolia's meeting us at the dim sum place, so she can come along," Rex said.

Olivia leaned into David.

"Oh," she said, surprising herself by starting to cry. "I'm a June bride."

A person doesn't have a right to so much happiness, Olivia thought. But here she was, filled with it. Everything that had come before seemed small and distant now. She imagined riding this happiness through the years, through the rest of her life.

"Next," a woman called.

She was tall and skinny with too-white skin and stiff black hair and red lipstick that bled past her lips, all of it together giving her the look of a vampire. Her clothes were black and clingy, her shoes thick cork-soled platforms that made her fall slightly forward as she walked toward them in a cloud of tobacco and lily of the valley perfume.

"I've come to suck your blood," David whispered into Olivia's neck.

The woman thrust papers at them and motioned for them to follow her into the justice of the peace's chambers. His name, according to a removable plaque on the door, was Rolioli. Vince Rolioli. Like the woman, he had stiff black-lacquered hair like the Dave Clark Five dolls Olivia had had as a little girl. Behind her, Winnie giggled.

"You got your witnesses?" Vince Rolioli asked.

Olivia nodded, waiting for him to stand. Then she realized he was standing, all four feet something of him.

Winnie was holding Arthur in his top hat, and Olivia squeezed her arm. "You look beautiful, Winnie," she whispered, because it did work—the chocolate brown crushed-velvet minidress and the big black *Breakfast at Tiffany's* hat that let just enough of Winnie's blond bob show and the Prada shoes Winnie got at a *You!* shoe giveaway.

Olivia looked around, trying to memorize everything: Vince Rolioli and his assistant, and Winnie and Arthur and Rex, grinning in his faded jeans and beat-up leather jacket. And David. He had on Levi's, too, with a white button-down shirt and a vintage fifties tie. Olivia studied his brown curls, his beautiful nose, his eyes—brown and a little too small for the rest of his face. She even made sure to look at his ears, and the sliver of his neck that showed above his collar.

Then, satisfied, clutching the small bouquet of daises from the deli, she took a deep breath and said, "Let's go."

The Honorable Vince Rolioli read his part with great feeling, as if he had once aspired to the stage. Olivia and David's vows sounded almost childlike beside his thundering words.

It was Rex who had remembered to bring a camera, an old Polaroid. Vince Rolioli's assistant agreed to take a picture.

"Smile big," she said, demonstrating how, showing off her own lipstick-smeared teeth. The four of them obeyed, arms around one another's shoulders, lips parted for wide, eager smiles.

The camera flashed and then spit out a snapshot. Olivia found herself holding her breath as she watched the black fade and the colors appear—David's tie first, and then the pink flowers on Olivia's hat, and slowly each of them growing vivid and sharp. The assistant urged them out of the chambers, shooing them, saying, "Good luck! Congratulations!" as if she really meant it.

The line waiting to get married was still long. More bikers, more pregnant brides. Olivia walked past them, saw flashes of bright blue eye shadow, colorful tattoos, beaded dresses, pierced eyebrows and lips. This was her receiving line, studying her, the new bride, the one who had finished what they were about to begin.

Later that summer, she and David would buy that small purple cottage at the beach in Rhode Island. One hot August day there they would decide to start a family. They would hold all the promise and expectation and hope that two people in love can hold. So much came later that summer that all of it would seem to Olivia a blur of happiness.

But on their wedding day, a sunny, breezy Friday in early June, Olivia wanted nothing more than to begin their life. She stopped at the door that led out and turned to the line of waiting brides.

"Good luck!" she shouted. "Happy lives!"

She felt that all the women standing there—pregnant and pierced, foreign and frightened, hopeful and eager—all of them looked at her and understood.

She turned again to leave, hesitated, then tossed her bouquet of daisies over one shoulder. Someone squealed, delighted. All the brides-to-be cheered. Olivia looked to see who had caught it: a teenager, pregnant, round-cheeked, and nervous. The girl raised the bouquet to Olivia and grinned. Olivia flashed on a vision of herself one day: beaming and pregnant. And then even further in the future: an old married lady.

David pushed the door open, and arm in arm he and Olivia stepped out into the blinding sunlight, into their future.

Alone in her shop, Olivia stared at the pieces of felt and ribbon and trim. But she had no plans, no ideas. Her mind was blank. Like snow, she thought. Like blinding sun. Without David, she could not think of what to do next. Their apartment with the view of the Hudson River out the small kitchen window—and the Eames furniture that David had collected, and Olivia's own flea-market finds and castoffs from interior-design shoots at *You!*—seemed foreign, the way airports feel when you emerge from an all-night transatlantic flight.

She had no refuge. Over their months together, she and David had fought and made up and planned a future; they had become each other's refuge. The beach house they'd bought sat empty now, unfinished, untended. Olivia could not even think of going there, of driving past the spot where David had been killed, of returning to the bed where she had slept so foolishly while he died.

And then there was this: the morning he died, he had come out of the bathroom and gotten back into bed. He had kissed her, not even minding her morning breath. He had slipped his hand under the T-shirt she wore and found her breasts, sighing as he rubbed the nipples.

"Go away," she'd said. She had rolled away from him then. "I'm tired."

He hadn't gone easily. He had pressed himself against her. He had moved his erection between her thighs. He had lifted her hair and kissed the nape of her neck.

"Why don't you go jogging?" she said.

This time, his sigh was one of defeat rather than pleasure. "Good idea," he'd said, leaving the bed. "Better than a cold shower."

He had not even seen her grinning at that. From her half sleep, Olivia heard him walk down the creaky steps and out the door. She heard him move toward his death a quarter of a mile away.

Now, sitting alone in the Rose Tattoo, she once again thought about how making love that morning would have kept him safe. He would not have been on that curve, in that bright sun, at that very moment that Amanda drove her Honda Civic around it.

Dear Amanda, she thought. But if she told the girl that it wasn't her fault, Olivia would have to admit that she was the one who had sent her husband out that morning. No, she thought, the smell of falafels turning her stomach, it was better this way. Better to share the blame than to carry it all alone.

The week between Christmas and New Year's, as the city took on a sad holiday look—dirty snow, abandoned trees with tinsel still clinging to their branches, lights blinking foolishly—Amanda showed up at the Rose Tattoo. She came with two other girls, friends or sisters—Olivia did not know or care to know.

"I'm in bad shape," the girl said. "I don't know what it is I want from you, but all week I've been thinking about you all alone. With the holidays and stuff."

She was so plain, a medium-sized girl with medium-brown hair. She wore painter's pants and a pink ski jacket with lift tickets dangling from the zipper. Olivia saw a bright blue turtleneck, the top of the yoke of a blue-and-white Fair Isle sweater. An ordinary girl who had happened to kill David.

One of the other girls, dressed similarly—green ski jacket, pink turtleneck, dark green sweater beneath—nudged Amanda.

"I'm taking next semester off," Amanda said. Olivia could see that the girl was trying to fight back tears. But still they spilled out, streaking her cheeks. "I'm going to stay with my aunt in Seattle. Maybe it will help to get away. I don't know what to do."

Olivia wished she could find some words, but the only ones that bounced around her brain were: *Why don't you go jogging?*

"Amanda," she said, her voice like a croak.

The three girls in front of her seemed to hold their collective breath.

"I don't know, either," Olivia said finally.

They waited, but she had nothing to say. She did not forgive the girl. Or herself.

"I brought you this," Amanda said.

She placed a small loaf of bread, wrapped in plastic and tied with red-and-green ribbon, on the counter.

"It's cranberry," she added.

"Thank you," Olivia said. They both stared down at the bread until one of the girls took Amanda's elbow.

"I've got to go," Amanda said.

Olivia nodded.

But Amanda didn't go. She just stood there, still.

"I keep thinking about you," she said again.

Finally, she turned and left, off to Seattle, to some life for herself. Olivia took the bread from the counter and pressed it against her nose. She smelled orange and cinnamon, the bitter scent of cranberries. The bread was still warm. Olivia breathed in its holiday smell; then she took it out back to the Dumpster and threw it away.

. . .

Sometimes, Olivia looked out her kitchen window at the Hudson River and New Jersey beyond and imagined taking a bus out there, to Morristown, where Amanda lived. It hadn't worked out in Seattle, the girl had written her. Now she was back home, taking Prozac, working at a bookstore. Olivia could go out there and find Amanda's house, knock on the door, wait until she saw the girl's bland face. But then what? She always came back to that question: then what? After all, what could a teenaged girl possibly give her that she could not give herself? How in the world, Olivia wondered, could someone so young and troubled possibly help her?

chaper two

Nouns Are the Part of Speech That Hurts

Olivia jogged.

It was June. Hazy, hot, and humid. "The three *h*'s," the vapid weatherman had said on the sunrise weather report. He had grinned as he pointed to a drawing of a sweating yellow sun. Olivia added weathermen to her list of things that annoyed her. The list was long and growing fast. Just that morning, after driving through the night alone to get up here finally and close up the beach house, put it on the market, do what everyone had been telling her to do since David died—"Get on with your life!"—after drinking so many bitter take-out coffees that she'd been unable to sleep and instead had smeared paste on the kitchen wall and flung everything she could find up there, when she finally fell asleep on the couch, the phone woke her.

"I hear you have a house for sale?" a young woman said.

Olivia had yawned into the phone, closed all the shades against the day, and said, "Who told you that?" in a tone that was less than nice. She didn't care. Even from the now dark living room, Olivia could see the mess she'd made of the wall where she had once planned to stencil the William Carlos Williams poem about plums.

"Uh," the woman said—stupidly, Olivia thought. "Your sister? Amy?"

"Figures," Olivia mumbled. Her sister, Amy, four years younger, bitter, divorced, a single mother, had been trying to take charge of Olivia's life since David died. Amy was, Olivia had decided, almost relieved that she and David's sudden romance and marriage had ended so soon and so tragically. "It's time," Amy kept reminding Olivia, "to grow up."

The woman took a big, impatient breath. "My name is Kim Potter-Franco and my husband is Joseph Franco," she said, and when Olivia didn't give her a how-do-you-do, she continued, "Anyway, my husband and I—we're newlyweds, you know?—we're renting over by the college, in the graduate-student apartments, and they're just awful. So when I met your sister at the gym and she said you wanted to sell your house, or maybe even rent it first, I said, I just have to call. We're both getting Ph.D.'s," she added, her voice full of idealism and hope, "in literature."

Olivia could see it, Amy and this idiot side by side on treadmills, walking hard and fast and going nowhere.

"This is our house," Olivia said. "And it's not for sale yet."

"These apartments," Kim Potter-Franco said, lowering her voice, "are not so great. We moved here from Ohio and we had this darling little place. We just want somewhere nice."

"Our house isn't nice," Olivia said. One of the witches from the occult store next to the Rose Tattoo had given her a book on feng shui and some smudge sticks to chase out the bad spirits and bad karma here. "Bad spirits," Olivia added.

"It's just that a house would be so nice," the woman said, "what with all our new things—the wedding china and crystal. We're newlyweds," she said again.

"We don't want anyone in our house!" Olivia shouted. "It's ours. We bought it so we could put our toes in the ocean whenever we wanted. We bought it so that we could grow old here. We don't want anyone with a stupid hyphenated name living here with china and crystal and big dreams. Do you hear me, you stupid fucking newlywed? You happy person?"

But Kim Potter-Franco had hung up already.

Olivia jogged down the scenic route, careful to run on the side facing traffic, to stay close to the edge of the road. She jogged past blue hydrangeas and old stone walls and houses hidden behind large trees—weeping willows, evergreen, oak, and maple. She jogged until she reached the spot. Then she stopped, panting, and waited.

The spot was on a curve. The policeman had called it "a blind curve," had said it in a way as if to abdicate it of any responsibility. The policeman had seemed like a schoolboy, fresh-faced and awkward. So awkward, in fact, that Olivia had comforted him, placed her arms around his trembling shoulders, brought him a glass of water, told him *she* was sorry. Sorry that he had the terrible job of showing up at the little purple beach house that she and David had bought and telling her that her husband had been hit by a car on Route 1A and was dead.

Olivia stood in the spot where it had happened and made herself think about all the details she had tried to forget over the past nine months. How she had made a big pot of coffee so they could take some in a thermos for the ride back to New York. How she had sat at the small green patio table with its wavy opaque glass top and looked out the window and wondered if she was pregnant. She'd let herself think of names for their baby, writing different combinations on a scrap of paper, the way in fifth grade she had written her name in various forms with Paul McCartney's: Olivia Bertolucci McCartney, Olivia McCartney, Mrs. Paul McCartney. She had sat and written names at the table, sipping Tanzanian peaberry coffee, the sunlight streaming through the window and bouncing off the glass tabletop almost playfully.

She had imagined many things as the morning stretched on and David did not return from his run. That he went to the good bakery for fresh croissants. That he had stopped to help someone who needed help. But she had not imagined even once that he was dead. They were too happy; life was going too right for them for something that bad to happen. He was, she'd thought fleetingly, hurt perhaps. She'd thought of twisted ankles or a wrenched back. She'd wondered if she should drive down the road to see if he needed help. But something kept her at home, at that table. So that when the too-young policeman appeared at their door, Olivia was smiling and ready to give him what he needed.

Now, standing here sweating in David's blue-and-gold Berkeley T-shirt, remembering these things hurt, but not in the doubling-over, all-consuming way they had at first. Everyone around her—even Winnie, even Rex—used euphemisms, cloaked language. They said in hushed tones that David had passed away, that he was gone. Didn't they know, Olivia thought as she began to work her way along the route, to move past the spot, didn't they know that verbs were harmless? To say the word *died* did not hurt her. Nouns were the part of speech that hurt. When she tried to speak his name out loud, she strangled on the syllables. When she dreamed of him saying her name, she woke up crying. When she had to say the word *husband*, she always choked.

Even now, jogging away from where Amanda's late-model Honda Civic had hit him, Olivia could not say his name. She had taken to calling him "Pal." It sounded sassy. It sounded like something a tough broad might say. They had loved old Barbara Stanwyck movies, and Olivia could imagine Barbara calling a guy "Pal." Even a dead guy.

"Pal," Olivia said out loud, into the early-morning June air, "this sucks."

She put on her Walkman, tuned to the local NPR station and "Morning Edition," and continued her run. In the distance, the ocean sparkled in the sunlight. Olivia moved slowly toward it. Slowly was how she did everything these days. Hadn't it taken her all this time to come back here and close up the house? She had met only half the orders for her hats since Labor Day, even though CNN and Winnie kept reminding her that hats were back. Even though Winnie had fanagled a blurb about Olivia and her hats in an article in the big summer issue of *You!* called "Hats Off to You!"

Olivia rounded each curve carefully, as if a blue Honda Civic driven by a college student might appear at any moment, "Morning Edition" fading in and out. Then, in a burst of strong reception, a reporter's voice shot through Olivia's headphones. The reporter was talking to a woman named Sheryl Lamont, whose husband had been tragically killed in a car accident the day after Labor Day last year, the very day Olivia's own husband had died. This woman, Sheryl Lamont, was now pregnant with her dead husband's child; she'd had the good sense to have his sperm removed and frozen for later use.

Olivia stopped jogging and leaned against the stone wall. Pink beach roses lined the other side of the wall. Bees hovered nearby.

"I knew," Sheryl Lamont was saying in a slow drawl, "that I was not ready right then, when he died like that, to handle a pregnancy, a little baby, all by myself. But as time passed and I grew stronger, I knew it was time to realize our dream of having a little Duane Junior."

As suddenly as they had come to her, NPR and Sheryl Lamont vanished. Olivia shook her head from side to side to reclaim them. She walked in small circles, hoping to move closer to them. But she found just static. When she fiddled with the dial, only the soft-rock station came through, Bette Midler singing "From a Distance" loud and clear.

Angry, Olivia turned off the radio and slid the headphones off her ears. She began to jog back in the direction of her house. Who was this Sheryl Lamont to come up with freezing sperm like that? She sounded young and uneducated; how had she gotten the idea? What about Winnie and all of Olivia's other supposedly savvy friends in Manhattan? They'd never heard of it. What about Olivia's mother, who found seemingly endless articles in *Reader's Digest* about how to grieve but none about freezing sperm?

She should be having David's baby, Olivia decided. Like stupid Sheryl Lamont. Two weeks before David died, they had decided to start trying to get pregnant. Like all of their decisions, it was spontaneous and surprising.

They were in their small yard, it, too, surrounded by fat blue hydrangeas and an old stone wall. David was grilling salmon and Olivia was stretched out on a chaise lounge, painting her toenails baby blue, the polish a gift from Winnie. She did not know what waited ahead for them in only two weeks' time. If she had, she would have looked up at him while they talked. She would have studied his back and arms as he brushed olive oil on the fish and placed it on the grill. She would have memorized how he looked from this angle, too: across a small yard on a late-summer evening, with the sun almost completely gone, the white Christmas lights they'd strung twinkling in the hedges, citronella candles beginning to spill light on the dimming day. But no. She had not looked up. She had taken his presence there beside her for granted and simply watched the small brush move across the smooth surfaces of her toenails, smearing baby blue.

David had said, "Should we eat the salmon first and then go inside and make a baby? Or should we just go inside?"

"Whoa, baby," she said. "A baby?" Because not knowing what lay ahead, she could be flippant.

"It came to me just now," David said, "that a little girl who looked just like you would be a very fine thing."

"'I don't know nothin' about birthin' babies,'" Olivia said, fanning her toes to help the polish dry. Between each toe sat a cotton ball, tipped with baby blue. She stretched her feet out and shook them.

"You know I hate that movie," David said.

"You know *I* hate that movie," Olivia said. Her heart was beating a little too fast, the way it did when she knew something was coming: her birthday present, a trip, a kiss. A baby, she thought.

"Also," David said, "a little boy who looked just like me would be a fine thing, too."

Olivia frowned at him. "Don't say 'also' and 'too' in the same sentence."

"Save me from redundancy," he said, dropping to his knees on the damp grass at her baby blue–polished feet. She opened her legs and he rested his head between them.

She should have studied him more carefully from this angle: his chin tilted up at her that way, his curls sparser than they looked upright, his teeth long and white and even.

But instead, Olivia did math.

"You know," she said, "if my biology of the female reproductive system is right, today would be a perfect day—"

"For banana fish?" he murmured into her thighs, where his tongue was making neat little circles.

"They are like fish, aren't they?" Olivia said. "Little fish swimming around inside a person."

His tongue had worked its way beyond her thigh, past the hem of her madras short shorts.

"Ah," Olivia said, her mind filled with thoughts of happiness and fish and David's tongue exactly where it was.

"So should we have dinner first and then go inside?" he said.

"Fuck dinner," Olivia said. "And who needs to go inside?"

He had caught her on the phone in the kitchen the next morning telling Winnie.

"We have," Olivia had said. "We've gone completely mad."

He had read somewhere that the best way to conceive was to have lots of sex. They did. All weekend. By the next weekend, Olivia thought she felt funny. Not sick exactly, but different.

"Do you think we actually did it?" she'd asked him that Saturday night back in Rhode Island.

"Of course we did it. We are blessed," he said. He had exactly ten days to live.

The next Saturday, Winnie and her new boyfriend, Lou, and Rex and Magnolia all arrived from the city to spend Labor Day weekend. All day, Olivia pulled David into the bathroom to help her search for traces of her period. But there were none. She stopped drinking the blender drinks that Rex concocted. She put her feet up. On Sunday morning, she told Winnie.

"Maybe you're just late?" Winnie asked.

But Olivia was sure that David was right. They had been blessed with each other, with the success of her hats and his new designs in plastic polymar. With a baby.

Things started to go bad early Monday morning when Winnie stumbled upon Magnolia and Lou screwing on the beach. She kicked sand in their faces, ran back to the house, woke Olivia up to tell her what she'd found, got in the car, and drove back to New York, leaving Rex to ride the train back with Magnolia and Lou, who claimed they had fallen in love.

As they were leaving for the train station, Olivia realized that

Arthur was missing. The five of them searched the house and yard, the beach and neighbors' yards, but no Arthur.

"Maybe he fell in love, too," Rex said.

Standing on the platform as the train pulled away, David took Olivia's hand.

"Let's not go back to New York tonight," he said. "Let's stay in bed and drink nonalcoholic beer and name our baby."

"And maybe Arthur will turn up," Olivia said.

"He will. He has to. He's part of our ever-growing happy family," David said. He had less than twelve hours to live.

Arthur never turned up again.

And after the policeman came and told Olivia, and drove her to the hospital to identify David, and after she had made phone calls from the pay phone in the lobby to Winnie and Rex and her parents and David's parents, standing by the entrance to the emergency room, waiting for her father to come for her, Olivia felt the warm gush of blood. No baby. No David. In just a few hours, everything had gone bad.

Running, her house in sight now, Olivia thought, I am thirty-seven years old. I am a widow. I will never meet someone I will love like that again. Her life stretched before her, sad and blank.

"Oh, Pal," she said in between breaths. "How could you?"

A cat meandered past her, and for a crazy minute Olivia thought it was Arthur. But Arthur was gone, too. She started to cry. It was easier to cry for Arthur than for her other enormous losses. It was easier to say his name as she ran, like a beat: "Arthur, Arthur, Arthur." Somewhere deep within her, it was a different name she called. But Olivia could not speak it out loud.

"Arthur," she said foolishly, crying. "Arthur."

Olivia could hardly make it up the dirt road that led to her own little house. She had run too long, too hard. Her dead husband's

T-shirt stuck to her like a hug. Inside, she would drink water from the jug in the refrigerator; then she would go upstairs, pull the shades, and get back in bed, where she would stay for hours, or even longer. Maybe forever, she decided, wondering how long it would take to starve or die of thirst or neglect. This was the type of thing David would have known.

A few feet from the kitchen door, Olivia noticed that it was open the slightest bit. She stopped, certain that she had locked it. She remembered growing frustrated with the old-fashioned key, pulling hard on the knob to be certain the door had locked. A robber was there, no doubt, convinced the house was empty. It had that look about it—neglected and unloved, like Olivia herself. She decided right then that she would let him kill her. In fact, she was almost relieved that it had come to this.

She yanked the screen door open, then pushed on the other door, the wooden one, and walked into her kitchen.

But it was not a man sitting there at the green metal table with the glass top.

It was a girl, a teenager.

She sat at the table, drinking a glass of water. Perspiration glistened on her face, which was pink and blotchy. Her hair was not quite red and not quite brown, but somewhere in between; long and thin, it hung in a sweaty tangle around her face, strands sticking to her neck. She had too many freckles, the kind that make a face look cluttered. She wore a nose ring, a small silver hoop in one nostril.

And, Olivia realized, she was pregnant.

Her T-shirt stretched ridiculously across her belly. Olivia could see her belly button pressing against the shirt. Her belly, round and big, made Olivia think of melons and bounty. Of life. The girl could be Sheryl Lamont herself. Or a figment of Olivia's imagination. So Olivia spoke in a loud, booming voice.

"What the hell is going on here?" she asked.

The girl's head jerked in Olivia's direction. Something flashed across her face—not panic, exactly, but something like it. Awkwardly, she got to her feet, in that way that pregnant women have. She was all belly. The rest of her was slender; her legs, poking out from cut-off dungarees, were a young girl's legs. She waddled, off balance, straight to Olivia, like one of the baby ducklings in that children's story.

"Stop right there," Olivia ordered, putting an arm up like a traffic cop. Her eyes scanned the kitchen counter for something she could use as a weapon, but there were only crumpled bags of junk food from her ride up here in the middle of the night. And the jar of paste she'd used when she arrived, to paste the things she'd found here to the wall: David's cracked Wayfarer sunglasses and unopened mail and the newspaper still unread from the day he died and Arthur's tiny straw hat that he hated to wear and dead flowers she'd found in a vase by the bed. Before her run, she'd pasted all of that to the wall. Oh, Olivia groaned inwardly now, how can you defend yourself with paper and paste? She remembered that childhood game: paper, scissors, rock. Rock always won, she thought.

"Look at me," the girl said with a nervous laugh. "I'm harmless." Taking a step closer, she added, "I'm desperate."

The smell of her own sweat slapped Olivia in the face. "Don't you come any closer, you little trespasser," Olivia said, sounding foolish rather than threatening. The Lord's Prayer ran through her mind for the first time since her childhood. "Forgive us our trespasses." Or was it "trespassers"? Olivia picked up the ruler she'd stuck in the jar of glue and held it up.

"Don't call the police or anything," the girl said.

"You bet your ass I'm calling the police," Olivia told her. "Breaking and entering and who knows what else." She tried to make a plan, to figure out how to call the police and keep the girl from running away.

"I didn't take anything except, like, eight ounces of water," the girl said, indignant. "Jeez."

Her voice was a teenager's, a voice that was capable of uncontrollable giggles and passionate sobs over small things like dead animals by the roadside or a Top Ten love song. Olivia knew this because she'd been that type of teenager herself. She saw something familiar in the girl's eyes. It was what Olivia had felt sitting in her room with the canopy bed and pink dotted-swiss bedspread and matching curtains and silver monogrammed hairbrush and hand mirror. Get me out of here, she used to think, begging the stars, the gods, whoever might be "out there" listening to a teenager's cry for help.

Olivia looked at the girl and remembered all this, but she thought, Still.

Still, she was a stranger. A stranger who had broken into Olivia's house.

"What the hell are you doing in my house?" Olivia said. "If you haven't taken anything, then why the hell did you break in? People don't break into other people's houses."

"I was just so hot." She shrugged, keeping her young arms—also covered with freckles—held out in surrender.

Olivia had to call the police. The phone, nestled against the far wall, seemed miles away. She could hear herself telling them, We have a B and E here. Barbara Stanwyck would be proud. But a pregnant teenager, she thought, how dangerous could she be? And she heard her own teenage self crying, Get me out of here. She had saved herself with Melanie records and cheap incense and rock concerts at the hockey rink that doubled as an auditorium. This girl had found sex. *Still.* Olivia considered everything. When she licked her lips, she almost tasted the black cherry lip gloss she used to wear, almost smelled the Love's lemon scent that she used to spray on herself after a bath.

"I found the extra key. Under the rock by the door." The girl let her arms drop, and she giggled, the way Olivia knew she could. "It's probably not a good idea to keep it there," she said. "That's the first place a burglar would look. My aunt, her name is Dolly—I swear that's her real name, not even a nickname or anything. She used to keep her money in her freezer because she thought a robber would never look there, but then she read in a magazine—I think it was *You!*—that the freezer is the first place a robber would look."

Olivia's eyes drifted toward her freezer, where she had twenties rolled into neat bundles, hidden behind the ice-cube trays.

"You have to go," Olivia said. The air between her and the girl seemed almost electrically charged.

"I'm not a robber or anything," the girl said, insulted. "Jeez. I just wanted to cool off. I think it's like a hormone thing or something." On the girl's arm, in the spot where children of Olivia's generation got their smallpox vaccination, was a tattoo of a butterfly.

"Cool, huh?" the girl said, grinning. "It hurt like hell, though. I'd never get another one. I hate pain."

Olivia nodded. This close, she saw that the girl's shorts were unzipped to allow room for the baby. Under her too-small T-shirt, they gaped open. This broke Olivia's heart.

"I guess," the girl said, "that having a baby hurts a lot." Her eyes were that odd yellow-brown that some redheads have. "Right?" she asked Olivia.

She looked like a child herself, Olivia thought.

"Oh," Olivia said, "I don't think it's really that bad."

"You don't have any kids?" the girl said, lazily scratching a mosquito bite on her arm.

Olivia got the feeling that the girl was sizing her up, taking some kind of measure of her.

"No kids yet," Olivia said with false cheeriness.

Then she had another, frightening thought. She had seen movies about teenaged girls who were ruthless killers. It was their youth, their seeming innocence that got them into the places they needed to be.

She swallowed hard, then forced herself to say, "My husband and I are working on it." She hoped the girl hadn't heard the way her voice caught on the word *husband*.

The girl narrowed her eyes. "No luck yet, though, huh?"

Olivia shook her head. "Not yet."

"I'm pregnant you know," the girl said. Then she laughed that adolescent laugh. "No shit, Sherlock, huh?" Her face clouded as quickly as it had cleared. "It sucks," she says. "It sucks big-time."

There was a moment of silence, less like the awkwardness between strangers and more like a settling in.

Olivia said, "Where's the father?"

She looked at Olivia blank-faced, then giggled. "Oh," she said, "*the* father. Ben. The asshole. He goes to college here and he was supposed to stick around all summer so I go there, to the college, to his fraternity house—which, I just want to say, is something I don't believe in. I mean, they're so fascist. Like they blackball people they don't like, and they're prejudiced and everything, and they drink until they puke, honest to God. But Ben said I could live in the basement during the summer and no one would even know because only like five people are even there at all in the summer and there's a bathroom there and everything."

Olivia wondered if the girl would even stop for air. She didn't. She kept talking.

"Except Ben, that asshole, was supposed to be one of those five people and sort of take care of me. You know. And then yesterday he tells me that A, he got a job at a camp in upstate New York and so he's leaving, and B, they're coming in to exterminate the place because it's infested with fleas or something and they have to bomb it and no one can go in for like three days because this bomb is really bad shit, chemicals and everything, and you can't breathe the air, especially me. Because if I breathe the air and the baby gets retarded or something, no one's going to want it."

Finally, she paused to twist a ring that she wore on her index finger, a silver star and moon, like a ring that Olivia herself might have worn when she was a teenager twenty years earlier.

"That's a fact," the girl said, her voice soft now, and distant. "No one will adopt deformed babies or stupid babies or HIV babies unless they're from someplace like Romania where they've been tortured really bad."

The girl looked up, away from her hands and right at Olivia. All those freckles and the tip of her nose sunburned made her seem even younger, like a little girl herself.

"Anyway," she said, taking a big loud breath, "thanks for the water." She picked up a tattered backpack, made from patches of velvet and sewn with thick gold thread. Again, Olivia thought of herself as a teenager, the vest she had that was made in the same ragtag fashion. She used to wear that vest for special occasions only—rock concerts, dates with older boys.

The girl moved past Olivia, who stood this entire time in the center of her empty kitchen, and toward the door, trailing pachouli.

"Wait!" Olivia said, and hurried to the girl, grabbing her by the shoulder to stop her from leaving. Was it that familiar scent that made her keep the girl there? Olivia remembered the jar of pachouli oil she'd kept on her dresser, how she'd carefully put droplets on her pulse points, the way it clung to everything. Or was it her own loneliness, her own desperation?

"Where will you go?" she asked. The girl's freckled arm under Olivia's hand was warm from the sun.

The girl shrugged.

"Where will you stay for the three days?"

She looked at Olivia, puzzled. Someone should tell this girl to use sunscreen on her face, to get her hair trimmed—the edges were all split ends. Someone should help her.

"While the fraternity house is getting bombed," Olivia said.

"Oh, that."

The girl twisted her ring again. Her fingers were swollen, Olivia noticed.

"I haven't exactly thought it through," she told Olivia. "But at the college, there's this whole street of fraternity houses. So I figure they must all have basements, right? And they can't all have fleas, right?"

"This boy," Olivia said. "Ben?"

The girl nodded.

"Has he given you any money? Have you seen a doctor?"

Questions bubbled up in Olivia's throat. Where was this girl's mother? Why didn't she get an abortion, get married, get help?

The girl was giggling again. "Of course I didn't go to a doctor. What's *he* going to say that I don't already know? And about Ben . . ."

Her eyes got dreamy, the way Olivia's own used to when she looked at pictures of rock stars in teen magazines, or when the older boy up the street would stop his white VW bug and talk to her on a summer evening.

The girl sighed. "If you've got a million years, I'll tell you all about him and me. But I have to warn you—it's a sad sad story. Honest to God."

Olivia decided it must be a Romeo and Juliet story. A girl from the wrong side of the tracks in love with a college boy—a fraternity boy, Olivia reminded herself. He was richer, and smarter, and older than she, and he made her all kinds of promises that he couldn't keep. Maybe he even really loved her, but his family had swept him away, to a camp in upstate New York, on a beautiful lake surrounded by pine trees and girls like him, rich girls who played tennis and sailed and were not pregnant, would not get pregnant. They were tanned and lovely in their white shorts and clean Keds. And now this girl, his girl, was alone and confused and still carrying in her, somewhere, the hope that he would come for her.

"Your parents—"

"Kicked me out," the girl said.

"But surely you could call them and—"

"I'd rather die!" she blurted, ferocious. "I'd rather get run over by like a tank or something. He's not even my real father," she muttered.

Olivia could hear her own father, his voice stern. "Olivia, we are so disappointed in you." He'd said those words over and over when she was a teenager, when she went to art school instead of a "real college," when she'd called to tell them she and David had gotten married. "Olivia, you simply aren't using your head."

"Stay here," Olivia blurted.

The girl, surprised, took a few steps back, away from Olivia, closer to the door.

Olivia laughed, a nervous, embarrassed laugh. "I mean," she said, "until you can go back to the fraternity house."

Again, the girl studied Olivia, sizing her up.

"Look," Olivia said, "I cannot send you out into the streets, scrounging around fraternity basements for a place to sleep." Olivia remembered her own college days, the damp, dark basements in those houses, the sour smell of old beer. "For God's sake," she continued, "you need to eat properly and get rest and take care of yourself."

The girl said, "What about your husband?"

Olivia had forgotten her lie. She considered what to say, but the girl didn't wait for an answer.

"I mean, what's he going to think when he walks in that door"—and here she pointed dramatically to the gaping door—

"and finds a knocked-up fifteen-year-old girl eating your food and wearing your clothes and sleeping in your bed? I mean, what will he do?"

The girl's words were a tornado in Olivia's head. Fifteen! And who said anything about wearing Olivia's clothes? There were assumptions and wrong conclusions everywhere, and still Olivia stood there, tongue-tied.

"I mean," the girl said, "I could be a crazy person. Or worse. A killer. Like Drew Barrymore in that movie where she goes on a killing spree with her boyfriend."

She leaned so close to Olivia now that Olivia smelled her breath—salt and vinegar potato chips, just like the ones Olivia had eaten on the ride up here.

"Like Ted Bundy," the girl added, giggling wickedly.

David had grown up in Berkeley—Oh! She could almost hear him say it: *the Bay Area*—in the 1960s. He once told her he'd dropped acid when he was only twelve. He used to go to see Jim Morrison and Jimi Hendrix live. A wayward teenager would not frighten him.

"My husband wouldn't mind," Olivia said finally.

The girl grinned. She stretched out her hand for Olivia to shake.

"Well then," she said, all teenager again. "I'm Ruby."

Olivia's mind had cleared. She managed to break all this down to the simplest of terms. She took the girl's small hand in hers, felt the delicate bones, the cheap silver rings, the swollen fingers. Olivia didn't shake Ruby's hand, but she didn't let go, either. She just stood there pressing it into her own and thought, Home. Baby. Ruby.

chapter three

Wouldn't a Person Be Surprised?

Olivia had not eaten Spaghetti-Os since she was a kid. But here she sat at her kitchen table, eating the stuff cold, straight from the can. The Cumberland Farms down the street only sold things like beef jerky and ranch-flavored chips. And Spaghetti-Os. Olivia had gotten up early this morning and gone there for supplies while the girl slept upstairs, hot and tangled in the sheets, frowning. Olivia had watched her, willing her—uselessly—awake. Giving up, she'd gone for some food and come back with all the junk she could afford.

"This is disgusting, Pal," Olivia said to the empty room.

Since her husband had died, she had started to talk to empty rooms. She had even started to hope for replies. She had started to make lists, to break things down to their simplest terms. Eating her Spaghetti-Os, waiting for Ruby to get up, she listed things she missed about being married to David. They loved to eat sugary cereal for dinner if they'd had a long day. They loved painting each other's toenails, Siamese cats, square cars, Eames chairs, reading Rod McKuen poems out loud to each other. They loved Leonard Cohen songs, Disney*land* but not Disney*World*, *The Twilight Zone*, Sam Adams beer. They loved each other.

The little round noodles slid around Olivia's mouth like worms.

"I will not cry," she told the empty room.

She waited.

"Cold Spaghetti-Os," Olivia continued. "For breakfast. Are you happy, Pal? This is what you've reduced me to."

Her friend Camille told her he wasn't really gone, that he'd just taken a new form. Olivia tried to imagine him: an angel on a fluffy cloud, a beam of light like Tinkerbell, a shadowy image of his former self lurking in this very room like one of the ghosts in Disneyland's Haunted House. But none of it worked. Olivia knew that if he were here, in any form, he would have pointed out that she had ended a sentence in a preposition.

So she added, "This is what you've reduced me to, *asshole*."

Anger, everyone told her, was a good thing.

She stood and smeared a good-sized section of the wall in front of her with artist's glue, the kind she'd used back in art school fifteen years ago for her mosaics of broken china and crystal that she titled *The State of Domesticity at the End of the Twentieth Century*. Then she stepped back and flung the can of Spaghetti-Os at the wall. The little round noodles sprayed out, landing haphazardly. Some stuck immediately. Others slid down a bit before resting.

Olivia stepped back and surveyed the results.

It worried her that she was starting to like the wall. That the happy fat fruit she'd imagined painting on it grew more and more surreal every time she tried to envision them.

Olivia decided that later she would shellac the Spaghetti-Os and spray-paint them gold. Which would do absolutely nothing for the resale value of the house. Which was why she had come: to pack up, clean up, and put it on the market.

She opened another can, sat back down at the table, and began to eat, reading the ingredients to avoid thinking about why she had come.

"There are carrots in here," she said out loud. She looked around the kitchen, hopeful, imagining David in some ghostly see-through form, as if he were made of organza.

David once ate so many carrots, he'd told her, that the whites of his eyes turned orange. That's when he was macrobiotic, back in the Bay Area. Even the mention of carrots could make him gag.

"Look," Olivia said, holding a spoonful of Spaghetti-Os out to the room, the universe. "Carrots."

But the room remained silent and empty. Of course. Dead people don't correct grammar or worry about eating food they don't like. Dead people, Olivia thought for the hundredth or thousandth or billionth time, were simply dead.

If she hadn't been mad at Winnie, this would have been a good time to call her. I'm going crazy, she'd say. I'm losing it. I'm eating canned food and waiting for David to appear as a bug or something. But Winnie had gone and fallen in love herself, at her twentieth high school reunion, which she had complained and complained and complained about going to. She had gone and ran into her old high school boyfriend, Jeff, and they had fallen in love and eloped during a weekend in Zihuatanejo.

Worse, Winnie had gotten pregnant right away, that very weekend, without even trying. Now she was big and lumbering, slow-witted and slow-tongued. She couldn't stop herself from talking about her breasts—large and veiny; her belly—also large and veiny; pregnant sex—intense and awkward even when she was on top, which she always had to be; her sonograms and amnio and due date.

Olivia hated Winnie.

Winnie had taken Olivia's life. The one she was supposed to have had with David.

Olivia's gaze settled on the stretched-out macramé bag that Ruby had left hung across the back of one of the kitchen chairs. Upstairs, the girl slept so soundly that Olivia had actually waited in the doorway of her room, watching until she saw Ruby's chest rise and fall. The last thing Olivia needed was a dead runaway. But Ruby was alive, even emitting a tiny snore before Olivia had made her way downstairs.

The bag, Olivia thought as she picked it up, could be from her own teenage closet. She'd had a belt made from the same stuff, with two cheap round metal circles for looping the ends through. It felt familiar in her hands, the bumpy texture, the bulky weight of it. The inside was lined with cheap shiny material that had been stained red from a spill of some kind. Olivia glanced up at the ceiling, waiting for a sound of Ruby waking. But the house was still and quiet.

"I have a right," Olivia explained to the empty room before she plunged her hand into the bag. "After all, a person could go to jail for harboring a runaway. For being an accessory."

An accessory to what, she wasn't certain. The word conjured Winnie, who had told her the last time they'd talked that citrus colors were in style now, and Jackie O sunglasses, and small handbags shaped like flowers. Winnie, who, along with Jeff, the investment banker, was living Olivia's life with the perfect accessories. She had bought a country house in Rhinebeck. She had started to take yoga for pregnant women. They had bought a station wagon to drive back and forth to their house in Rhinebeck.

Olivia took a deep breath, then looked through the bag in

earnest. She remembered her own outrage and betrayal at her mother looking through her things when she was Ruby's age. But the memory didn't stop her from snooping herself. Her mother had feared all the stories going around about teenagers smoking marijuana and taking the pill. "I have a right," her mother had said, indignant.

She hadn't found anything in Olivia's drawers or pockets; Olivia had been smarter than that. Apparently, so was Ruby. Two tubes of cheap lipstick, a pot of Carmex, a broken emery board, some loose pennies and a few French francs jangling around at the bottom of the bag. There was an address book, a cheap Hallmark giveaway, with all the names and phone numbers written in a loopy childish hand. Olivia flipped through the pages, but the name Ben did not appear there.

When a folded piece of paper fell out, Olivia opened it almost gleefully. She was disappointed to recognize it as a snippet of an Elizabeth Bishop poem that the girl had copied down: "Should we have stayed at home and thought of here . . ." Olivia tucked it back into the book, then continued her search. Her hand settled on another square object that could be yet another address book. But when she pulled it from the bag, she saw that it was a wallet, the kind one might give a child as a toy. Small and pink plastic, with a cracked image of the Brady Bunch on it, bulging with school photos of adolescents.

A fortune from a fortune cookie read: "You are special and will travel far." A daily horoscope cut from a newspaper: "Keep your eyes open today, Aquarius! You and your soul mate will cross paths!" Some mimeographed lavatory passes. Half of a letter setting up an appointment with the principal: ". . . *unexcused absences, cutting classes, and persistent tardiness.*" Olivia smiled in spite of herself. She thought of the term *wayward teen,* of movies of the week. With some makeup and better clothes, Ruby could star in one of those, and then she'd turn out all right in the end.

The last thing in the wallet was a library card. Olivia started to slide it back into its spot, but then she looked at it again "Ruby Grady," it read, "15 Strawberry Field Lane." The town, Olivia noticed from the stamp on the card, was the same one where her old high school friend Janice lived. Perhaps this was significant. Perhaps the fact that Ruby lived near Janice was a sign of some sort. A woman from the occult store next to her hat shop had once told Olivia that nothing was an accident. Take everything as a sign, she'd said, almost like a warning. Olivia replaced everything, then slipped the bag back over the chair. As she walked out the door toward her car, she sang softly to herself, the song "Strawberry Fields Forever."

Finally, Olivia thought as she studied the street map and formulated a route. Finally, she was taking charge of her own life again. Almost smugly, she navigated the secondary roads that would take her to 15 Strawberry Field Lane. Ever since David died, people had had advice for Olivia. At first, she took it. All of it. She had to; she was incapable of thinking on her own. Her brain had turned to oatmeal, thick and sluggish. There were decisions to be made about funeral arrangements and personal effects, about notifying work and filling out insurance papers. Slowly, those had turned into larger decisions, which all led to the same question: What was Olivia going to do now? She couldn't begin to imagine an answer.

So much advice, Olivia thought as she drove down a long stretch of empty road, from so many people who had never lost anything more than an elderly distant relative. She used to write it all down on the inside of her thigh in laundry marker: "You can't be alone." She'd written that on her thigh just before she got into the backseat of her parents Oldsmobile and let them take her home with them. After three weeks of Olivia mostly staying right there in bed and sometimes stumbling about the house at night like an intruder, her mother sat her down and told her that she had to get a grip. "Get a grip"—Olivia wrote that, too. "It's time to resume your life," her mother had said, so matter-of-factly that it seemed a simple task: returning to New York, to work, to nights out for all-you-can-eat sushi, to facials by the Polish woman on the corner. "Resume life," Olivia had written on her thigh.

While she tried desperately to make hats, alone in the back of her shop late at night, the woman from the occult store next door brought her tea made from roots. "It only tastes bad because you feel so bad," the woman told her. "It will start to taste good when you don't need it any longer." The tea left grainy sludge at the bottom of the cup, like the sand inside a wet bathing suit. The woman told her to look for signs.

Olivia tried. She looked for omens and guideposts everywhere she went. She copied the advice that screamed from the covers of copies of *You!* that Winnie brought her: YOU CAN SAY NO! and CONTROL YOUR BUTT NOW! She wrote the phone numbers from posters on the subway for laser surgery, lawyers, lab-technician schools, and even poems from the Poetry in Motion series on the insides of her arms, like a junkie. "Stop writing on yourself," Winnie told her, and Olivia wrote that down, too.

In the car now, she tried to find meaning in the random songs that played. But what was she to make of "Yummy, Yummy, Yummy, I've Got Love in My Tummy" or "I'm Henry the Eighth, I Am"? Instead, she switched from the oldies station to Lite Rock and started to count the roadkill she passed. So many dead animals! As a young girl, death had frightened her. She remembered Harriet Lindsay North ("Linzer Torte," they had called her behind her back), her Sunday school teacher at the Congregational church her family had attended. Harriet used to wear her hair in two long braids down her back. She had very thick glasses, the shadow of a mustache, and wore gauzy skirts and bracelets of bells. One day, Harriet took a group of them into the middle of the church and pointed to the ornate Tiffany windows on each wall. "The east windows," she told them, "represent life and birth; the west windows represent death."

Olivia had swung her head to gaze west, where fuzzy glass symbolized heaven and the unknown. Terrified, she had hyperventilated. The teacher stuck Olivia's head in a paper bag and forced her to breathe deeply, but every time Olivia glanced westward, her breath left her again.

Olivia added to her roadkill list: one squirrel. So far, she had seen two skunks, a raccoon, and something too squished to identify. At least David hadn't been squished. She passed another dead raccoon.

"Great," Olivia said into the empty car, "I am actually counting roadkill."

B.D., she would not have done this.

B.D. was a Winnie expression. *Before David.* Winnie liked to remind Olivia of her life B.D. B.D., Olivia had gone to art school, had lived for a million years with a man named Josh, had moved to New York and started to make her hats. Winnie was right: It just felt like that all belonged to someone else. *Her* life, Olivia thought, was about David.

"B.D.," Winnie had told her, "you were strong and funny and full of ideas about things to do with your life. You left Josh, didn't you? And you became a fucking milliner, which is not like the most common profession in the world. You didn't marry that guy who wanted to marry you so bad. What was his name? Chris? You didn't like that he said Feb-*u*-ary instead of February and li-*berry* instead of library. You were a person who had her limits. You raised a cat by yourself, for Christ's sake."

B.D., Olivia thought as she added another dead skunk to her list, she would not be on this road at all. She would not have let a pregnant teenager into her home. The kid was probably a professional thief. Or worse. If Olivia could call anyone right now and ask advice, she'd call David; he'd always given her good advice. He'd made lists, pro and con. He'd made graphs and time lines. He'd used logic. They used to kid that each of them operated from the opposite side of their brain, so that together they had one good functioning brain. Now here she was, stuck with just her half.

Olivia turned at the rotary that would bring her to the road that led to Ruby's parents' house. She needed to figure out what to say to them. What did she want, anyway? To save the girl? To save herself? Before David, Olivia had tried to save everything—Narragansett Bay, the Platte River, manatees and the great northern wolf. But saving babies and bad girls was different from saving bodies of water or endangered animals.

At this very moment, that girl was asleep in her house. Poking around. Robbing her, maybe. Forget B.D., Olivia thought. She had to decide what she wanted with Ruby.

Strawberry Field Lane sat in the middle of a development filled with streets named after fruit, not Beatles songs. Olivia would have preferred driving down Penny Lane or Day Tripper Boulevard. But here she was, navigating Pumpkin Patch Road and Apple Orchard Court, a crumpled street map on her lap. It was very hot. Rivulets of sweat trickled down her arms and back. All the houses looked alike: small and square, slightly run-down despite the cheerful street names.

Janice lived across the highway, in a newer part of town, one that was struggling to keep some of its rural flavor. Here, there were few trees, only parched patches of lawns and some cheap plastic swimming pools decorated with garish Barneys and Simbas. It was noisy from cars getting on and off the interstate somewhere behind the houses.

At last, Olivia reached Strawberry Field Lane. Number fifteen was painted the color of rust. On the front door hung a scarecrow dressed like Uncle Sam. A dog paced the length of a chain-link fence in the backyard. It was one of those dogs that eat children, a Rottweiler or Doberman. Olivia sat sweating in her car across the street, watching the house, the dog, trying to figure out what the hell she was doing there. Finally, she unstuck her legs from the seat and walked to the front door of number fifteen, where, up-close, Uncle Sam looked like a hanged man. She could hear the drone of a television inside, the laughter of a studio audience.

Olivia knocked.

The woman who answered looked remarkably like Ruby, younger than Olivia. An older sister maybe, dressed in a nurse's uniform with a name tag that read DENISE. She didn't open the door very wide, just enough to get a good view of Olivia. The smell of fried food hit Olivia and made her swoon.

"We don't want anything," Denise said in a tired voice. "And we don't want to give anything."

"No!" Olivia said too loudly and too fast. She was afraid the woman would close the door and that would be that.

"What? Lost cat? Dead dog?" Her voice told Olivia she had heard it all.

"I wanted to talk to someone about Ruby?" Olivia said.

The woman glanced over her shoulder, and Olivia followed her backward stare. Two pajamaed boys watched television. The room was small and square, like the house itself, the blinds drawn, the room cluttered with plaid furniture and some sort of over-sized reclining chair and tables stacked with magazines and news-papers. Before Olivia could take more in, the woman was outside, too, the door firmly shut behind her.

"I don't want to wake up Bobby," she said. "If he knows I'm even talking about her, he'll go nuts." She took a big preparatory breath. "She okay?"

Olivia nodded.

The woman sighed, relieved. Out here in the bright light, Olivia saw that she was older. Her face was ruddy, full of tired lines caked with makeup. Her eyes were a pretty shade of blue, but flat, and the bright blue lines she'd penciled in beneath them gave her a clownish appearance. There were thick clumps of mascara on her lashes, and her hair was overpermed, overcolored. Olivia took in all of this. She tried to imagine the girl here, moving about the tiny house with her big belly and her dreamy eyes.

"I work the eleven to seven today," Denise was saying. She pointed at the Timex on her plump wrist.

Olivia nodded again. The woman did not want to waste time. Neither did Olivia.

"You're her mother?" she asked.

"I hate to say yes, because who knows what trouble she's in now. But yes."

"When did you see her last?" Olivia asked, choosing her words carefully. All right, she thought, the girl is a real troublemaker. A bad seed. That really didn't surprise her. The mother surprised her. But Olivia tried to get past that, to find out what exactly the mother knew, what she was willing to relinquish here.

"The day I walked into her room and saw that little bulging gut and knew she got herself knocked up, I said, 'Get out here and talk to Bobby and me about that bun you got in your oven, and don't be denying it.' And she came out and started running off at the mouth about love and Ben and everything we didn't know about everything. But you see, lady—"

"Olivia."

"Olivia. Pretty name."

Somehow, the way the woman said her name made Olivia want to jump into a hot bath.

"You see, Olivia," Denise said, rolling all of Olivia's vowels around her mouth, "I was there myself. All in love with Ruby's father. Sixteen years old and stupid as a stone. My head was all full of love and sex and fairy tales. Then he left and I was stuck with a kid. Don't get me wrong—I love her, but I didn't know my ass from my elbow. We didn't have a pot to piss in. My mother threw *us* out, we got the welfare and I used most of it to buy something to make me feel better. Beer or whatever." She bent her head, embarrassed.

When she looked back up, she said, "Olivia. See, that's a classy name. I didn't even know how to pick a name right. Ruby sounded so highfalutin to me back then." She laughed at her own foolishness.

"The thing is," Olivia said, because she, too, was embarrassed by the woman's talk-show story. She wanted to get to the point. "The thing is, Ruby is at my house, and she's pregnant and needs some care. From a doctor and from an adult."

The woman squinted at Olivia in the same way that Ruby had, sizing her up, figuring her out.

"And you want to be that adult?" the woman said.

"No. Not exactly. It's just that she's been sleeping in basements and—"

"Where's Ben? Took off already? I think he's got Ray beat there. Ray at least waited until Ruby was born and he realized he couldn't stand the crying and the shitting and the spitting up."

Now it was Olivia who sighed. The sun beating down on her back and head made her dizzy. That, and all the information she was getting about this woman Denise's life, and about Ruby's predicament. Olivia thought briefly about her own life, which seemed dull by comparison: the big brick house where she grew up, with its Oriental rugs and six-burner stove and parquet floors, the private school she hated and scorned, her dreams of escape, lying in her room reading poetry, sketching, playing her stereo too loud and burning incense. Olivia realized that until David's death, she had not known unhappiness. Not really.

"Will you take her back? Help her out?" Olivia asked, hoping the answer would be no. How could this woman help Ruby?

Denise laughed, a short barklike laugh. "That's why you came?" She laughed again, then glanced down at her watch. "Look, that girl is no good. She started fucking like a rabbit way before it was sensible, and I told her to get herself some birth-control pills, to use condoms so she didn't get VD or AIDS or whatever, but she went ahead and did whatever she wanted. The drugs, the sex, the 'nothing can happen to me' attitude. I went there myself, and lady, it sucks. When the sex wears off and the high is gone, you got no money, no food, and a kid to boot. I wised up, and so will she."

"But—"

"You think she needs some TLC, be my guest. Give it to her. In there, I got a husband and two boys who are all better off without a knocked-up wiseass kid to screw everything up."

"I don't want her so much as I want to help her," Olivia explained.

"She's in good hands, then, Miss Good Samaritan, Miss Holier Than Thou," Denise said. "You got yourself a nice name and a car with New York plates and probably some good sense. God bless you."

Before Olivia could protest, Denise slipped back inside. Olivia heard the door lock. She stood there a minute longer, not waiting for the door to open, but forcing herself to shape her plan. It was true. Olivia saw that now. She did not want the girl. What she wanted was that baby.

Olivia made the phone call from a phone booth at Big Ed's, the local breakfast joint near the beach. She got the number from the Realtor, who was eager to sell the house. "I can't wait to see what an artiste like yourself did with that little gem," the Realtor said.

An image of the wall flitted across Olivia's mind. "Well"—she laughed nervously—"you'd be surprised." Then she asked for the number of a good family lawyer in the area, and the Realtor happily gave her one.

"Time to tidy up affairs," she'd said with forced sympathy.

The Realtor wore suits she bought from the Victoria's Secret catalog and heels so high, they made Olivia feel off balance. Her nails, sharp and painted colors like coral or bright pink, drummed across everything she touched—the steering wheel of her Miata, papers that needed signing, her desktop. Olivia thought she could hear them drumming even now. She thanked her for the number and called the lawyer. The smell of bacon frying wrapped itself around her while she listened to the phone ringing in her ear.

"This is Ellen," the lawyer said when she answered. "What can I do for you?"

Olivia had to speak above the breakfast noises to explain the situation. The old man at the grill—Big Ed himself? she wondered—listened and frowned.

"Well," Ellen said, "in Rhode Island, a minor can consent to a private adoption if the father doesn't object."

What was it that Ruby's mother had said? That Ben had taken off already? He wasn't likely to object, Olivia thought. But still, she wanted assurance.

"Since '95," Ellen explained, "a father can assert rights and go to family court to acknowledge and prove paternity, or he can do it in writing if the mother doesn't object. But he can also give up rights the same way."

"It sounds so easy," Olivia said.

"Private adoption is the way to go," Ellen told her. "It *is* easy. Come to the office and get all the papers signed and you're on your way."

"On my way," Olivia repeated. "Good."

Big Ed scowled at her when she hung up. But Olivia didn't mind. In fact, she sat at the counter and ate a Hungry Man's

Breakfast: three eggs, bacon, sausage, and three buttermilk pancakes. She paid and overtipped, then stepped outside into the bright summer day, moving toward home.

Of course, there was a moment of panic when Olivia imagined that Ruby was gone. Or that she was still up in the room where Olivia had left her, maybe dead or comatose. But in fact, Ruby was standing in the kitchen, eating Spaghetti-Os from the can, studying Olivia's wall with great interest.

"I like it," Ruby said when Olivia came in. She didn't look at Olivia, just kept eating and staring.

"It's just a crazy thing," Olivia said, wanting to distract Ruby from the wall where the truth hung—David's obituary was there, the newspaper story, all of it.

"That's why I like it. I decapitated all my Barbies, you know, and then I stuck their heads in empty tuna fish cans, in plaster of paris."

Olivia waited for an explanation, but none came.

"Where have you been?" Ruby asked, turning now to face her.

"Errands," Olivia said.

"Like the post office and stuff?"

Olivia shrugged.

"I just got up," Ruby said proudly.

Olivia decided that Ruby needed nutritious food, from all four food groups. "I was thinking we could go out to lunch. Are you still hungry?"

"Always," Ruby said, grinning. "I eat tons and tons of food."

"Good," Olivia said. A baby needs protein at this point, she thought, for brain cells. Despite her Hungry Man's Breakfast, Olivia's own stomach felt empty and needy.

Ruby said, "You want to see something cool? If I drink a glass of real cold water fast, then lie down flat, the baby will kick like crazy."

Before Olivia could respond—she wasn't ready for the baby to kick!—Ruby guzzled a glass of water and dropped to the floor.

"Come here," she ordered Olivia.

Olivia hesitated. Come here and what? she thought. She tasted bacon and syrup in the back of her throat. Sour.

"Quick!" Ruby shouted.

Olivia found herself scrambling to her knees beside the girl, suddenly eager for the baby's response. She let Ruby guide her hand to somewhere on her big belly.

"There," Ruby whispered, awed. "Feel?"

Olivia nodded, unable to say anything. All she could think about was what she was feeling.

Life.

Ruby watched houses. She walked with great purpose, sometimes making marks in a little notebook as she went. The houses did not seem to be in any special order. For a few days, she sat across the street from a plain bungalow in a development named Eastward Look. The house had aluminum siding, fake white brick along the lower third, a mailbox shaped like a lighthouse, and a profusion of marigolds growing in fat circles across the yard.

Then she watched a redwood and glass contemporary that was isolated down a dirt road next to the seminary. After that, it was the stone guest house of one of the mansions that sat perched on rocks above the ocean. And then she returned to Eastward Look and watched a small Tudor-style home with a playhouse in the backyard that was an exact replica of it. Ruby watched all of these houses, made notes in her notebook, then moved on.

The first time Olivia saw her doing it, at the bungalow, she had wondered if Ruby was planning to rob the house. She had imagined her making note of when the family was away, their daily routine, the possibilities of the goods inside: big-screen TVs, video cameras, fine jewelry.

But her pattern wasn't consistent with that, Olivia realized. She didn't watch them in a way that would allow her to know the family's comings and goings. And she never went to the windows to look inside. She just sat at a safe distance, sometimes halfway smiling as she watched, sometimes her lips moving as if she was telling a story to someone.

Once, Olivia looked for that notebook. But Ruby always carried it with her. What could the girl possibly be doing? Olivia wondered. She was convinced there was an ulterior motive, and that it was not a good one.

Ruby sat on the low wooden fence that ran across the yard of a house kitty-corner to the one she was watching. That one, *hers*, was painted a happy yellow with green trim and shutters. There was a tangle of bikes of all sizes in the driveway, and tomatoes growing plump and red on vines in a fenced-off square in the side yard. Olivia watched Ruby watching, saw her scribble in her notebook, frowning in concentration as she wrote. The house was on a road that was a good shortcut to the beach, so it seemed natural that Olivia might be walking past, even though she had followed Ruby here, had watched as she headed carefully to this spot and took her place on the fence that gave her a clear, uninterrupted view of the yellow house.

"Hey," Olivia said, "funny meeting you here."

Ruby squinted up at her, suspicious.

"How did you find me?" she asked, closing her notebook firmly and holding on to it.

Olivia shrugged. "I don't know. I was going to take a walk on the beach."

The girl was still studying her in a way that made Olivia feel caught. She sat beside her on the fence and then she, too, had a good view of the yellow house.

"Cute, huh?" Olivia said, nodding her chin in the direction of the house.

Ruby turned her attention back to the house, too.

"Do you know what I think?" Ruby said. As usual, she didn't wait for an answer. "I think the owners went to Brown or somewhere like that. And the mother, she played field hockey and the father played lacrosse and they got married outdoors somewhere, under a big striped tent, and there were lots of hors d'oeuvres, fancy ones, not pigs in a blanket or anything wrapped in bacon, but something else, like maybe baked cheese. You know they do that. They wrap it up and make the crust all fancy, with little leaves or something on it, and they bake it and you spread it on little pieces of bread. And I think they worked hard at solid jobs, maybe in a bank or someplace, and then they had three children in a row, all boys, and the mother stays home and makes sauce from real tomatoes and maybe even her own pasta." She looked at Olivia, blinking. "You can do that, you know. In a special machine. Cut out different shapes and everything. I saw it on the Home Shopping Network."

Olivia laughed. "Now how do you figure any of that just from sitting over here looking at a house?"

Ruby shrugged and then got off the fence. "Have fun at the beach," she mumbled.

"Do you want to come?" Olivia asked her.

"Got to go," Ruby said.

As Olivia watched her walk away, she couldn't help but think that somehow she had disappointed Ruby.

. . .

She gave the girl a hat, a pale pink straw hat with a short brim and a top that resembled a muffin. It had a black ribbon around it that ended in a triple loop. Olivia had named the hat "Nicotiana." It was from her flower series; she named all of her hats.

The girl took it reluctantly. "A hat?" she said. "I don't know." She twirled it around and around in her hands, studying it.

"I made it," Olivia said. "That's what I do. I'm a milliner."

That seemed to worry the girl even more. "A milliner?"

"That one is called 'Nicotiana.' It came in a light blue, and off-white, too. I have series, you know. This was from my flower series."

"Like nicotine?" Ruby said, brightening.

"Yes."

"Cool," she said, and put it on.

It was really the wrong hat for her. Pink was a bad color on her, and the small brim made her face look too round and too big. "Perfect," Olivia said.

Ruby went into the tiny lavatory downstairs and stared at herself in the mirror. "God!" she gushed. "It's great. It's so cool. Sophisticated, huh? Don't you think?"

Olivia grinned and nodded, only feeling a little guilty at how bad the hat looked.

"*Oui, oui,*" Ruby said, strutting out of the bathroom and into the living room. "*Voulez-vous coucher avec moi ce soir?* Oo là là and humma humma. Jeez. I wish my mom could see this. Every time I came home with something new, even if it was on sale or something, she'd be like, 'Well, la-di-da,' even though it would be nothing. Maybe a pair of jeans or something. But this"—Ruby shook her head and patted the top of the hat—"this is so fancy."

Olivia was due at her friend Janice's for dinner in twenty minutes. But she wanted to stay here with the girl. They were making progress. Ever since she'd felt that baby move under her sweaty hand, Olivia knew there was no going back. But how could a girl—even this girl!—feel that every day and still give the baby away? She thought of all the teenage girls in the news lately who had their babies in motel rooms or bathrooms somewhere and then killed them. Would Ruby do something like that? Maybe in some crazy way killing the baby was easier than handing it over to someone else.

Olivia needed a plan, a plan that would convince Ruby that giving the baby to Olivia was the smartest thing, the best thing, the only right thing. She would show Ruby how charming she was. She would convince her that she could give a child a wonderful life. She would show Ruby her credentials—not diplomas and résumés, but charm and sophistication and wisdom and anything else Olivia could think of to impress this girl. She would make it so that Ruby could not do anything except sign over the baby to her.

Already, Olivia had laced her conversation with words that she thought could seduce a teenaged girl looking for a certain kind of life: "Symphony," she'd said. She'd said, "Greenwich Village." Ruby's eyes had widened at all the right times. "Wow," she'd said, "you've been there? You've done that?" And now there was the hat, Nicotiana. It was too soon, Olivia knew, to lay it all out for the girl, to tell her she'd talked to her mother, to a lawyer, that they could settle this so easily. It was too soon because Olivia didn't trust the girl yet. And she knew the girl didn't trust her, either.

"I wish we could go somewhere tonight," Olivia said. "You could wear the hat."

Ruby flopped onto the sofa, looking even more ridiculous with her stomach up in the air and the hat perched on her head.

"Whatever," she said. She started to flip through a copy of *You!*, ignoring Olivia.

But as Olivia walked out the door, Ruby looked up and said, "Like maybe if you have time, you could teach me how to use chopsticks sometime."

The girl had tried to sound casual, but Olivia knew that it was not a simple request. Show me, the girl was saying. Show me what you know.

Olivia couldn't shake the image of Ruby in the hat. She sat in Janice's kitchen, watching her three-year-old daughter, Kelsey, methodically tear out all the pop-up pieces of a storybook and thinking about Ruby. Olivia and Janice had been friends since seventh grade. They had double-dated at their junior prom, lost their virginity in the same week of November during college, and then drifted apart, Olivia to New York, Janice here, to Rochester, the same small formerly rural town where Ruby's family lived right across the highway. The town was being developed in a frenzy of mismatched architectural styles and economic classes. The family next door to Janice raised chickens; Olivia could hear them now, clucking away.

Still, Janice and Olivia were friends of sorts. Olivia had worn an embarrassing emerald green bridesmaid's dress at Janice's wedding and Janice made a yearly weekend trip to visit Olivia in Manhattan. When she came, they drank pink zinfandel, the way they had when they were younger and trying to be sophisticated. Once, Janice brought her old Ouija board, and the two of them sat on Olivia's bed, asking it the same questions they used to at overnights in junior high: "Who will I marry? Where will I live? How many children will I have?"

Olivia looked around Janice's kitchen with its slate blue cupboards and ornamental copper molds hung along one wall. She had never thought she would one day envy Janice's ordinariness, but, Olivia realized, she did in a way. Janice's husband, Carl, was stretched out on a recliner in their family room, watching CNN and enjoying a beer; Kelsey was entertaining herself, humming "Frère Jacques" as she tore up a book; the baby, Alex, stood in the playpen, throwing measuring spoons onto the linoleum floor; and Janice herself was at the stove, frowning over a recipe that was too complicated for someone who could not cook very well. It made Olivia feel bad that her old friend was trying so hard for her. But then Olivia was gripped by an even stronger pang of envy for the things that Janice had.

Across the state, the country, the world even, families were operating in this very way, Olivia knew. Even Winnie, who was up in Rhinebeck painting a mural of a cow jumping over the moon on the nursery wall. Olivia imagined Jeff, Winnie's investment banker husband, downstairs cooking spaghetti just the way Winnie liked it: so al dente, it crackled slightly when she bit into it. They could hear chickens, too. And the low mooing of cows at the farm across the street. They drank milk from that dairy, milk so rich and fresh, it lay heavy on your tongue all day.

And what do I have? Olivia asked herself.

She was surprised by the answer that popped into her mind: Ruby. Ruby's baby.

The girl was back at Olivia's house, in Olivia's bed, wearing Olivia's white cotton nightgown. Before she left for Janice's, Olivia had given Ruby extra pillows, warm milk, an iron pill, and a stack of the magazines that her sister, Amy, had left for her to read. "They'll help you get a grip," Amy liked to say. "Look at what's going on in the world. Put things in perspective." Surely the girl needs iron, Olivia thought. Six months pregnant—"I guess," Ruby told her. "Something like that. I wasn't ever too regular, you know? My girlfriend Betsy told me just not to do it fourteen days after your period and you're fine. Ha!"

Olivia had cringed. Didn't they teach birth control in schools these days? Even she and Janice had suffered through a course euphemistically named Health when they were in high school, lessons about ovulation and condoms and how long sperm could live. She thought again of Sheryl Lamont, happily pregnant in Texas, and Winnie, fat and happy in Rhinebeck, and she sighed.

"I know," Janice said, appearing beside her to refill her wineglass, "dinner's taking forever. Carl told me just to make steak, but I told him a lot of people don't eat red meat anymore. You know Carl, though. Steak, potatoes, and ranch dressing." She rolled her eyes so that Olivia would know that she, Janice, was better than that.

Olivia reached out and patted Janice's arm, a gesture she meant as something kind but which came out wrong.

Janice squinted and said, "Is the wine okay?"

The wine was an expensive one. Too expensive, Olivia decided. Overhead, a ceiling fan churned the hot air around. Earlier, Carl had explained that the house never got hot because of all the ceiling fans. But Olivia was sweating and miserable, hungry for air and food.

"*Bon Appetit* recommended it," Janice was explaining. "Carl wanted to get a jug of something horrible, but I wanted to splurge. Here you are, a New Yorker now. A city girl. I want you to know that not everybody here is such a hick. I want you to know that you're not all alone."

Olivia decided she would drink too much tonight. She had let a stranger into her house; she was reckless.

"When you were pregnant," she blurted out, "did you have to take iron pills?"

It occurred to Olivia that maybe she had done the absolute wrong thing giving Ruby iron tablets. Maybe she should race home this instant and be sure Ruby and that lovely kicking baby inside her were fine.

Janice was back at the stove, frowning over a recipe. "Probably," she said. "But I threw up everything, so eventually I stopped taking stuff. Even the prenatal vitamins. They say you really need that folic acid, but I didn't take it, and my kids came out fine."

Olivia glanced over at the kids. Alex was banging his head against the side of the playpen; Kelsey was eating Play-Doh. She stopped when she discovered Olivia watching her.

"It's nontoxic," Kelsey said.

Three years old and she knew words like *nontoxic.* What other words did they know? *Nuclear waste? SCUD missiles? Safe sex?* Not my baby, Olivia thought, her hand jumping a little at the memory of those glorious kicks. She would go to some special school where they taught the ABCs and long division and none of the bad stuff.

Kelsey was staring hard at Olivia. She had brown hair cut in a sort of pageboy—short, straight bangs and the rest in a bob. Her eyes were oddly big—not in a charming wide-eyed way, but in a way that reminded Olivia of Marty Feldman.

"Is your husband still dead?" Kelsey asked.

"Yes."

"You're never ever going to see him again?"

"No," Olivia said.

"Never never ever?

Olivia decided she didn't like this kid.

"Never," she said.

"Not even in a million years?"

"I'm not going to be alive in a million years myself. No one lives that long."

Kelsey considered this, then ate more Play-Doh, the blue.

"Are we going to eat anytime soon?" Carl bellowed from the family room.

He was a bellower, a backslapper, a man who used *party* as a verb. Whenever Olivia saw him, he said, "You still living in that shithole city?" Since David had died, he backed off a bit, but Olivia still didn't like him very much. She studied Janice's back at the stove—her ass was too big, her jeans were too tight, and she was making a bad dinner. Sadly, Olivia wasn't even sure she still liked Janice.

Janice was talking about babies. Should she have a third? she asked, not expecting an answer, and, silently, Olivia said, Hell no.

Something was burning. Olivia got up and poured herself more wine. She was slightly drunk already. *Good,* she thought. She wondered if Ruby still had on the hat. There was something almost exciting about sharing her home with this girl she didn't know, this stranger, for three days. Ruby thought David was away on a business trip, in New York. For a while at least, Olivia could pretend that her life was different, the way it was supposed to be.

"Okay," Janice said. "Carl?"

Olivia sat at the table, but Kelsey shook her head no. "We're eating in the dining room," she whispered, pointing through the archway to a room that held Janice's parents' old furniture—made of heavy dark wood with years of furniture-polish buildup. It was too big for the small room. But there were fresh flowers in a vase, and candles lit, and what Olivia recognized as Janice's wedding china. The pattern, Olivia remembered, was named Strawberry Field, just like the street where Ruby lived, cream-colored plates with small ruby strawberries in the center, dusted with gold flecks. Olivia thought of that small house, of Ruby's mother, and tried to picture the girl there, sullen and hostile and desperate to go. The image comforted her; she knew Ruby wouldn't go back.

Carl seemed especially awkward in here, with his faded jeans and large gut and flannel shirt. He gripped a bottle of beer in one hand, the edge of the table in the other.

"We've never eaten in here," Kelsey whispered.

Janice laughed nervously. "Of course we have," she said.

Kelsey looked at Olivia with great seriousness. "Honest to God, we never eat in here. Not in a million years."

"Well," Olivia said, watching Janice bring in steaming plates of food, everything either undercooked or overcooked, "it's lovely." This ceiling fan seemed even more sluggish, and Olivia felt as if she were getting a facial with all the hot air and the steam rising from the platters.

When she'd finally brought all the food to the table, Janice surveyed everything nervously. Olivia was reminded of the way Janice had acted when presenting oral reports in school: flustered, like she was now, blushing slightly, almost giddy.

"Since it's June," Janice said in her oral-presentation voice, "I made summery things. Like risotto primavera and stuffed chicken breasts with spinach and sun-dried tomatoes."

Janice pointed to the food as she talked. Carl and Kelsey glanced at each other. Back in the kitchen, Alex was in his playpen, grunting. Olivia wondered if maybe Janice should have been more careful with that folic acid.

The food was passed around in silence, with a forced formality that sent Olivia straight for more wine. She was embarrassed for everybody. She wished she hadn't come. She and Ruby could have rented movies. Movies about babies. *Baby Boom* and *Look Who's Talking* and *Three Men And a Baby.* They could have sat together under a quilt and eaten popcorn and watched movies, the way people do.

"Don't you think?" Janice was saying.

Everyone was looking at Olivia, who just shrugged and laughed a little. People excused her for everything these days, rudeness and absentmindedness and for not listening when she should.

Janice spoke louder, slower, like Olivia'd gone deaf instead of drunk too much wine. "Don't you think summer is a good time for fresh starts?"

"I suppose," Olivia said. "Starting over" was a phrase people always used around her. They told her to "start over," how important "starting over" was. But Olivia still wasn't sure what it entailed. Moving away? Getting remarried? Dyeing her hair red? Learning to tango?

"Carl?" Janice said with a "Come on, do it already" look.

"Yeah, well," Carl said.

Olivia noticed that Carl unrolled his stuffed chicken breast and scraped the stuffing from it. He picked all the vegetables out of the risotto primavera.

He stroked his scraggly beard and said, "You remember Pete?"

Olivia shrugged again.

"Of course you do," Janice said with strained gaiety. "From our wedding."

Olivia almost said something about how badly she'd looked that day in that screaming green dress and with her ridiculous French curls, but then she remembered that all of that had been Janice's doing, so she tried to look as if she was straining her memory. "Pete," she muttered. "Pete . . ."

"I work with him," Carl said. "Pete Lancelotta."

Carl sold clothes hangers, of all things. To clothing stores. He also sold the racks to hang clothes on and the spinning racks that makeup and panty hose often sat in.

"He's bald," Kelsey said.

"Bald*ing*," Janice interjected. "And very tall."

"Big," Carl said.

"Not fat," Janice added quickly.

"I didn't say fat," Carl said. "Jesus. He's a big guy."

"Big sounds like fat," Janice said. "I don't want Olivia to think he's fat, that's all."

"I don't think he's fat," Olivia said.

"See?" Carl said. "Jesus."

A vague image was forming. A tall, bald, fat man who acted like Carl.

"I can't place him," Olivia said. She wondered if she would get salmonella poisoning from the undercooked chicken.

Janice leaned toward her, across the scorched risotto—Olivia now knew what she'd smelled burning—and said in a low voice, "He got divorced recently. The wife is a nightmare. She got his credit cards up to something like ten thousand dollars and stopped working and only watched the O.J. trial. I mean, that's how she spent her time. Shopping and watching the O.J. trial."

Olivia shook her head, tried to look sympathetic. She was officially drunk and she wanted to leave.

"Not ten thousand," Carl said. "Eight thousand."

"I think it was more like ten, Carl," Janice said. She said it in the voice of someone who would argue this small point to the bitter end.

"Maybe nine," Carl said.

Janice rolled her eyes. "It was close to ten thousand dollars. Pete told me so himself."

Carl looked at Olivia. "Isn't nine close to ten?" he asked her.

"Either way," Olivia said, "that's a lot of clothes hangers."

"Do you know why six is afraid of seven?" Kelsey asked no one in particular.

"The point is," Janice said, "I think you two might hit it off."

"Because seven *eight* nine," Kelsey shouted. "Get it?"

"No romance necessarily," Janice continued. "Go slow. You've both been burned."

"Well," Olivia said, "yes, in a way. He was burned by his ex-wife and I was burned by God."

Everyone was silent.

Olivia realized that even Alex had stopped making noises out in the kitchen.

Then Kelsey said, "God burned you? Like with matches?"

"To tell you the truth," Carl said, "I don't think he's even going to like you. He's a nice guy. A regular nice guy."

"Carl," Janice said, "you're making it sound like David wasn't a nice guy."

"No," Olivia said, "he's implying that *I'm* not a nice guy."

"Gal," Kelsey said. "Girls aren't guys."

"Will it hurt anybody if Pete and Olivia go to a movie?" Janice said, stretching her arms out like Christ on the cross.

"I'm just saying," Carl mumbled.

Olivia stood up too fast, banging her knee on the screw that opened the middle of the table so that someday, if they ever ate in this room again, a leaf could be added.

"It's late," she said, though she had no job to go to in the morning, no husband waiting at home.

Janice looked stricken. "There's cheesecake," she said.

But Olivia was out of the dining room, moving through the kitchen, toward the Dutch doors that led out to the driveway and her car. The getaway car, she thought. Alex was in a crumpled heap on the floor of his playpen. Seeing him like that was the only thing that slowed Olivia down. She considered stopping and doing something. CPR, maybe? She wondered if it was too late for folic acid, and she made a mental note to get some for Ruby.

"We just keep him there," Janice explained. "Otherwise, he'll wake up when we pick him up, and then he's awake all night." She was right at Olivia's heels. Somehow, she had retrieved the cheesecake from the refrigerator and was following Olivia, holding it out.

"How interesting," Olivia said as she pushed her way outside.

The air smelled like pine trees and shit. Chicken shit, Olivia assumed, given the noise next door. The way Winnie's air must smell in Rhinebeck. On the other side of Janice's, a house resembling a castle was being built. Even in the dark, Olivia could make out turrets and large arched doorways. Her car looked familiar and safe.

"Thanks for dinner," Olivia said, climbing into it. She breathed in its smell happily.

It was not until she had the headlights on, the car in reverse, that she saw Janice's face peering in her window.

Reluctantly, Olivia rolled it down.

"He's a nice guy," Janice said, shoving the cheesecake at Olivia. "Pete."

"I know," Olivia said. "I remember. Big but not fat." She backed away, the cheesecake sliding around on the seat beside her.

She had enough wine to make driving difficult. Olivia sat too close to the wheel, stared too hard at the road. Drunk like this, she could hit someone and kill them. Someone's husband.

She pulled over at a Dunkin' Donuts for coffee. While she waited inside, she thought about Ruby. What if she was not as Olivia imagined her? What if she *was* like that Drew Barrymore character, a killer? A thief? Not that Olivia had anything valuable in the house. Her good jewelry and bankbooks were all back in New York. But she had cash and credit cards in the beach house. Her grandmother's pearls. Her most valuable possession was worthless to anybody else: the answering-machine tape with David's voice on it. She had not played it since he'd died, not once. Instead, she put it in her jewelry box, the place where valuable things should go.

On the stools at the counter were some teenagers, kids around Ruby's age, Olivia guessed. They all looked stoned, gobbling sugar doughnuts and laughing too hard about nothing at all. They all had tattoos and pierced body parts; one girl even had a small hoop earring jutting from her tongue. How is she eating so many doughnuts with that thing in there? Olivia wondered. These kids reminded her of Ruby, and they looked scary, dangerous.

What if Ruby was a criminal? In some kind of burglary ring, maybe? What is wrong with me? Olivia thought. She had let a strange girl—maybe even a criminal—into her home. I am a woman so desperate for—love, company, what?—that I put myself in jeopardy. Are you happy, Pal? For a frightening instant, Olivia thought she had spoken out loud, but, no, it was just that her lips were moving, and one of the pierced girls was looking at her as if maybe Olivia was crazy or dangerous. Olivia smiled at the girl, who stared back at her blankly.

Maybe the pregnant stomach is fake, Olivia thought. Something to garner sympathy and gain entry into people's homes. And Olivia had told her she was there alone, that her husband was away. Instead of a poor kid from the wrong side of the tracks knocked up by some rich, callous college boy, Olivia imagined Ruby as streetwise, a runaway. She'd seen a documentary once about street kids who robbed for a living. They slept on park benches and beaches; they ate from garbage cans behind restaurants.

Olivia could see Ruby this way, with her tattoo and pierced nose. She was disappointed in her own suspicious nature. But then she remembered the careful way Ruby had studied her, the tough way she talked, not unlike these kids, who were eating too many sugar doughnuts and saying things like "Fuckin' right, man" and "I'll get that cocksucker."

It was taking forever to get one simple cup of black coffee. While she waited, some kid was robbing her, vandalizing her house.

"Excuse me," Olivia said to the kid closest to her, the one who had looked at her before. "Do you know someone named Ruby? She's got a boyfriend at the college? She's—uh—kind of, you know, pregnant?" Olivia clutched the slippery counter, drunk and scared and dizzy.

They all turned their red-rimmed eyes on her. They smelled like mothballs and sweat and marijuana. None of them answered. But they, too, narrowed their eyes and studied her.

"As a matter of fact," Olivia continued, unable to stop herself, "she *is* pregnant." Her own sour wine breath wafted up to her.

The girl closest to her had on black nail polish; her pupils were dilated, her lips chapped.

By the time the coffee came, Olivia was trembling with fear. What if Ruby was like them, a drugged-out kid who would stop at nothing? A desperate kid. Olivia didn't want her things touched, gone over, examined by this kid. In a shoe box in her closet were pictures of David, a video Rex had made of a sailing trip to Block Island. What if Ruby took those?

She went back out to her car. The coffee burned her tongue as she gulped it, hoping to get clearheaded. She checked behind her to be sure the kids weren't coming out to the parking lot. They weren't. They were still in there, eating, laughing. Olivia drove the rest of the way home too fast, hugging the scenic route's curves, keeping her high beams on the whole way to warn people's pets and bicyclists and joggers that she was there. The cheesecake on the seat beside her was sliding around dangerously but never fell.

Her tires squealed on the gravel of her driveway. Too many lights were on in the house. It looked the way it might if someone had ransacked it, turned everything upside down. Olivia could not remember if she had put those lights on before she left. She could not even at this moment remember Ruby's face. If she had to go to the police, she would be able to describe only the belly—large and round, with a protruding belly button. "If she drinks water fast," she would have to tell them, "the baby kicks like crazy."

Olivia stumbled up the few steps to the door and burst in, ready for anything.

But the kitchen was empty, untouched.

"Ruby?" Olivia called.

No answer.

She made her way through each room, turning off the lights as she went. Everything was in its proper place.

She climbed the creaky steps and called again. "Ruby?"

Still no answer.

But in the doorway of her bedroom, Olivia stopped, slumped against the frame. Ruby was there, in her bed, the hat still perched on her head. She was propped up against all the pillows, reading magazines. She smiled up at Olivia when she saw her there.

"These are great," she said, and held up some chocolate truffles.

They were a gift from Winnie, who had started sending Olivia all the castoffs from the *You!* kitchen.

"You eat weird stuff," Ruby said. "It must cost a fortune, huh? It's good, though. I liked that chutney a lot, with all those chunks of—what, pears or something? I put most of it on the crackers with the cracked pepper. Not bad. I mean, all pepper is cracked, though, right? Unless it's in those little balls like at restaurants when they come over and grind it up for your salad. They always do that in movies." She licked the chocolate from her fingers, then asked, "Are you like a gourmet cook or something?"

Her face was blank and innocent. She was not a robber. She was just a teenager in trouble.

Olivia wasn't sure whether to laugh or cry from relief.

"My friend works for a magazine," she told Ruby.

"Cool," Ruby said. "I love magazines. You don't have to concentrate on them the way you do on books. I'm not a big fan of books."

Realizing its potential power, Olivia added, "She works for *You!*"

"No shit? That is like so cool."

"You must have been starving," Olivia said. The bag of food that Winnie sent was nearly empty.

"I'm always starving. I bet I've gained fifty pounds. No joke. Ben told me I look like I swallowed a pig. He said I'm like a snake. You know, there're these snakes in South America that swallow pigs whole. So they're like skinny on top; then they bulge out in the middle because there's this whole pig inside them, and then they're skinny again." She grinned a toothy, chocolate-smeared grin. "Ben says that's what I look like. One of those snakes."

Ben.

Olivia wondered if she should try to find him next. Or his parents.

"Do you think those snakes kill those pigs first? Before they eat them?" Ruby was asking.

Olivia shrugged. "I don't know. I would think so." Ben's parents should be notified, she decided.

"There is *so* much I don't know. It blows my mind," Ruby said, shaking her head. "And nature," she continued. "Nature totally freaks me out. Like tornadoes and typhoons and hurricanes." She ate another truffle, studying it after each bite. "And babies," she said finally. "The way they get made. I mean, they come out of just a gob of come. A whole baby."

"And an egg," Olivia said stupidly.

"Remember Betsy?" Ruby said suddenly. "My friend who told me that if I didn't do it on the fourteenth day, this *wouldn't* happen? She also thought that you couldn't get pregnant if you did it standing up, because the come just like falls out of you. That's how *she* got pregnant. But Planned Parenthood made her watch this tape that explained stuff, which is supposedly where she got this other misinformation."

Olivia did not know where to begin with Ruby. She sat on the very edge of the bed and tried.

"I don't think Planned Parenthood gives out misinformation," she said.

Ruby nodded. "Uh-huh. Betsy says so."

"What did Betsy do with her baby?"

"Abortion," Ruby said offhandedly, chewing her truffle. "Get this. They ask her if she wants like liquid Valium or if she just wants to do it without anything. And so Betsy says, 'Oh, liquid Valium? Like I drink it?' And they go, 'No, it's an IV.' So Betsy says no thank you, even though she loves a good high for free, like anybody, because her boyfriend paid for everything—the abortion, and even for a year of the pill. So anyway, she doesn't get the IV, because the thing about Betsy is, she is terrified of needles. Once she even bit her doctor when he gave her a shot. And another time, she puked when she got a needle. She asked this lady if it hurt a lot—you know, the abortion—and the lady said there might be a little cramping, so Betsy figures big deal, right? A little cramping's better than having a baby, right? So they don't give her anything, and it hurts so bad, she freaks out. I mean, she really freaks. And she sees everything. She says there wasn't really anything to see, not like a whole baby or anything. But there was something. They called it 'tissue.'"

Ruby's voice went all soft and she said, "That's why I didn't do it. I was too scared." She blew a long stream of air out through her teeth. "Except now I'm more scared. It would have been over, you know? Now it's like there's a baby in me. It is so creepy."

Olivia realized that the girl was gulping back tears.

"And you know what? Betsy did it again. She had another abortion, and this time she got the IV, and she said it was a piece of cake and a good high and everything." Ruby took a breath. "Of course by then, it was way too late for me."

Olivia tried to sort through everything Ruby had said. The girl talked like a speeding train; it was hard to catch it all. There was a mention of drugs as a good thing. There was this Betsy, full of trouble and bad advice—two abortions! And she was probably only fifteen herself. And then there was Ben.

Ruby brightened quickly. "But they'll give you drugs when

you have a baby, so that you don't feel anything. And then it's over and I just move on." She sat back against the pillows, satisfied. "Boy," she said, "you get a lot of phone calls." Ruby read from some writing on the palm of her hand. "Your mother. Amy. Winnie, twice, who wants you to know she's in Rhinebeck in case you need anything. And your friend Janice, who said to tell you that she talked to Pete—"

"Already?" Olivia blurted.

"He's going to call you tomorrow."

Ruby dropped her hand and studied Olivia's face.

"What?" Olivia said.

"Well, your husband didn't call."

Olivia said, "I call him right before I go to sleep. That's our routine."

"That's sweet," Ruby said.

And Olivia was sure the girl knew she was lying.

The clinic Olivia took Ruby to was thirty miles away, a dull drive on a new highway that had gobbled up all the trees and farms that had once lined the road. Ruby looked straight ahead, bored.

"Our apartment in New York," Olivia told her, "is right in the West Village. In an old brownstone, so there's just one apartment on each floor. We're on the third. And in the back we have a terrace where we can barbecue and eat dinner outside. Last summer, I grew lilacs out there." She took a breath and said, "They smelled so lovely."

Ruby only grunted.

Olivia waited, then changed her tack. As a kid, she had taken sailing lessons, and sometimes now she found herself comparing the simple act of human communication to negotiating wind and waves: When do I head straight into the wind? When do I come at something from different sides? Ruby required a lot of tacking.

Olivia thought of the girl watching those houses, writing her bad poetry or her robbery plan. With Ruby, it could be anything.

"Do you know anything about gardening?" Olivia asked Ruby. "It's one of the most relaxing hobbies. Really. Figuring out what blooms when, where to place each plant."

Finally, Ruby looked at her. "I swear to God," she said, "my mother even killed cactus. Like they don't need water or anything, right? They grow in sand, in nothing. They don't need any attention at all, and she still managed to kill them." Ruby stared out the window again. Olivia saw her breathe air onto it and draw something quick before it disappeared.

"It sounds like you miss her," Olivia said, even though she couldn't imagine missing that woman.

"Ha!" Ruby said. "Like I would go grocery shopping with her, and do you know what she bought? Everything frozen. Fish sticks and chicken nuggets and this really bad pizza that is so bad that once when I was really stoned, I actually microwaved part of the box and ate it, and I didn't even know because it tasted just like the crappy pizza. That's the truth. And you know what she said when I told her? I'm like, 'Mom, I just ate a box that tasted practically better than that shit pizza you buy,' and she goes, 'Ruby, I smell pot. I know what pot smells like, and don't try to lie to me.' And I'm like, 'Mom, this is about the junk you put into my system that you call food, okay?'" She looked at Olivia, all serious concern. "I mean, would you ever feed a kid of yours a cardboard box?"

Olivia shook her head. She thought, I would feed your baby organic baby food, the kind that costs way too much money. I would puree vegetables from the farmer's market. I would bake my own bread. I would do whatever you want.

Ruby sighed. "A good mother bakes apples in the autumn and things like peach pie in the summer. Families need stuff like that. They say that my father was famous for his whole-wheat pizza. He used to make it from scratch. Knead it and everything."

"You should see my family," Olivia told her. "My mother used to weigh our food. Six ounces of chicken. Ten green beans. I was the only kid who used to visit my friends and ask for a glass of milk, because she used to give us half skim and half dry milk. She read somewhere that dairy was bad for you."

Ruby brightened. "Really? That's crazy."

"My sister," Olivia continued, "is a workout addict. Her entire wardrobe is Lycra. She's thirty-four years old and she's already had liposuction and a lip job. You know, collagen."

"Like a movie star," Ruby said, impressed.

"Like a crazy person. Now she's talking about getting an eye tuck."

"Really?" Ruby said. "That is so cool. Like fucked up and cool, you know? I heard that Cher even had ribs removed. I don't know if I'll do it when I'm old. Are you going to?"

Olivia glanced at Ruby. Her face was open, her eyes shiny with excitement. And Olivia sighed with relief; she'd gotten her back again.

When they got back from the clinic, Ruby announced she was going for a walk.

"I have been poked and prodded and measured too much," she said, cranky. Her face was too pink from the heat, and she'd put her hair up in a messy knot that revealed one ear pierced from lobe to tip, each hole filled with a cheap stud: turquoise, rhinestone, silver butterfly, something baby blue and something yellow, a silver heart, a silver star—an array of bad earrings.

Olivia tried to convince Ruby to stay. She offered lemonade, iced tea, Popsicles. But Ruby refused.

"I need air," she mumbled.

From the kitchen window, Olivia watched her walk away, head bent, her pocketbook bouncing against her hip. She walked toward the water, where the large houses sat perched above rocks, each with a shaky wooden stairway leading to a small stretch of private beach. What if the girl hurt herself? The thought made Olivia shiver. Those rocks. And the way Ruby waddled so awkwardly. What if she *wanted* to hurt herself? Olivia rubbed her arms, the flesh there covered with goose bumps at the thought. That doctor had been cold, harsh. He had shaken his head in disgust more than once. He had insisted on giving Ruby an AIDS test, tests for gonorrhea and syphilis. Embarrassed, Ruby had closed her eyes and given herself over to him. Was it what she had done with other men, closed her eyes tight and let them do what they wanted?

"Ruby!" Olivia called as she ran out the door. The girl is capable of anything, Olivia thought. And why not?

"Ruby!"

She tripped slightly as she scrambled over some rocks, imagining how difficult it had been for Ruby in her cheap flip-flops and big belly. Olivia thought of her splayed on one of those small beaches. She thought of her looking the way David had, the sheet pulled up to his chin, his expression one of confusion rather than peace. She had imagined his last thought to be something like What the hell is happening here?

Panting, Olivia was just about to call the girl again, when she caught sight of her. She was sitting on the edge of one of the dirt paths that led to the rocky cliffs, staring at the large house across the path, writing in her blue notebook. When she heard Olivia approaching, she looked up sharply.

"I said I needed air," she said.

Olivia had to catch her breath. She inhaled once, then again, erasing that image of David. For months after he died, she would wake up from a dream in which he was alive, but his face was bluish and confused. She had to get rid of that, think of him another way, how he had looked that first time in the doorway of her shop. Olivia did that now, fixed that David in her mind before she turned her attention to Ruby.

She flopped down beside her and said, "What do you write in that thing?"

Ruby considered for a moment, then sighed and pointed to the house. It was enormous, a rambling house with weathered shingles, dark green shutters, and on one side almost all the windows faced the ocean. From here, they could see all the way to Block Island.

"A doctor lives there. Not like the doctor today, a different one. This one is a pediatrician and he loves kids, and he loves his wife, too. Marjorie. She was a debutante. Southern, you know? They have five kids and some of them already are in college, and the oldest daughter is going to get married right here, on the lawn. Under a tent."

The house stared blankly at Olivia. "I don't get it," she said.

Ruby sighed. "They're a family. At Christmas, they only put up white lights and fresh boughs of fir and these big red velvet bows. That's it. She lay down and looked not at the house but up at the sky. "When the kids were young, the father had to leave and go take care of an emergency for one of his patients, but now the younger associates get to do that and the father stays home and makes his special eggnog and carves the turkey and everything."

"Oh," Olivia said softly, as she saw that what Ruby did when she watched houses was to make up families. And maybe to wish herself a spot in each one that she invented.

"They're a nice family," Ruby added. "Good people."

Since Ruby had arrived, Olivia had stopped answering her phone. Instead, she watched as the counter on the answering machine accumulated messages—three, then six, then eight. It rang and rang as Ruby watched for Olivia to pick it up. But she didn't want to. She didn't want to explain Ruby to any of them. Not yet. It would be more important to explain later, after everything with the baby was settled.

But after their slow, silent walk home from the large weathered shingled house, when the phone started to ring, Olivia simply picked it up. Immediately, she wished she hadn't, but it was too late. There was a man on the other end, sounding relieved to hear her curt hello.

"Well, good," the man said, instead of hello. "Now I can tell Janice you're okay. When I told her I'd left you three messages and hadn't heard back, she said that was impossible. She said you hate to go out." The man lowered his voice. "To tell you the truth, she was worried sick."

"Excuse me," Olivia said as she watched Ruby gulp orange juice straight from the container. "Who are you?"

The man chuckled. "Oops. I was so excited to find you alive, and, well, I forgot the appropriate introductions. Pete Lancelotta. Carl's friend."

Olivia almost groaned out loud.

Now Ruby was watching her.

"I'm sort of busy right now," Olivia said.

"Oh, no you don't," Pete said. He chuckled again. "I swore two things to Janice. One: If I found you, I'd let her know you were okay. And B: I would buy you dinner tonight. At Spain. We'll share a paella and some sangria and call it a night."

One and B? Olivia thought, and groaned.

"Not tonight," she said. It was supposed to be Ruby's last night here. Unless Olivia convinced her to stay until the baby came. Unless she convinced her to *give* her the baby.

Ruby had a way of staring at Olivia that was almost creepy. Olivia turned her back to Ruby, but she still felt her eyes on her.

Another chuckle. Olivia couldn't stand chuckling. A nervous habit, maybe, but still.

"This is not optional," Pete was saying. "I promised Janice." Then he added, "Look, if we can't stand each other, then at least our duty to Janice is done. Right?"

Olivia wanted to tell him she had no duty to Janice. The day she walked in front of three hundred people as a bridesmaid in emerald green taffeta with French curls that rivaled Marie Antoinette's was the day she'd paid off any debt to Janice.

But Pete said, "See you at seven," and hung up before she could argue.

There was Ruby, waiting. Olivia had planned a seduction of sorts—dinner out, a movie, an effort at camaraderie that would make it impossible for the girl to refuse Olivia's offer: stay here until you have the baby. Then let me adopt the baby. She would make her strongest pitch of all: I am a good person, too. I will give this baby a family.

But now Pete Lancelotta was coming at seven and there was no time for Olivia's grand plans.

"Going somewhere?" Ruby said, raising her eyebrows.

"No. Yes." Olivia took a breath. "Look," she said, "I want you to stay here. I'll do all the things you need, make you good food and make sure you're comfortable. Whatever it is you need. I want you to stay until you have the baby."

They both knew how long that was: The doctor had told them Ruby was twenty-eight weeks pregnant. "I'd estimate your due date at"—he'd swung a little dial around, matching up lines and numbers, then looked up, grinning—"Labor Day. Ironic, huh?"

Olivia took a deep breath. "And if you're going to stay here for three months, we've got to come clean with each other. About Ben. And everything." Asking for the baby was harder than she'd imagined. How do you ask someone for something like that?

Ruby leaned against the wall. Olivia thought, If it wasn't for her stomach being so big, she'd look cocky standing there like that—head tilted up, shoulders pushed back, legs apart.

"Okay," Ruby said. "You go first."

It's best to just say it, Olivia decided, and did. "My husband," she began. The words were scratchy in her throat, like broken glass, like threads of fiberglass. "He's not away," she said. "He's dead. He died."

"So your husband is dead," Ruby said flatly, "and you want my baby."

This startled Olivia. It was true; she did want that baby. But wouldn't a person who thought David was in New York on business say something else? Wouldn't a person be surprised he was, in fact, dead?

Ruby's eyes flickered, just for an instant, toward the wall covered with fragments of Olivia's life. How long has she known? Olivia wondered. And she realized that she could not toy with this girl. Ruby was too smart. Maybe smarter than Olivia.

"Yes. I want your baby," Olivia said. "Yes."

Ruby waited, expressionless.

"You don't want it," Olivia said. "You said so yourself." She tried not to sound too desperate.

"Sometimes I do," Ruby said.

"But you always say—"

"I say I'm scared. I say I wish I wasn't knocked up. But I mean, this baby moves around inside me. You know what happened this morning? He got the hiccups. I felt them, little gasps of air."

Now it was Olivia who waited.

"I think I could make this kid something really great. Like my mother had all these opportunities to make a real family for me, but she couldn't get her act together." Ruby's hands rested for an instant on her stomach. "I'm different from her. I could do so much."

Olivia's heart was pounding hard enough to send blood pulsing in her temples. Ruby is just a kid, she thought. She shouldn't have this baby. I should. I need someone to love more than Ruby does.

Ruby will have other chances. She couldn't say the same for herself.

"On the other hand," Ruby said, slumping into a chair, "sometimes I don't. Most of the time. In Home Ec, they made us carry around an egg for like three days. We always had to watch this egg. We couldn't put it down. We couldn't break it. We had to take care of it. Like a baby."

No wonder this kid's pregnant, Olivia thought. What kind of teaching is that? An egg. Jesus.

"I hated that stupid egg," Ruby said.

And when she said it, Olivia felt, for the first time in months, hope.

"Why don't you stay and we'll see how you feel when the time comes," Olivia said, forcing her voice into steadiness. There were counselors and professional people who would urge Ruby to give this baby to Olivia. She thought of Ellen, the faceless lawyer whom she'd spoken with on the phone yesterday. Ellen would be on her side. Things were stacked in her favor.

"If I stay here and you take me to that doctor and feed me and stuff like that and then I keep the baby, you can't do anything about it," Ruby said.

"Right," Olivia told her. But what she knew was that Ruby would never keep this baby. "I hated that stupid egg," she'd said.

Pete Lancelotta was balder than balding, heavier than big, with a beard. Olivia never liked facial hair much, except for the scratchy feel of David's face on weekends when he didn't shave. She used to like how he would rub his cheek on the inside of her thigh. That was the only facial hair Olivia liked. Also, Pete smoked. He'll be dead in twenty years, Olivia thought. Once a widow was plenty for her, thank you.

But the paella was good, overflowing with fish and lobster and clams and sausage and chicken. It was as if Olivia hadn't eaten seafood in years; the salty taste almost excited her.

"Jeez," Pete said, watching her. "You can really eat."

Time was moving differently for Olivia. Instead of the plodding, slow-motion feeling of these last months, she felt something pulling her forward, toward something she was not yet ready even to think of as a future. But she could think: In twelve weeks, I will have a baby. And when she thought it, she could see past those twelve weeks, to some point where Ruby was gone and she, Olivia, was holding an infant. It was cooler and drier in that future. The long, hot summer was over, and the tips of leaves had turned color. Seeing that made her lighter, as if she might float away like a balloon that had been let go. Or like that puff of smoke she'd imagined David had become. The sangria, too sweet, clung to Olivia's teeth and tongue. Delicious.

Since she would never fall in love with this man, Olivia even entertained the thought of having sex with him. Lately, she'd begun to think of it again, and thinking of it made her wet enough to put her own fingers there between her legs, to bring herself some pleasure. Hadn't Winnie been urging her to find someone for that kind of companionship at least? "You're a widow," Winnie had told her, "not a nun." Olivia tried to think of Pete naked, inside her, and the image made her want to laugh and cry at the same time.

It made her want to leave. She stood, abruptly, foolish in her backless summer dress and the sandals she'd found in the closet, left there since last summer. When she'd found them, fine strands of cat hair stuck to the straps, and she didn't have the heart to wipe them away.

On the curvy silent ride back to her house, Olivia knew that Pete Lancelotta was absolutely the wrong man for her. He had lived in Rhode Island his whole life, had only journeyed as far as Montreal to see an Expos game once. He didn't like to read.

There was the smoking and the weight, making him a candidate for horrible things: stroke, heart attack, worse. But she had Ruby and the baby. She felt generous and risky and optimistic. So when they pulled up to her house and he asked her if she'd see him again, Olivia said, "Sure, why not?" His quick scratchy kiss was almost pleasant, but not quite.

She'd been disappointed to see the door to Ruby's room closed—she had moved a cot into the nursery that afternoon for her. Olivia had half-expected to tell her all about the date. And now, alone, in her own bed, Olivia was struck by a sadness so extreme that she got jittery. She felt as if she could jump right out of her skin. And into what? she wondered. Some other form, like David?

It was not that she wanted to be with Pete Lancelotta. In fact, Olivia was certain that she did not. But she remembered how often she'd gone on dates with men before David—B.D.—that were fun and without potential but somehow made her aware of all the men out there with potential. Was that it? Was that what was making her so nervous? If she could have a kind of fun with one man who wasn't her type, what would happen if she met a man who was her type?

"And then what, Pal?" Olivia said out loud. She thought of that morning when he'd wanted to make love and she'd refused. She had sent him to his death, jogging down that road when he should have been with her. Would it always come to that, her last act with her husband, her rolling away from him? She did not even have a final image of him. She had not bothered to watch him go.

Olivia paced.

She went downstairs to get a glass of wine. She decided to take one of the pills that Winnie had given her months ago, back in winter, a pill that Winnie had told her would help take the edge off things. In bed, she drank the wine and took the pill—thought fleetingly of Karen Ann Quinlan and wondered if she would want that, to be nowhere, suspended between life and death. Olivia decided no, she wanted to be here after all. But she had already taken the pill; there was nothing to do about it. Even now the effects of it were grabbing at her; the room and everything in it floated nicely around her. She did something her mother had advised her to try: "When you're feeling bad, try to remember all the good things you still have."

Olivia thought of Ruby sleeping across the hall. She thought of that baby hiccuping inside her.

That baby could be hers.

She held tight to that thought, brought it with her into a restless sleep. Olivia dreamed of sex, not the act so much as the sounds of it: squeaky bedsprings and stifled groans and ragged breaths. She dreamed of footsteps and giggles and falling out of windows.

When she woke up, slightly hungover and headachy, the house was still, too quiet. Olivia had one thought: Something is wrong. When she got shakily out of bed, the first thing she saw was that her jewelry box, the one that held her passport and pearls, the one that held David's voice, was gone. She ran from the room on quivering legs, calling to Ruby, wondering what else had been taken.

"Ruby!" Olivia called in a hoarse voice. "Ruby, we've been robbed."

It wasn't until she flung open the door to Ruby's room that the truth of what had happened hit Olivia. *They* hadn't been robbed; *she'd* been robbed. Ruby was gone, and she had taken everything with her.

chapter four

Karma Is a Boomerang

That morning that she discovered Ruby gone, Olivia drove straight from her house to the college. She didn't realize until she was almost there that she still had on her white cotton nightgown. "Underwear as outerwear," Winnie would say. She could be counted on for tips like that. And counted on to steal Olivia's life, the one she should be living at this very moment instead of chasing after a horrible thieving kid. Maybe this was one of the signs the woman from the occult store was talking about; maybe genetically this baby would grow into a teenager who stole things. Maybe Olivia should just turn around and forget the whole thing.

But the big granite sign with the college's seal gleaming gold in the sunlight loomed before her and Olivia turned onto the campus. She couldn't go back to that in-between life. She had to find the girl and get that baby. She had to reclaim the new life she'd imagined for herself, omens or no omens. The school had lots of trees and ivy-covered buildings and winding roads. David and Olivia had gone to a dance performance there and a James Dean movie festival, but she didn't really know the campus well, so it was by sheer coincidence that the road Olivia turned down was the one where all the fraternities were located. Where else could Ruby have gone except back to the subterranean safety of one of these houses? Olivia would walk from door to door, looking for Ruby, not stopping until she found her.

Olivia parked, then threw on her jeans jacket over her nightgown. Feeling like an overgrown Nancy Drew, she found herself thinking about Winnie again. Winnie would be strangely pleased by the fact that barefoot, Olivia was snooping around college fraternities this early in the morning, wearing her white cotton nightgown and the same jeans jacket she had owned since college. Underwear as outerwear, Olivia thought again. Maybe these kids would find her amazingly hip. Maybe they would hand Ruby over to her without a fight.

It was the same at every house—and there were more than Olivia had thought, a dozen or more, all big and white, with Greek letters hanging on their fronts. No one, none of the sleepy-eyed, musty-smelling boys who leaned in the doorways, staring out at her, had heard of a Ben or a Ruby. One said there was a Ben there, but he was not from New York and did not work at a camp upstate; in fact, he lived in Westerly—another seaside town right in Rhode Island—and worked with his father at the boatyard. All of the boys were sorry they couldn't help. Some offered her a soda; it had gotten very hot and they could see how Olivia was sweating in the heavy jeans jacket. One offered her a yearbook to look at. Happy to step into the cool basement, she accepted. But she did not know whom she was actually looking for. None of the faces meant anything to her.

This boy, the one who showed her the yearbook, worried that somehow drugs were involved. He told her that a fraternity had been kicked off campus for dealing drugs. The boy's face, smooth and tanned and so young, almost broke Olivia's heart. His fraternity, he told Olivia earnestly, was a good one. They sang at a nursing home at Christmastime. They cleaned up the beaches at season's end. Good kids, he insisted.

"Why do you need these folks?" he asked finally, finished with his pitch.

At first, Olivia considered lying: Ruby was her daughter. She had run away and her family wanted her back. But Olivia was too hot and angry and weary to shape the lie convincingly. Besides, the boy's innocence disturbed her. Standing there with him, Olivia could not reach far enough back to remember herself this way—open and innocent. Trusting. She actually started to hate the boy for all those qualities he possessed that she had lost.

He grew impatient, glancing over his shoulder into the cool darkness of the fraternity house.

"So," he said, shifting his weight from foot to foot in an annoying hop.

Olivia told him everything. About her great love story and their City Hall wedding, about how she'd sent him off that morning so she could sleep and how he'd died, that her best friend had eloped and Ruby had robbed her. She told him about the answering-machine tape, how that was gone now, too.

His eyes, a muddy blue, opened wide with surprise. He could not believe that life could be so bad, that husbands could be killed jogging, that a young girl could rob the woman who had taken her in. For a moment, Olivia was sorry she'd told him the truth;

she felt like she had taken something from him, too, robbed him. But then, as she handed the heavy yearbook back to him, she was glad she'd told him. Maybe he wouldn't be so foolish to think that life would always be beer parties and cramming for tests and trying to get laid. He knew something important now.

She wished him luck, then walked away quickly from the look that spread across his young innocent face. It could be a look of horror at what happened to her. But Olivia was afraid it was something else, something worse. She was afraid that the boy pitied her, a woman in her nightgown whose husband was dead, who had been robbed by a girl she'd been stupid enough to trust.

"It will make you forget your troubles for a while," her sister, Amy, had promised. "Reading takes your mind off things." If Olivia still wrote everyone's advice on her thigh, Amy's would take up a lot of room. "Book clubs feed your mind and soul," Amy'd said. The she reminded Olivia of how in second grade she had read every Nancy Drew book, in order, right up to *The Mystery of the Ninety-Nine Steps.* It was true that until David died, Olivia read a book a week. Good books, the kind the *New York Times* reviewed. And that since then, she'd read nothing except true-crime paperbacks, savoring the grisly details of mutilated bodies hidden in cellars and the tricks killers used to lure their victims into their cars.

When Olivia climbed the wooden stairs to Amy's condo that night, she was sure that nothing was worse than a book club that consisted of Amy, who used to boast that the last book she'd read was *To Kill a Mockingbird* back in ninth grade, and three other divorced women. Nothing except getting robbed by a fucking juvenile delinquent, which was the term Olivia had settled on by the time she'd returned home that afternoon.

Amy's condo was new, built across the street from the beach

but sitting right on the scenic route. Occasionally, there was the sound of waves or a foghorn, but mostly it was just traffic noises that filtered inside. The stairs leading to Amy's had open spaces between them, so that Olivia felt as if she might fall through at any moment.

She saw her sister and two other women through the sliding glass door that led to a small terrace. They were inside, putting food on the table. Olivia paused, watching. The women were all laughing. They took the time to style their hair, to put on lipstick, to choose what they wore—jewelry and sundresses and headbands. Olivia had put on the same backless dress and sandals covered with cat hair that she'd worn out to dinner with Pete Lancelotta. Everything about her and coming here felt so wrong that Olivia turned around and began to go back down the stairs.

But it was too late. The sliding glass door slid open and Amy said, "No way. You're coming inside and you're going to have fun."

"You know, Amy," Olivia said, "I've had a really shitty day."

"Me, too. My darling ex-husband and his bimbo girlfriend want to take Matthew to the Galápagos fucking Islands to watch turtles hatch. And P.S., they'll be getting married while they're there." Amy pointed overhead. "The bug zapper's dead," she said. "Come in so I can close the door."

Obediently, Olivia followed, but her legs felt like tree trunks, heavy and unwilling to be uprooted.

Inside, Amy introduced the other two women: Pam, who not only sounded like Snow White but looked so much like Snow White that Olivia found herself staring at her, and Jill, who was tall and lean and too sexy—pouty full lips and a tousled shag haircut, thin hips and large breasts. Olivia looked from them to her sister, who wore her usual Lycra to show off her overly worked-out body, and thought, I don't belong here. Amy was explaining that the other woman, Mimi, was always late.

Amy handed her a glass of white wine and, as if she had read Olivia's mind, said, "I'm glad you came, sis."

Snow White shook her head. "Amy told us what happened."

For an instant, Olivia thought she meant about Ruby, about having everything stolen. But then she realized that of course the woman was talking about David.

They led her into the living room with its black-lacquer furniture and Erté prints, the tiny white brick fireplace with its Duraflame log. Olivia settled into a mauve suede chair.

"Sometimes," Snow White said in a near whisper, "I think I would have preferred it if Phillip had died."

Amy, who always found it difficult to sit and stay seated, as if she had to do aerobics constantly, jumped to her feet. "I said the same thing. I mean, being left for a bimbo completely out of the blue is so humiliating."

Snow White nodded. "It's like none of it meant anything. Twelve years, three kids—"

"And you had those miscarriages," sexy Jill said, taking a slow puff on a cigarette. She looked at Olivia. "You have no idea what she's been through."

"And he leaves me for a woman he met on business in Finland."

"A Finn!" Amy said, as if it were the craziest thing possible.

"Her name is Hickie," Snow White said. "You know. Like a hickey? And the worst part is, he's moved there."

"To Finland!" Amy said.

"And he wants the kids to go to Finland to visit him four times a year." She leaned back, weary, disgusted.

Jill leaned forward. "Don't they believe in trolls there?"

She seemed to be asking Olivia this. "I have no idea," Olivia said. *Trolls!* She looked around for some books; weren't they going to talk about *The Celestine Prophecy?* But there was nothing except *People* magazines fanned out on the glass coffee table.

Amy hopped around in front of Olivia. "Jill's story is even worse," she said.

"My ex-husband," Jill said, stretching each word out carefully, "is a fucking faggot."

"He fucks men!" Amy said.

"I know what a faggot is," Olivia snapped at Amy. She sank into the suede chair, realizing what her sister was up to: proving that Olivia wasn't the only one with a terrible story to tell. But Olivia knew that already. She couldn't imagine anything worse than sharing sad stories, trading regrets.

They were all looking at her, the sympathy in their eyes enough to make Olivia puke.

Olivia said, "I honestly don't care what happened to you and your marriages. Dead is worse."

The other women looked at her, round-eyed. She was not like them. She had been to a place none of them had ever been.

"Dead is worse," she said again. "Trust me."

After dinner and wine and cigarettes, the talk finally turned to the book. Olivia hadn't read it. The size alone wore her out. Still, she tried to listen to the discussion, but it was useless. Olivia had drunk too much wine—again. She tried to remember those questions you're supposed to ask yourself to determine if you should go to AA. But the only one she could think of was: Do you ever drink alone? What a joke; she did everything alone.

When she tuned back in, Snow White was saying "Do you think Mimi's okay? She isn't here and it's so late."

"And she has dessert," Jill said.

"Cheesecake," Amy added. "She always brings cheesecake."

Snow White said, "Whose turn is it to choose the next book?" Turning to Olivia, she added, "We take turns choosing the book every month."

Olivia looked around. The book discussion was over already?

"Like I chose *Men Are from Mars, Women Are from Venus*," Snow White said.

"Which sucked," Jill said.

"*She* chose a book about sex abuse that was so depressing!"

"Bastard Out of Carolina," Jill said to Olivia, as if somehow they were on the same wavelength. "Didn't it win the Pulitzer Prize or something?"

"I'm not sure," Olivia said. Why did this woman think she and Olivia were so alike? Is this what I've become? Olivia wondered. A comrade in abandoned womanhood? Someone who reads the book review alone at night, wears sexy clothes to the supermarket, is desperately needy?

Snow White continued, "And Amy had us read *Prozac Nation*, which was a real eye-opener."

"So now we're all on Prozac," Jill said to Olivia in that same confidante's voice.

"What do you like to read?" Snow White asked Olivia.

Olivia wanted to tell them about Ted Bundy and Charles Manson and some woman in Washington State who tried to kill her daughters because she loved a man who didn't want children. But she knew that if she opened her mouth to speak, she would cry instead. She would cry because these women were all friends and she had lost her best friend to love and domesticity, because the only title that she could come up with was *Drinking: A Love Story* and that seemed like the only safe love story there was; because they had ex-husbands, at least, in Providence, in Finland—remarried or gay, they were out there. These women could touch them, call them, scream at them, look at them, hate them, and Olivia had lost the last piece of David, his voice, coiled tightly in plastic, safe and cozy as when they slept side by side spoon-fashion.

Crying had become so second nature to her that Olivia did not realize that she was indeed crying until Amy was by her side, stroking her hair and explaining with such hopelessness in her voice, Olivia cried even harder. "She just does this sometimes," Amy said. "Out of the blue."

The sliding glass door opened noisily, and a woman—Mimi, Olivia assumed—burst in. She was short and squat—like a Jeep, Olivia thought—with a head full of blond ringlets and a floral baby-doll dress. Unlike the others, who were tanned and well toned, Mimi had very white skin that was soft and unmuscled. Olivia decided she was more like a woman made of dough than a Jeep. A Pillsbury dough woman, a Michelin baby all grown up. She was also out of breath.

"You're not going to believe this," she said, gasping. "I was robbed."

"I was, too!" Olivia blurted, jumping to her feet.

"You were?" Amy said. "When?"

Even though Amy had asked Olivia, Mimi answered.

"This afternoon. I went to get the cheesecake"—and here Olivia saw all of the others sneak a glance at each other, but Mimi didn't seem to notice—"and when I got back, everything was gone."

"Everything?" Snow White asked. "Like what?"

"You name it! Both TVs, the VCR, the stereo. And get this, selected CDs. They only took certain ones. They left all the classical and jazz and pretty much took everything else." Her bottom lip quivered as she took a deep breath. "They took my Beatles *Love Songs* album. And you know that one—'In My Life'? That was the song from our wedding and the song we played when Trey was being born. I mean, it was our defining song."

Olivia closed her eyes to try to regain her own composure. It wouldn't do to break down now, what with Mimi needing solace of her own. But she couldn't stop thinking of her tape, discarded somewhere. She imagined it in the sand, seagulls uncoiling it. She imagined it tossed carelessly into a Dumpster beside garbage.

Worse, she imagined Ruby in a dark basement with her loser friends, playing it and laughing. She could hear her: Hey, a dead guy's voice. Cool.

"The weirdest thing," Mimi was saying, "and this is what has me so upset—they took my wedding gown. I mean, it's useless, right? It only means something to me. Not to Frank, that's for sure. Just me. I mean, you can't sell it or anything. It sat in the same dry cleaner's bag since 1981, for Christ's sake. You know?"

Mimi was crying now, and Olivia wondered if that was what always happened here, if it was a chance to cry with someone instead of by yourself, the way you usually did.

Amy let the other women console Mimi. She took Olivia by the elbow and pushed her into the galley kitchen.

"God," Olivia said, forcing a laugh. "Thanks for the rescue. I feel like I'm on *Geraldo* or something. 'Women Who Got Left Behind.'"

Amy refused even to smile. Or to let go of Olivia's arm.

"Would you believe 'Women Who Got Robbed'?" Olivia asked.

"What do you mean you were robbed?" she said, not letting go of Olivia's arm. "When?"

"Last night. This morning. I don't know. While I was asleep." Even now that the girl had taken everything from her, she still wanted Ruby to be a secret.

Amy was waiting for more, so Olivia said, "I woke up and everything was gone."

This was exactly what Mimi had said, and it felt right to Olivia, until Amy said, "You didn't have anything to take. Your house is basically empty."

With great clarity Olivia remembered what was on that answering machine tape: "Hello, you've reached the summer cottage of Olivia and David. We're outside playing croquet right now, but leave your name and our butler will get back to you." It had been funny, she remembered. A joke for Rex, who liked to tease them about having bought a summer house. In fact, David had ended the message with: "Unless this is Rex. Then our butler's butler will call you."

"Olivia?" Amy said, and by the way she said it, Olivia realized her sister had been trying to get her attention.

"I had some jewelry and stuff."

Amy's face went all sad. "Like your wedding ring?"

"And Grandma's pearls."

Amy, so much shorter than Olivia, tried to hug her, but it felt awkward, her head pressed into Olivia's breasts and their legs knocking together.

When they got back into the living room, Mimi had stopped crying. "This is so embarrassing," she said. "Trey," she began, then, to Olivia, added, "That's my son."

"He's a JD," Jill said.

Amy jumped in. "A juvenile delinquent. Ever since the divorce."

Jill took over. This time, when Olivia could relate, Jill avoided meeting her eyes. "There's a group of kids who are real trouble. High school kids. They run away from home and live in abandoned houses here at the beach or at the college in summer. And basically, they rob people. Break into houses and wipe them out. Trey has been caught twice already. He runs away for a couple weeks, until Mimi finds him and brings him back."

"Where do these kids hang out?" Olivia asked. She thought of Ruby sitting at her kitchen table that day. She thought of how long her house had sat empty, inviting these kids, these J fucking Ds in. She thought about how stupid she was. Even as she waited for their answer, she was getting up to leave.

"At the A&W past the college," someone said.

"Olivia," Amy said, following her, "these are not nice kids. Don't go down there thinking you can get your stuff back or anything crazy like that."

But Olivia could not stop to explain. Ruby's face floated in front of her, sure and smart-assed. Olivia held that image, and she let it lead her as she ran now down the wooden steps toward her car.

There was something creepy about this part of Rhode Island. Too far from the beach, too far from the orchards and chicken farms in the western part of the state, too far from the city or the suburbs, and too far from the college to be quaint or historic. It was, Olivia thought, nowhere. The road was dark and straight. Here and there, behind the trees that lined it, were some new housing developments, like Janice's, and a few older ones, like Ruby's parents'. There were also trailer parks and the remnants of communes. Then, out of nowhere, the old A & W, its sign slowly spinning, bright white and orange.

The parking lot was full of dented cars with rusty paint jobs and souped-up cars that sat on oversized fat wheels. In the darker corner of the parking lot, a group of teenagers sat around on hoods of cars, or on the asphalt itself. Amy was right—these were not nice kids. The boys had greasy long hair that reminded Olivia of the bad boys when she was in high school in the seventies. Some tied it back in loose ponytails. They wore faded jeans jackets, leather vests, tight jeans stained with grease. Their skin looked sickly, too white.

The girls were either waiflike, skinny and pale, with tangled long hair and wide eyes, or tough-looking, all large breasts and wide hips and too much makeup. Olivia watched them from the safety of the brighter area near the building. She didn't see Ruby among them. In a way, Olivia wanted this to be a dead end. But there was only one way to find out. Olivia forced herself from her car, toward the group at the far end of the lot. She felt, walking toward them, as if she were in a Stephen King novel, that at any moment some sort of inhuman force would leap out at her. She remembered why she'd stopped reading Stephen King novels; they scared the hell out of her.

They all watched her approach. Olivia wished she recognized the music that was coming from one of the cars. Familiar music would soothe her. But this—a woman shouting above an electric guitar—was even more unsettling than the fact that these kids, up close, looked like they might have guns or switchblades. They looked stoned. They looked angry.

"I'm looking for a pregnant girl with reddish brown hair and freckles," she said, stopping in front of them, placing one hand on her hip. And she was pleased by how her voice sounded—strong and tough.

None of them answered.

A girl—one of the waifs—lay flat on her back on the asphalt, her eyes half-opened, a thin line of drool at the corners of her mouth. Before she asked the crowd if the girl needed help, Olivia watched the girl until she was certain she was breathing.

They all laughed at the question.

Olivia thought she heard raccoons in the dark area behind the teenagers. But it was two kids, rooting around in the trash bin, handing half-eaten french fries and bits of hamburger buns to the others.

The girl on the asphalt made a strange sound, a kind of laugh, and Olivia realized she was simply stoned, so out of it that she could not hold herself upright.

"Look," Olivia said, wanting nothing more than to get the hell out of there, "this girl, Ruby, she has something of mine and I want it back. She can keep everything else."

"Gee, lady," one of the big girls said, "we don't know no pregnant teenagers."

"No, ma'am," another one said. "We practice safe sex."

"We practice abstinence," still another one added, and everyone laughed.

She wanted to be forceful and threatening. But these kids didn't care about her. About anything, she supposed.

"If you see her," Olivia said, "tell her Olivia is looking for her."

"Oh, yes, ma'am," one of them said from the darkness. "You bet."

They were still laughing—even the girl on the asphalt was laughing in an odd stoned way—when Olivia turned her back on them. Someone came running up behind her, and Olivia let out a little yelp, turning around fast to face off whoever it was. But it was just one of the waifs, a little skinny girl who didn't seem to be more than thirteen.

"They're bad, aren't they?" the girl said. She wore a gauze dress with a soft floral print that Olivia liked—pale blue and orange flowers floating on an off-white background. Still, she turned her back on the girl and kept walking. The girl hurried to catch up and walk beside her.

"That girl on the ground," she said to Olivia, her voice squeaky. "She did crack for the first time and it knocked her down. That's what it does the first time."

Olivia glanced over her shoulder and saw the girl getting shakily to her feet.

She slowed down and looked at this girl beside her.

"Crack?" she said, feeling stupid. She remembered her mother's horror at discovering she was smoking pot in college. "Marijuana?" her mother had gasped.

"Oh," the girl said, shaking her head, "they're bad."

"You should stay away from them," Olivia told her. "You should go home." She glanced back again and saw the girl leaning against two of the boys. For an instant, Olivia wished she were that girl, numb and oblivious, here but not here.

"I know who you're looking for," the girl said. She walked right in front of Olivia, forcing her to stop. "Ruby."

Olivia swallowed hard. Her heart raced. Ruby, Ruby, she thought, but she didn't want the girl to see how important this was to her. So she said, "What about her?" as casually as she could muster.

"I can find her for you," the girl said, and Olivia saw in the brighter light that the girl was not sweet or innocent or any of the things her little flowered dress and squeaky voice made you think.

"Okay," Olivia said.

"Twenty bucks," the girl said.

Olivia pushed past her. "Forget it," she said.

But the girl didn't leave. She walked right beside Olivia, matching her step for step.

"Look, kid," Olivia said, weary now, "just leave me alone. Okay?"

They had reached the car by then, and Olivia wanted nothing more than to be inside it, heading home. The girl said, "I guess you don't want to find her very bad."

Olivia opened the door, climbed in. "Oh," she said, "I'll find her."

The girl stood under the restaurant lights, looking small and, from this distance, young again. The lights shone right through the thin fabric of her dress. She didn't have on any underwear; Olivia saw her flat breasts, dark nipples, a thatch of blond pubic hair. She needs a flesh-colored body suit under there, Olivia thought, turning the car toward the road. That's what she used to wear under a dress she had like that. She stepped on the brake, then sat there, watching the girl in the rearview mirror.

"Shit," Olivia said, pushing the shift in reverse. That was *her* dress the girl was wearing.

Her tires squealed when she turned around and jerked into the same spot she had just left.

"I'll give you ten," Olivia said.

The girl came to the car and held out her hand. When Olivia counted ten dollars into it—two dollars' worth of change she had to scrounge around the floor and in her pockets for—the girl smiled and pointed at the restaurant.

"What?" Olivia said, thinking that this kid better not fuck with her.

The girl just pointed again.

Then she set off in a full run back to the far corner of the parking lot.

Olivia got out of the car, shielding her eyes from the bright restaurant light reflecting off the wide glass window. Inside, there were skinny men in baggy clothes sitting at the counter. And there, in one of the bright orange booths, pregnant and laughing, sat Ruby. Olivia pressed her face to the plate-glass window, looked right in Ruby's face. Ruby stopped laughing and looked her right in the eye.

Olivia moved forward, opened the door, and stepped inside. She was hit in the face with the overwhelming smell of grease and a blast of cold air-conditioned air; she had not realized until that moment that the humidity that was forecasted for that night had actually arrived. She had not realized how sticky she was until the cold air sent goose bumps up her arms.

Moving toward Ruby, Olivia remembered something the girl had told her on their ride to the clinic: "Karma is a boomerang," she said. "You do something bad, it comes right back at you."

Here I am, Olivia thought, coming right back at you.

Ruby was waving at her, happily.

"What a surprise," she said, practically chirping.

The girl had nerve. "Brass balls," David would have said. She sat there, smiling and waving and chirping at the person she'd robbed less than twenty-four hours earlier.

"I know why you're here," Ruby said.

Olivia was right in her face now, no plate glass between them. She could smell her, she was so close, a smell of smoke and sweat and—Olivia flinched—sex. The boy she was sitting with—Ben, maybe?—had the flat stoned look of those kids in the parking lot. Between them on the bright orange table were onion rings, french fries, empty packets of catsup, and grease-splattered wrappers.

Despite the cold air in there, heat rose in Olivia; she felt her face flush, felt the hot grip of anger tear through her.

"You little shit," she hissed.

She had Ruby's fleshy freckled arm in her hand and she gripped her so hard that she knew there would be bruises when she let go. Olivia tugged Ruby right out of the tight booth. When Ruby was on her feet, Olivia recognized the Japanese baseball shirt she wore, and the khaki drawstring shorts: They were David's.

"Those are his clothes, you stealing little shit," Olivia said, and then she was tearing at the clothes, at the girl. She felt the sweaty tangle of Ruby's hair in her fingers, the familiar way those clothes felt under her hands. How she had struggled to untie those shorts, to pull them off David and release his penis to her waiting body. "You fucking shit," she said, and started to drag Ruby out of there, and the girl, too pregnant to slip from her grasp, let herself be pulled away, into the hot night air.

Outside, Ruby managed to free herself. She didn't run. She just stood under the fluorescent lights and tried to pull herself together—straighten the shirt, smooth her hair, wipe her face. Olivia heard her own ragged breath. She could kill this kid. She really could.

Ruby held her hands up in front of her face.

"Look," she said. "Okay. Jesus. Calm down."

It was those words—"Calm down"—that sent Olivia at Ruby like a football player tackling an opponent. She slammed into her, and the two of them tumbled to the ground, awkwardly flailing at each other, rolling around on the hot asphalt. Ruby hit back, but her blows were so ineffective, they seemed almost comical.

Thinking this, how silly Ruby's soft punches were, Olivia was struck by how comical all of it was—the eerie lights, the shabby A&W, the pregnant girl wearing Olivia's dead husband's clothes, and Olivia herself, rolling around like this, scraping her knuckles against the gravel and tasting the iron tang of blood in her mouth—and so Olivia stopped hitting and rolling and settled instead into an awkward hug, lying spoon-fashion with this girl, this thief, this JD. At last, their breathing slowed to a normal intake of air. That was when Olivia realized that she was still holding on to Ruby, holding on tight, not about to let go.

chapter five

Who Could Hang a Name on You?

Olivia sat on the rocks above the ocean, the rocks where college kids came to watch storms, where every year at least one got swept away by a wave. Beside her sat Ruby. Olivia did not want to take Ruby back into her home. Not yet. She knew that she should have taken her to the police. She should have pressed charges. But she could not do it. She wanted something from the girl, something big, and important: that baby Ruby had inside her. Olivia could not let it go. Instead, she let good judgment and common sense go. Instead, she had brought Ruby here.

They sat on the rocks and drank Coffee Coolattas from

Dunkin' Donuts. "This is awesome," Ruby had told Olivia at the drive-through window. But it wasn't; it was too sweet for Olivia.

"Isn't this just the yummiest thing you've ever had?" Ruby said happily.

She slurped the last of her Coffee Coolatta, then stretched out on the rocks as if she was about to take a nap. She closed her eyes, squirmed around until she found the most comfortable position.

Olivia tried to shape her demands, but before she could say anything, Ruby said, "You know how Pooh says, 'I have a rumbley in my tummbly?' That's what I have." She opened her eyes, squinting up at Olivia. "You know. Winnie-the-Pooh. When I was a kid, that's all I wanted. Pooh sheets and jelly that came in a Pooh glass, but my mother was always like, "Oh sure, Ruby, let's give Walt Disney money to advertise for him. That makes a lot of sense. He should pay us to wear clothes with Pooh or Peter Pan or whoever.'" Ruby sighed and closed her eyes again. "I guess she was right. But I want my kid to have like a huge stuffed Pooh. And Tigger—"

"This isn't exactly what I wanted to discuss," Olivia said.

Ruby propped herself up on her elbows. "You going to drink that?" she said, pointing to Olivia's Coffee Coolatta. "Because it's melting and it's not good melted. You need to drink it when it's all slushy."

"Here," Olivia said.

Ruby grinned and took a big swallow, then winced immediately. "Oh," she said. "A cold headache. Man, I hate those. I told you I hate pain, remember?"

"Look," Olivia said, "the thing is, I want my stuff."

"Your stuff is gone," Ruby said. "Really, I'm sorry. I am. But I can't undo it."

The heat was becoming oppressive. But up on these rocks, there was something like a breeze, and the air from the ocean was clean and soothing.

"I want it back," Olivia told her. She was surprised that actually she didn't want it back. Not really. The image of that girl in her dress, taking her money, kept Olivia from wanting any of it. Except the tape. That was her most valuable possession. But she trusted Ruby so little that she worried if she told her the thing she most wanted returned, it would be the thing she was least likely to get.

"To tell you the truth," Ruby said, "I was surprised how little you actually had. I mean, no offense, but it was pretty slim pickings. I kept the guy clothes because, let's face it, I'm a fucking whale and nothing fits me anymore. Except his clothes. I like the drawstrings on the pants, so I can make them even bigger." She sighed. "Because I'm out of control here. Growing like crazy. At first, it wasn't so bad. Three pounds the first three months. Then I had like a growth spurt, you know? But I was cool about it. This is fucking out of control, though." She lowered her voice. "I looked in the mirror yesterday and I cried. I mean, I'm only fifteen years old. I look like John Candy or somebody."

Olivia was still seduced by the rise and fall of this girl's voice. Her stories took Olivia in. But she had to keep her head now. She knew better. So she said, "Where is everything? We can drive around and get it all back."

Ruby laughed. "Like duh, Olivia. I stole your stuff to get money. I didn't like go to the Salvation Army and give it away. I don't need a—what's it called? A charitable contribution on my tax return or anything."

How much money could she have even gotten for such a measly group of things? Olivia wondered. It wasn't even worth stealing.

"What a joke," Ruby continued. "I mean, I hardly got anything for it. The pearls were okay. But that was about it."

At the word *pearls*, Olivia's heart lurched. They were in the jewelry box with the tape. She imagined Ruby's hands grabbing at the stuff—tape, pearls, all of it—and Ruby quickly judging what was worthwhile, what was worthless.

"Oh," Ruby said, "and you had this ring with like a purple stone in it—"

"Amethyst."

"Right. That was okay, too. Antique."

Olivia swallowed hard. The ring had been a gift from her old boyfriend Josh, and although she no longer wore it, she liked having it, knowing she had it. There had been a time when she had worn it every day.

"We'll buy it all back," Olivia said. There's a ridiculous notion, she thought. Buy back stolen goods. She rotated her left hand; it might be sprained, from their wrestling match earlier.

"I know you'll never believe this," Ruby said, "but I'm not a total moron. Like I even got *A*'s and stuff in school. Some of my teachers consider me a total disappointment. My English teacher even told me I had potential."

"You're right," Olivia said. "I don't believe you." Who knew? Maybe Ruby was the class valedictorian, a bundle of contradictions, a good girl gone bad.

"It's true!" Ruby said, insulted.

"Fine," Olivia said. "You're a genius and you and Ben are madly in love—"

"We are!" Ruby shrieked. "What do you think? This was like the Immaculate Conception or something?"

"Hardly." Olivia laughed.

Oh, she imagined there could be a dozen potential fathers, all of them like those stoned boys in the parking lot. Boys with greasy hair and fast cars.

"I get it," Ruby said. "You think I just screw guys randomly." She hesitated, then added, "*Indiscriminately*, right? Well, for your information, I have only been with nine guys—"

Jesus, Olivia thought. Nine guys and she was fifteen years old.

Olivia couldn't help but think of her own fifteen-year-old self, with her John Lennon glasses and Indian-print skirts and her one true love, Peter Hershey. They hadn't had sex until senior year.

"And I love Ben," Ruby said, her voice passionate now. "I love him desperately. I never got pregnant before. I didn't just fuck anybody anytime, so there."

"Okay," Olivia said. "Okay."

"It's not okay. Who do you think you are, anyway?" Ruby leaned back, weary, her stomach rising like a whale on the horizon. "I like sex," she said dreamily. "I do. It's hard to believe it can cause you so much trouble. The first time I had sex, I was like thirteen years old—"

"Thirteen!" Olivia blurted.

"And drunk, of course."

"My God," Olivia said. She knew nothing about anything, she decided. She was certain that when she was thirteen, she had not even known for sure what a French kiss was, or exactly how babies were made.

"The guy's name was Guy. Can you believe it? I guess it's like a French name, except they say *Gee.* But we all called him Guy, you know. And it was a Halloween party and I went as Scarlett O'Hara because I had just seen that movie for the first time, and I swear I watched it like fifty times in a row because I loved it so much. It's still my favorite movie, and I thought, Why can't I be her? Why can't I have Tara and Melanie and Rhett and all of it, you know?"

That stupid movie again. Here was the kind of young girl who fell for all that romantic gibberish. Olivia shook her head. How could she have seen so much of herself in Ruby? Maybe she was just hoping for that sameness, hoping for a kindred spirit to fall into her lap.

Ruby sighed again. "Where was I?"

"Gee," Olivia said.

Ruby laughed. "Right. Gee. So I go to the party and I drink only bourbon because that's like a big southern thing and I wear this hoop skirt and these gross green curtains my mother had in the basement. In case you don't know, that's what Scarlett O'Hara does—she makes a dress out of these curtains. And I get drunk as hell, and of course whenever I smoke pot, I get really horny because it like gives me a buzz down there, like I've got an electric current down there. And Guy comes as Ike Turner with like a Nehru jacket and this Afro wig and bell-bottoms and he has his face painted black and I'm so drunk that when I lie down, I can't pull myself back up because of the hoop skirt and everything and Guy and I are making out and laughing because I can't get up and then he makes some stupid joke about doing the horizontal waltz or something, but I know what he means and I think, Why not? Why not just get it over with? He's cute and everything, so I go, 'Let's do it, yeah' and he goes, 'Really?' and I go, 'Sure,' because by this time we've smoked a joint, too, and I'm buzzing down there and so we do it."

"Just like that?" Olivia said. She thought about how much she and her friends had discussed it: "Should we? Should we?" She thought about how terrified they all were.

"It was so nice, too," Ruby said.

"It was?" Olivia said, surprised.

"I guess if I didn't like it so much, I wouldn't be in this predicament, right?" Ruby laughed.

Olivia closed her eyes and imagined her own first time, Peter Hershey pushing into her on the golf course behind his house. He kept his jeans on, just pulled out his dick and slipped her panties off, lifted her denim skirt, and did it. She was afraid of getting caught. The zipper on his jeans made tiny welts on the inside of her thigh.

"After Guy, I would think about doing it with other people, you know? Like I wanted to do it in a bed. And be naked, too.

But it wasn't like a slutty thing. Not like some girls, who go to parties and blow everybody or something."

When Olivia didn't answer, Ruby said, "You think it is, though, right?"

"What?"

"You think it's slutty to have sex like I did?"

Olivia hesitated and then said, "Not slutty exactly. But not right."

This was hypocritical; she knew that. Certainly she'd had sex *indiscriminately.* She'd made love with strangers. Sometimes she'd even sought it out. But somehow what she'd done was different. She was older, after all. An adult. Ruby was fifteen. *Fifteen!*

"All I know is, I don't want this baby," Ruby whispered. "And Ben doesn't want it."

Olivia reached across the cold, hard place between them.

"I do," she whispered back to Ruby.

They had picked out names, Olivia and David, for the child they would have. They had wanted just one child, so they could stay in New York, in their apartment on Bethune Street, and send their child to a good school, to summer camp, to ballet class or piano lessons or gymnastics. They would have one child and give it everything they could. "What a lovely, lovely life we're going to have," David whispered to her the night before he died. He died not knowing if she was pregnant or not. He died hoping, maybe even believing that she was.

Olivia lay in her bed, thinking of all these things.

Ruby was back, on the cot in the room that was going to be the nursery. That *would* be the nursery, she reminded herself. Because they struck a deal: Olivia would take care of Ruby so that Ruby would not have to rob anyone, or sleep in abandoned university buildings, or lie anymore. And Ruby would give Olivia the baby. Olivia knew she was crazy to trust Ruby. But she wanted to trust her. She wanted to believe that Ruby would live up to her end of the deal. If I don't have that, Olivia thought, what do I have?

She would name it the name they chose.

She would send it to a good school, to summer camp, to ballet or piano lessons. She would give this child everything.

"What a lovely, lovely life we're going to have," Olivia whispered, pressing her lips to the wall. On the other side, growing in a young girl's stomach, was her baby. Her hands fluttered above her own stomach, as if the baby were there instead of resting inside a fifteen-year-old girl who didn't want it. Olivia had traveled in her lifetime from being the Protestant girl her parents raised to being an atheist, then a Unitarian, an agnostic. After David died, she was, she supposed, a nihilist. But now she believed that someone—God, maybe?—had brought Ruby to her. That she was meant to have this baby. "Karma is a boomerang," Ruby had told her. And Olivia was certain that the good she'd done in her life had finally bounced back to her.

Winnie called from Rhinebeck.

"You have to get that house on the market and come up here and stay with us," she said. "Jeff insists. *I* insist. We're spending the whole month of July here and we want you."

Olivia watched as Ruby ate the stack of pancakes she'd set before her. Syrup glistened on her chin, all sticky and sweet.

"July?" Olivia said. "I don't think I'll be ready by July."

"Not ready? What is there to do there?"

"Actually," Olivia said, "I'm not selling the house. I've changed my mind."

Winnie sighed. "This isn't good," she said. Then she let out a little squeal. "Oooh," she said, "the baby's foot is right in my ribs."

Olivia waited for the familiar pang of jealousy that came with every conversation she had with Winnie these days. But there was nothing. Instead, Olivia watched as Ruby picked up her empty plate and licked every last drop of maple syrup from it. Then she sat back and rubbed her belly in a lazy circular motion.

"It's the most incredible thing," Winnie was saying. "Watching a baby grow inside you. Did you get the sonogram picture I sent you up there?"

"Mmmmm," Olivia said. Somewhere sat a huge pile of unopened mail, much of it addressed to David or "Resident."

"Doesn't that profile look exactly like me?" Winnie whispered. "I think Jeff's kind of pissed off about that."

"I've got to go," Olivia said.

"I've upset you, haven't I? The baby and Jeff—"

"Bye," Olivia said, and hung up almost happily. Winnie wasn't living her life. She'd made one of her own.

"Once," Ruby said, "I went away with a married man for a whole weekend." She pulled out a tin of Scottish shortbread from one of Winnie's baskets, opened it, and started to eat. "My French teacher," she added—wickedly, Olivia decided.

Olivia tried not to act shocked. When she was in ninth grade, she and Janice had a crush on their French teacher, Monsieur Levesque. They used to stay after school for special tutoring and do extra-credit projects. But they never even considered sleeping with him. It wasn't how they thought. Once, Janice got a ride home with him in his convertible MG, and it was all they talked about for weeks—the way Monsieur Levesque's hair blew in the wind, how his knuckles whitened when he downshifted, how he took off his tie and unbuttoned his top button for the ride.

"And how old was this married man?" Olivia asked.

"I don't know exactly. He wasn't my official teacher. He was like a student teacher. So in college. Twenty-two, maybe? And his name was Michael, so we had to call him 'Michel,' which was a real trip. You know, a man named Michel. So for our midterm, we had to give an oral presentation, and I sang that Beatles song 'Michelle,' except it was like the masculine form and I changed the words so it fit, like *'Michele, mon beau.'* You know. Goofy, but he blushed and everything and he liked it a lot and he stopped me after class and said it had kind of turned him on, having me sing him a love song like that."

"He *said* that?"

"Not in so many words, but yeah, basically. And then he like brushed up against me and squeezed my hand when he left. This was a Friday, so all weekend that's all I can think about, you know. And then I stay after school on Monday and tell him I need help conjugating irregular verbs, and after about fifteen minutes of conjugating, he's got me pressed up against the blackboard and we're making out like crazy."

Olivia decided Ruby was a liar. Every time that thought crossed her mind, she saw the promises the girl had made to her start to crumble. She found herself wanting to believe Ruby. But a teacher with such a young girl? Even a student teacher would have more sense.

Out of nowhere, Ruby laughed. She pointed a cookie-crumbed finger at Olivia. "You don't believe me."

"I just can't imagine that a teacher—"

"*Student* teacher—"

"—is going to make out with a fifteen-year-old—"

"—Fourteen, actually, at that time."

"—in a classroom where anyone could walk in on him."

Ruby grinned. "Crazy, isn't it? I mean, he's got his hand up my dress and he's poking at me down there, inside and everything, and he says, 'I've got to have you. I've been wanting to fuck you since you walked into class the very first time.'"

"Uh-huh," Olivia said. This kid is too much, Olivia thought. How far will she go, anyway? "He said, 'I've been wanting to fuck you.' And you said?"

Olivia looked in the basket for something sweet and found dried Mission figs stuffed with nuts—hazelnuts, walnuts, pecans. Funny how living with Ruby had given her a sweet tooth. Briefly, she thought of David and how he used to forgo white sugar, white flour, red meat. "I'm a California boy," he used to say, throwing his arms in the air as if surrendering to his roots. He would give her golden seal when she had a cold, tea made from fresh ginger root when her throat hurt, lavender baths for stress. She bit hard into a fig, the sweet fruit making her teeth ache slightly. They were incredible.

"So I take the bus to Cape Cod," Ruby was saying. Olivia realized she has missed part of the story. "And he picks me up at the bus stop and drives me to this house on the beach and we go inside and he's got like a pound of cocaine—"

"He gives drugs to you, too?" Olivia said. "Sex and drugs with a minor. Interesting. Is this guy actually teaching somewhere now or is he doing time at the ACI?"

Ruby leaned back in her chair, her hands folded on her stomach.

"I wouldn't know," she said. "He's probably still married, living in a renovated historic house, like on Benefit Street. That's his style, you know?" She narrowed her eyes. "What are you eating?"

"Stuffed figs," Olivia said. She was enjoying them so much, she didn't want to share them with Ruby. Still, she handed her one.

"I do admit I miss snorting a few lines of coke from time to time. Even though it got me in trouble," Ruby said, chewing thoughtfully. "Coke makes me so horny."

"I thought pot made you horny," Olivia said. The girl could be a screenwriter—with these crazy stories of hers.

"Coke makes me different horny. Not the buzzing down there, but like you want something inside you all the time, you know?"

You're lying, Olivia thought, and it felt good to think it—better than imagining all of this to be true.

Ruby smiled. She closed her eyes. "What a weekend that was," she said. Then, abruptly, her eyes opened and she was digging through Winnie's basket of food again. "Made French class interesting for the rest of the quarter. Then he was gone, back to college, I guess. I used to pretend he would leave his wife and come and get me and take me away. We would talk French all the time, you know? Maybe even live in Paris."

Ruby was walking across the kitchen as she talked, trying to keep her feet on a line in the floor. She's walking the plank, Olivia imagined. Or taking a sobriety test. She was somewhere else, that was for certain. Softly, Ruby hummed. Olivia recognized the tune. "Crazy." In her head, as Ruby hummed, Olivia filled in the words.

They settled into a routine, Olivia and Ruby: walks on the beach and visits to the obstetrician and videos to rent. Olivia began to feel as if she was entering the real world again. Whenever she and David had been apart, for a night or a weekend or a week, they called those first few hours of coming back together and catching up on each other "reentry." It was how she thought about this time with Ruby. Reentry. Olivia saw the beach differently, the oiled bodies stretched out before her in the daytime, the radios blaring, all on different stations, the smell of clam cakes and seaweed. In the evening, it was quiet, with salty air and treasures on the shore—beach glass and shells and pieces of oddly shaped driftwood.

There were long talks, too; Olivia heard about eight of Ruby's nine guys. She did not hear about Ben. But Ruby told her about each of the others in great detail: Jay, the football player and student council president, who used Ruby to defy his parents—"He smashed my teeth when we kissed, like I thought they would fall out or something"; Rollo, the local drug dealer—"He like never came because he rubbed coke on his dick; I swear to God"; all of the stories horrible and sad in some way, even though Ruby always made them funny, always made herself the ironic onlooker instead of the lonely girl desperate for love that Olivia suspected she really was.

At night, when Ruby was asleep—and she went to sleep early now—Olivia watched her. She went over in her mind how foolish she was, how crazy, really, to take in this girl. How foolish she was to want Ruby's baby so badly. What did she know about raising a child? She had never even held a baby, not a newborn. Olivia thought she should be terrified. She thought she should be cautious. She thought she should stop all of this before Ruby did something worse than robbing her. But mostly, she thought that some little part of her had come back to life. Mostly, she sat across the room from Ruby and kept an eye on her until all the late-night talk shows were over and the local news had been replayed and television finally ended. Then Olivia roused Ruby, led her up the stairs, and put her to bed. That was when Olivia slept, too.

It was the first of July, relentlessly hot, and Ruby was in her seventh month. Her face was blotchy and bloated; she no longer looked like a kid. She was uncomfortable, complaining about a foot in her ribs, indigestion, sinus trouble. On the phone, Winnie reported the same kind of things to Olivia, but Olivia lived them every day with Ruby. Their due dates were exactly three weeks apart. Whenever Winnie told Olivia a new symptom or development, Olivia would say, "I know. I know."

Olivia started to make hats again. She ordered supplies from New York and got to work on a new series, all of them straw the color of the sand on different beaches: Bermuda pink, wet sand, black volcanic sand, the sand of the beach Olivia walked with Ruby here. The hats had wide brims, contrasting trim, and flat, tight bows—beach hats like women wore in the twenties and thirties. She sat on the lawn, shaping them, naming them for famous beaches: Cape May, Truro, Captiva. Ruby watched from a chaise longue beside her, wearing her own funny pink hat.

That was how the Realtor found them one hot afternoon.

She teetered toward them on her too-high heels. She wore a suit the color of cantaloupe, the jacket's underarms damp.

"Hello," the Realtor said, with so much cheerfulness that Ruby laughed and answered with a big false hello.

"Just checking on your progress," the Realtor said, frowning at Ruby and Olivia and the house.

Olivia spread out her arms. "Well," she said, "here we are."

"Yes." The Realtor chewed on her bottom lip.

"I'm thinking," Olivia said, "that maybe it's not time to sell."

"No, it is! The market is up, up, up. You'll make a killing."

"Not that," Olivia said, aware of Ruby watching her, aware of the Realtor's thick perfume, and the grass itching beneath her, and Ruby's obviously pregnant self, and her hats spread before her. "I'm not ready to sell yet. That's what I mean."

The Realtor bent down as best she could in her tight cantaloupe miniskirt. "It's a hard thing. I know that. To sell your dream house. But when you let go of it, you'll be able to move on."

"The thing is," Olivia said, looking right into the Realtor's eyes, "I'm not ready." The woman's mascara was caked in the corners and made little dots where she blinked.

The Realtor stood and cleared her throat. "When you're ready, you'll call. You can't rush things like this. I know that. I understand that."

She held out her business card and Ruby took it from her.

"You're?" the Realtor asked.

"The pregnant teenager," Ruby said.

"It made me sad," Ruby said as the Miata drove away. "When she called this your 'dream house.' Dreams always get smashed, huh?"

"Who do you know like that?" Olivia asked her.

"My dad. My real dad, that is. Not the loser my mother married. I haven't talked to him in like five years. But he wanted to be a writer. He wrote like three novels that never got published. Then he's got to pay child support and pay a mortgage and stuff and he's forced to take shitty jobs." She swallowed hard. "He maybe drank too much because he was so far from what he wanted. I don't see him anymore. He tried AA and NA and every other A. But they never quite fixed him, you know? And we sort of lost touch. Maybe he's even dead. Maybe he died in some real tragic way."

This last would make Ruby happy, Olivia realized. A father who gave his life for art.

"Can I ask you something?" Ruby said. "I mean, since you're older and everything, maybe you can help me out here."

Olivia shrugged. "I'll try," she said.

Ruby lay down on the grass, which was only green in spots; mostly, it was brown from lack of water. There was a drought.

"Did you ever wish you could take something back? Like totally change something you did?"

"Like what?" Olivia said. But already her gut was twisted with regret. Already she was imagining a different day last year, a day when she turned toward David and his unshaven face, his searching hands, and saved his life. A day when she kept him away from that blue Honda Civic.

"Like why didn't we just use a rubber?" Ruby said. "I just want to, like, go into a time tunnel and play that one time over, except this time do it different, you know?"

"It doesn't get you anywhere to beat yourself up about a mistake," Olivia said, without much conviction. It was advice Winnie had given her often enough. Advice she was still not able to take.

"Yeah, yeah," Ruby said, waving her hands dismissively. It was foolish advice for someone ridden with guilt. "I have this moment frozen in my brain and I keep replaying it, you know? Here we are, in Ben's room at school and slightly stoned, good stoned, not like totally blasted, but just riding this high and like totally into what we're doing, you know, and he goes inside me and he says he'll pull out, you know? He says, 'Just this once, don't make me put on a rubber,' and I know in my brain that it only takes one fucking microscopic sperm and I know one can leak out before he even comes. I know everything, but I think, What are the chances?"

Bingo, Olivia thought. What are the chances that you go back to sleep instead of making love with your husband and he gets killed by a college girl driving a blue Honda Civic?

"I guess," Olivia said, "the chances were pretty damn good."

"No shit," Ruby said.

Usually, Olivia did not let herself think about the girl who had done it. A college sophomore on her way to get a few things for the house she was renting with three other girls. Milk and toilet paper and M&M's. Olivia knew these details because the girl had come to the house, shown up there the next day with her roommates to explain. "We like M&M's. While we study, you know?" she'd said. She had explained about the bright sunlight, about the curve, how David had appeared out of nowhere. But of course that wasn't right. He had appeared straight from Olivia's side. He had shaved and had a glass of orange juice and then gone out and run smack into the girl's car. "I didn't know what I'd hit," she'd said, still awed by what she'd done. Later, a letter had come to Olivia in New York. "I can't sleep at night," she wrote. "I keep thinking, If only I'd stayed put. If only I'd taken the main road instead of the scenic route. But it was such a beautiful day. And now I'll regret that decision the rest of my life."

"Regret," Ruby said, "is the worst thing, don't you think?"

For a moment, Olivia wondered if she'd spoken aloud.

"What do you mean?" she asked stupidly, because as much as that girl had regrets, had dropped out of school for a semester and gone home to New Jersey and taken Prozac, as much as her life was now shaped by regret, so was Olivia's.

"Take my mother," Ruby said. "My mother regrets that she let my father go. That she didn't fight harder for him. And like I regret some things. Little things. Like robbing you. I regret that."

"That's not such a little thing to me," Olivia said.

"Come on," Ruby said, laughing. "That pile of junk? I did you a favor, honest to God." She sighed and got her dreamy look. "My grandma?" she said. "She was like the one person who made me think I really mattered, you know? I used to pack my stuff in a garbage bag and tell my mother I was moving to my grandma's. She always used to keep animal crackers for me, in this big cookie jar she had that was shaped like an apple. But the thing is, I never ate them. I played with them. Sometimes I'd pretend I was a kid whose parents took her to the circus for her birthday and I'd march those stupid little cookies around the floor and I'd go, 'Animals on parade' in this fake announcer's voice. The thing is, I never went to the circus, so I never really knew what a kid would see there."

Impulsively, Olivia reached out and took Ruby's hand, but the girl recoiled.

"Don't," she said sharply.

"I'm sorry," Olivia said. "I just—"

"No one feels sorry for me," Ruby said, her tough-girl voice back again, all hard and edgy. "I mean, the fucking circus chains animals to cages and totally mistreats them, so who would want to go anyway? It was just a stupid little kid thing. I'm sorry I even brought it up."

Olivia nodded. "I know," she said, because she was sorry for trying to comfort the girl, for thinking about the one who had killed her husband; she was sorry for so much.

"My grandmother has lungs like Swiss cheese," Ruby said, "honest to God. I saw the X rays and they blew my mind. Emphysema." She pointed at Olivia. "But she says she has no regrets. She would smoke a cigarette in a flash if it wouldn't blow up because of the oxygen she's on. She says she loved every smoke she ever had. She doesn't even believe smoking causes all this shit. She thinks that's just propaganda. My grandma says regrets get you nowhere but feeling sorry for your own sorry ass." Ruby smiled. "So I don't regret being pregnant. I mean, I wish it was different and stuff, but you can't imagine what it feels like. I mean, it sucks. Yeah. But on the other hand, it's almost like a mystical experience. Like when you drop acid. Some people freak out, but I always liked it, you know. This other reality. That's what this is. A baby rolling around inside your stomach. It blows my mind." Ruby shook her head, amazed. "It can hear us," she whispered. "It can see bright light." Her hand moved to her stomach and hovered above it like a bee. "It blows my mind. It really does."

"Good idea," David had said when Olivia sent him off to his death. If only she had held him. If only she had opened her arms and her legs and let him in, she would not be sitting here with this pregnant teenager worrying. She would be with David. She would be talking to her own baby inside her stomach. *Good idea.*

"The thing is," Ruby said, "giving away your baby can certainly be one of those things. Major regret factor, I'd say. You could walk around the rest of your life wondering if you would have been happy together. You could make yourself crazy imagining a future that can't be, you know?"

. . .

For some time now, Olivia had considered writing to that girl and telling her to move on with her life. It was an accident, she wanted to tell her. She wanted the girl to feel absolved from what she'd done. But Olivia had been unable to write the letter. If she absolved the college girl, then it really was all her fault.

Still, she tried. She sat at the kitchen table and wrote, "Dear Amanda, I hope you remember me. . . ."

That was a foolish start. How many guys had Amanda killed, after all? How many widows were writing her letters?

"It has been almost a year since the accident and slowly I am moving on with things. I have started to make hats again. . . ."

More foolishness.

"Also, I am going to adopt a baby . . ."

She paused, then wrote: "You stupid idiot, why didn't you look where you were going? Why didn't you have on sunglasses if the sun was so fucking bright? Why didn't you see a guy over six feet tall in bright orange running shorts—"

"Ooooh," Ruby said, appearing out of nowhere and looking over Olivia's shoulder. "Is that a poem? Ben's a poet, you know. Did I tell you that? He writes these incredible poems. He won't give up, either. No matter what it takes."

Olivia folded the letter carefully, nodding at Ruby as if she, too, believed that Ben was a real poet, someone who would make it someday.

"We might go and live in Indonesia," Ruby said. She stood by the sink and let the water run to get it cold. "It's really cheap to live in Indonesia. You can get a house and cook and a maid and a nanny for next to nothing."

"Really?" Olivia said, swallowing hard. "In Indonesia?" She had not heard this fantasy before. The word *nanny* caught in her throat. "When did you decide all this?"

"It's not decided. It's just an idea. Something to think about.

Like the Greek islands. Ben has been to these places. He's been everywhere. And he says that's the thing to do." She put one hand under the faucet to test the water, deciding it still wasn't cold enough.

"Go and live in Indonesia?"

"Or Greece or Costa Rica." Ruby was measuring her words; Olivia could tell. "There's so many better places."

"When did you talk to Ben, anyway?" Olivia asked, trying to sound offhanded.

Ruby shrugged. "Oh. You know. Whenever." Again, she tested the water.

"Either drink some of that or turn it off," Olivia said angrily. "There's a drought, you know. You don't stand and let water run and run when people aren't even flushing their toilets or taking baths in order to save it. Do you ever think of anyone other than yourself?"

Without even getting a glass, Ruby turned off the water.

"Have you done anything to get my stuff back, for instance?" Olivia said. The letter was just a piece of crushed paper now, wrinkled and moist in her hand.

"It's gone," Ruby said. "I told you that."

Olivia nodded. "I know. But what about the stuff no one wanted?"

"Can you be more specific?" Ruby said.

"The jewelry box."

Ruby held up both of her hands. She no longer wore the cheap rings, and seeing them plain like this reminded Olivia of a washerwoman's hands: rough and red and swollen.

"I'm sorry I said anything about your stupid poem," Ruby said. "I only saw like three words or something."

"Forget it," Olivia said. She pretended to clean up the kitchen just to have something to do.

"Like I saw the word *baby.* Was it a poem to the baby?"

Olivia concentrated on wiping the counters.

"Can I pick the name?" Ruby said. "I know it's a big thing, but I wanted to put my two cents in."

"What name?"

"The baby's. Can I pick it out?"

Olivia didn't want Ruby to name the baby. She felt uncertain again; Ruby might take this baby and go away somewhere. Somewhere far. *Indonesia.* Then she would have nothing. No baby, no minicassette of David's voice.

"What names do you like?" Olivia asked.

"I just like one. Sage. For a boy or a girl."

"Sage," Olivia said, hating it, hating Ruby. "Interesting."

"I've liked that name forever," Ruby said. She gently rubbed her hand across her stomach in that circular motion. "That's what I always wanted to name my baby. Even when I was little and I'd pretend I had a sister, I'd call her Sage. I mean, she was invisible and everything."

"It's a good name," Olivia said. If you want to name your kid after an herb, she thought. Or a Simon and Garfunkel song.

"I can tell you don't really like it. But would you consider it? I don't want this baby saddled with Jennifer or Elizabeth or something."

Reluctantly, Olivia said, "I think you should name the baby. Sage."

The baby is mine, Olivia thought. She put her hand lightly on Ruby's stomach, too. Beneath the tight drum of belly, the baby kicked back at them both.

Olivia tried not to leave Ruby alone too often, but sometimes she was happy to be away from the girl. Ruby liked to go off by herself, to the beach—"Not where anyone can see me like this!"—or to a movie, where it was air-conditioned and dark. That was where she was going tonight, the movies, while Olivia and Pete had dinner with Carl and Janice.

Olivia had gone out with Pete one other time, to the lobster fest in Point Judith, where they sat and drank beer and ate chowder and lobsters under a tent one Saturday afternoon. Their time together that day had been brief, and Olivia quickly put it out of her mind. This isn't a date, she'd kept reminding herself. It's just two people eating lobster and coleslaw under a hot tent. Thinking this, over and over, had helped her relax. She'd almost had fun.

But this dinner with him felt all wrong. Janice called, too often, all chatty and excited, as if they were back in high school and getting ready for a Saturday-night double date.

"This is just dinner," Olivia told Janice. It was a good way to remind herself, too. "Not a date."

"Whatever," Janice said.

Olivia frowned. That was an answer Janice had used for as long as they had known each other. In high school, it had sounded sassy, even cool. Now it was simply irritating.

"Pete Lancelotta is not my type," Olivia told Janice during one of the calls. "I would never date him, even under the best of circumstances."

"Whatever," Janice said, and launched into a one-sided discussion about what to wear that night.

Now that she was actually on her way to the dinner, Olivia reviewed all the reasons why she would never date Pete Lancelotta. No matter what she added or subtracted from the list, she always ended with the same thing: Pete was not David.

When she pulled into the parking lot of the restaurant and saw Janice and Carl's car parked right beside Pete's, she had to fight the desire to turn around and surprise Ruby at the movie. She sat in her car and looked at the name of the restaurant: Angel's. Maybe, Olivia thought, David had sent Ruby her way. Maybe he was in heaven, or wherever it was people went, and he'd found Ruby for her. She imagined David screening potential people to help her get along without him. Certainly he had eliminated Amy and Pete Lancelotta. But then he'd come across Ruby. A pregnant girl who did not want her baby. And David had said, Yes! You! As crazy as Olivia knew this was, she almost believed it. Sitting there in that parking lot under a sign that said ANGEL'S, Olivia finally felt David's presence.

A loud knock on her car window startled her.

There stood Janice, peering in.

"Are you okay?" Janice shouted, loudly enough for Olivia to hear through the closed window and above the car's air conditioner.

Olivia didn't turn the car off. She rolled down the window, swallowing a mouthful of muggy summer air.

"I am," she said. She struggled to explain it all to Janice. David had sent her Ruby. He had sent her the baby they never got to make together. But she couldn't find the words to say to Janice, who was standing there in her pink dress and white sandals, all dressed up for a dinner out.

Instead, Olivia said, "Pal?" softly into the summer night. "Thanks." Her voice was a whisper. Despite the heat, a shiver ran up Olivia's spine, making the back of her neck tingle.

"Uh," Janice said, glancing over her shoulder, "we're all inside waiting."

"You know what?" Olivia said, almost lightheartedly. "I can't do this."

"You can," Janice said. "It's just friends. A dinner." She glanced back again. "They have really good calamari."

Olivia shook her head. "The thing is, I'm working on this project."

She would go home and paint the nursery the way she and David had discussed once, with murals—a cow jumping over the moon, Jack and Jill tumbling down the hill, Humpty-Dumpty. "You'll paint it the way a kid's room should be," David had told her, and she'd imagined it, the brightly colored walls depicting a child's world. He'd had faith in her to do it right. And she would.

Janice was reaching in to take her arm, to lead her out of the car and into the restaurant toward Pete Lancelotta and the good calamari, but Olivia resisted.

She said, "I'm sorry, Janice."

Janice stepped back. On her face, Olivia read a whole world of emotion—Poor Olivia, she was thinking; Olivia was certain of that.

"I'm okay," Olivia said. "I am."

What Olivia imagined was that she would sit down and plan the room. She would go home and dig through her portfolio, the one she used to carry in the trunk of her car, the one full of graph paper and different points for her drawing pens, the one that had been under her bed since last September. She would sit at the kitchen table and begin. When Ruby came home from the movie—and Olivia could see the moment, Ruby's face shiny from buttered popcorn, and her breath sweet from an extralarge soda—she would find Olivia there, drawing, and together they would construct the room for the baby.

But instead, Olivia came in and heard the television upstairs. Ruby was home already. Or perhaps she had been too tired to go to the movie after all. The theater was a short walk from the house, and Olivia had seen Ruby start off. But she must have turned around. She got tired so easily.

Olivia rushed up the stairs, eager to begin.

She expected to see Ruby in Olivia's bed, in Olivia's nightgown, all the pillows behind her and food strewn everywhere and some silly sitcom on—Ruby loved them, all of them, with their fake versions of life in New York City and ridiculous friendships and canned laughter.

But what she found was this: Ruby large and naked—and Olivia had not seen her naked, was unprepared for the large misshapen belly and jutting belly button and blue-veined breasts—sprawled out on the bed, her cheeks flushed, her face pink. Beside her, also naked, was a boy, a teenager, with long blond hair to his shoulders and a dark tan and the kind of muscles that stand out even when the person isn't trying to show them off. They were lying together, tangled, familiar, eating the gourmet popcorn that Winnie had sent—jalapeño.

Olivia stood in the doorway, too shocked to be embarrassed.

The bluish lights from the TV screen made them look otherworldly; as if a very pregnant naked teenager and a naked boy weren't otherworldly enough. Olivia thought she smelled marijuana. There was the canned laughter, and then the two of them laughed, too, a beat behind.

That was when Ruby saw Olivia in the doorway.

"Oh," Ruby said, not the least bit nervous. Did the girl ever act embarrassed or surprised or guilty? "Hi," she added, as calm as ever. Like a hostess introducing guests at a cocktail party, she held an arm out to Olivia, palm turned upward. "Olivia," she said, "this is Ben."

chapter six

Ruby, Ruby, Ruby, Will You Be Mine?

At the kitchen table, Ruby and Ben huddled together on one chair, Ruby half on Ben's lap and half off, clinging awkwardly to the edge of the chair. They were the type of teenagers who gave each other hickeys, French-kissed at their lockers, made out until their chins and mouths grew red and raw; Olivia saw this about them right away. Even now, dressed but tousled, they nuzzled and petted one another, stroked and rubbed enough to embarrass Olivia. Rather than look at them—and they sat right in her line of vision, right across the table from her—she looked at a place on the wall beyond them where one strip of wallpaper met another, making the faded teapot pattern look fractured.

"See?" Ruby was saying. "He's real. You thought I made him up, didn't you?"

"Well," Olivia said, "he certainly is real."

Ben had pulled his long hair into a ponytail held in place with a piece of rawhide. He had a beautiful face, good strong cheekbones and a fine jaw, the kind of eyes that reflect the color of the sky or the sea. He was, Olivia knew, a boy a young girl would fall in love with too easily.

He grinned at Olivia, the slow, lazy grin of a charmer. A charmer who's stoned, Olivia added, because the strong smell of pot clung to him, filled the air around him. Olivia thought of Pig-Pen from the Snoopy comic strip, who traveled in a cloud of dirt.

Ruby looked at Olivia, suddenly all wide-eyed. "You're not *mad,* are you?" she said. "That Ben's here?"

Olivia thought that indeed she was mad, as in crazy. Mad because her life was this unpredictable, uncontrollable *thing.*

"Because I never said I wouldn't see Ben. I mean," Ruby said, "I love him."

When she said this, her eyes actually teared. Only teenaged girls loved that way; Olivia remembered it, remembered sitting at her bedroom window waiting for the boy up the street to drive by in his white VW bug. Just a glimpse of him could make her dizzy. She used to stay in her room and play Crosby, Stills & Nash records until her mother begged her to turn them off. She remembered all of it and she still thought Ruby could turn on those tears without any problem. A real actress, this kid. A real winner.

"You lied about going to the movies. He smoked pot in my house. And you had sex in my bed. That's what I'm angry about," Olivia said.

Each point forced her voice a bit louder, until she was practically shouting. The kid was such a liar. How could she ever have believed anything Ruby told her?

Ruby grinned at her, a big goofy grin, as if she had access to some secret that Olivia couldn't begin to understand. And she was right, in a strange way. Here she was with her ponytailed boyfriend, in love.

"Maybe you should just go," Olivia said, her voice low again, defeated.

"Don't make her go," Ben said.

His voice was smooth and deep and made Olivia think of chocolate ice cream, espresso, molasses. What a heartbreaker he must be. She wondered if he was going to break Ruby's heart. Immediately, she thought, Of course he is.

"See," Ben continued, "I have to be upstate for the summer—"

"I told you!" Ruby said to Olivia, bursting with righteousness.

"Like I'm teaching tennis at this totally bourgeois camp for rich kids when I should be here with Ruby."

He stopped talking long enough to kiss Ruby some more and long enough for Olivia to imagine him there, at the camp. She could see him with his thick blond hair, his strong arms and legs, in tennis whites. All the girls in love with him, whispering his name when he passed by: *Ben Ben Ben*. All the girls doing anything to get his attention. She imagined starlit nights, a still lake, the smell of pine trees and clean air. Poor Ruby, she didn't stand a chance against these rich, unpregnant girls. Worse, she remembered that Ben fancied himself a poet. Teenaged girls loved poets, longhaired boys who played the acoustic guitar and wrote love poems and taught tennis. Poor Ruby, she thought again.

Ben said, "But we need the money so we can go to Greece or Bali or somewhere to live."

"See!" Ruby said, smiling, redeemed.

"So I have to do it. As much as I'm going crazy being away from her and the little one." He rested his hand on Ruby's large belly, but he kept talking right to Olivia. "It's so amazing, isn't it?

She's got a life in here. A baby growing inside her." He shook his head. "It blows my mind."

Olivia's mouth went dry. He wasn't talking like a person about to give his baby away. She could picture the fantasy that Ben had: he and Ruby and their baby—Sage—the three of them on an exotic island, feeding each other olives, swimming naked, drinking local wine, the baby in a papoose on his back, sleeping in a hut with a thatched roof. A poet, Olivia thought again, scoffing. He probably was in love with Rilke. Her fantasy didn't stand a chance against his.

Ben cleared his throat. "I mean, we made a baby together."

"By accident," Ruby said.

His hand rubbed her stomach now like a man rubbing a lamp with a genie inside.

"Still," Ben said. "We did it."

Olivia said, "You want to keep the baby, then?"

The silence stretched between them.

"Of course I want to keep the baby!" Ben said. "It's got my genetic code. And Ruby and I would have the most awesome kid."

Olivia hated him, Ben the poet and his genetic code.

"But," he added, "I'm only nineteen years old. I can't keep it."

Ruby grinned at Olivia, satisfied, as if to say, *There!*

"Look," Ben said, "I have twenty-four hours off. That's all. And it took me nine hours to get here. And nine to get back. Then it's back to the fucking Adirondacks and a bunch of spoiled brats who couldn't serve a tennis ball or lob a shot if their life depended on it." He nuzzled Ruby's hair. "It's back to life without Ruby."

"Can't he stay, Olivia?"

She wanted him gone; Olivia wanted Ben out of her house.

"I didn't lie about the movies," Ruby said. "I'm on my way and I look down the street and it's like I see a mirage or something.

Ben. Coming toward me. And I blink like a hundred times. But he's still there, coming toward me."

"I surprised her," Ben added.

"He hitchhiked the whole way," Ruby said, sighing because, of course, hitchhiking was the most romantic way to travel.

"Because I'm saving every penny I make up there for our tickets out," Ben said again.

Could they have worked out this story so carefully? Olivia wondered.

"And I told him everything that's happened. How you'll keep the baby for us," Ruby said.

Olivia focused on the word *keep.* This baby was not going to be on loan until they got older and were ready to take it themselves. You kept someone's cat while they were out of town. You kept their plants. But a baby was something else.

"We couldn't give it to strangers, you know. That sort of freaked me out," Ben said. "They could be anything. Republicans even."

"First thing in the morning, he's got to leave. And I won't see him again until August," Ruby said, frantic.

"She might even have the baby by then," Ben said. He was nuzzling again, stroking her arm.

"Stop!" Olivia said, startling both of them enough for them actually to stop and look at her.

Until now, she had avoided confronting Ruby about the legal end of all this. As much as Olivia was watching Ruby, wanting to trust the girl, she had also been trying to make sure that Ruby trusted her. Olivia wanted to prove that she was going to be not just a good mother to Ruby's baby but the perfect mother. She wanted Ruby to be absolutely convinced that this was where the baby should be, that there was no better choice for Ruby. She didn't want Ruby to change her mind. But now, Olivia realized, it was time to get to the legal details with Ruby. And with Ben.

"I'm going to have to get something in writing. An agreement that you two will let me have this baby."

They glanced at each other.

"And I have to know about your parents, Ben. Ruby's are out of the picture," Olivia said, and an image of Ruby's mother in the doorway of that rust-colored house drifted into her mind. Olivia took a breath. "But where do you stand?"

"Man," Ben said. "I thought you said she was cool, Ruby."

"I just can't take any chances," Olivia said. She could not keep her voice from trembling, sounding weak.

Ruby and Ben exchanged looks again. They were at that age and had that belief in romance that allowed them to communicate this way. They were pure, in a way—untouched by couple's counseling and broken hearts and catchphrases like "what I hear you saying." They were, simply, in love.

"Okay," Ben said. "That's cool."

And Ruby nodded.

Olivia tried to think of where to begin, but Ben was already talking.

"My parents know about the baby," he said. "They totally freaked and sent me up to that camp like a slave."

"They forbid him from seeing me," Ruby said proudly.

"Like I could stay away," Ben said, burying his nose in her hair.

"Where are they?" Olivia asked him.

"Westchester. Living their white-bread lives in a six-bedroom colonial. Driving their Mercedes-Benz into Manhattan every day to screw people out of money."

"They're lawyers," Ruby said, disgusted.

Olivia noticed for the first time that Ben wore two small gold hoop earrings, one in each ear. Girls must love that, too. Those earrings and all his talk about hating the bourgeoisie.

"And what do you do, Ben?" Olivia asked him, sounding the way her own mother used to twenty years ago when longhaired boys came to pick her up for dates. If Ben only knew that many of those boys, with their torn jeans and rolled joints and American flags sewn on their jackets, had become lawyers and businessmen and investment bankers.

"I go to school."

"I told you that," Ruby said. "Except he's not in a fraternity."

They both scowled over the very idea of that.

Then Ruby added, "But he did tell me to stay there."

"Figures they'd have fleas," Ben said, still scowling.

"So your parents are where in Westchester?" Olivia asked.

"Bedford Hills," Ben said. "I heard that's where that movie *The Stepford Wives* was based on. And that is my mother to a tee. Zombie Mom. She takes classes on how to arrange dried flowers or make wreaths. She sits around planning her garden on graph paper."

Olivia narrowed her eyes. "I thought she was a lawyer."

Ben didn't miss a beat. "That's my *step*mother who's a lawyer. You got to have like two sets of parents and all these stepbrothers and half sisters and shit. My old man is classic. He leaves my mother for a junior partner in his firm after my mother put him through law school and gave up her own life and blah, blah, blah. Then my mother marries our dentist. Can you believe it? He's been in all of our mouths."

"That is so creepy," Ruby said, wrinkling her nose. "When he told me that, I like almost puked, you know?"

Olivia tried to sort through the information, the lies from the truth. They were a good match, Ruby and Ben, full of wild ideas and large imaginations. Full of bullshit, too, Olivia reminded herself.

Ben said, "We're in the phone book. My father's John Adams—"

"They're related to the *real* John Adams," Ruby said, and again her voice swelled with pride.

She had a name and a town. Tomorrow, she would get to the bottom of this. She was comforted by the John Adams part; no one would make up something as ridiculous as that.

"I didn't believe him when he told me that," Ruby was saying. "I was like, 'Right. You're related to a President. And I'm the Pope.' But it's true."

"Abigail Adams brought ice cream to the United States," Ben said. "Did you know that? She tasted it in France."

Olivia wanted them to stop talking, to stop plying her with information. She had read somewhere that liars gave too many details, to convince you they were not lying.

"Listen," Ruby said, suddenly serious. "I won't tell you where my parents are. They kicked me out when I told them I was pregnant. They don't want me or this baby. You got to believe me, Olivia. You know the A&W? Where you found me? I lived near there."

That was true. All of it. So why didn't she feel any relief? Maybe that wouldn't come until she actually had that baby in her arms. Until she saw the last of Ruby.

Ruby kept talking, adding details, answering questions that Olivia didn't even ask.

"The way Ben and I met was so cool," Ruby said. "We used to buy pot from a guy in Ben's dorm. And one day, Betsy and I are waiting for this guy and I see Ben and, like, I almost die. He's so gorgeous, right?"

Ben laughed, obviously pleased with this description of himself.

Ruby said, "Then the guy comes and everything and I keep thinking about Ben. I mean, I didn't know his name or anything, but I'm like, I've got to meet him. So we get high with this guy and he tells us he's going to this poetry slam and do we want to go—it's in Providence—and we figure that sounds cool, so we go. And Ben reads *his* poetry. I almost died when I saw him. It was like karma. And then I heard his poem and I was like, This is it."

Ben took over the story. "And while I'm up there, I see her with Jamie—"

"The guy," Ruby said.

"And I see her and I start hoping she's not *with* with him, you know. She had this green leotard thing on, and these turquoise beads, ropes and ropes of them, and her waist was about this big." Ben made a small circle with his hands.

"Can you believe it?" Ruby groaned.

"No," Ben whispered to her. "Don't say it like that. You are so beautiful like this. With our baby."

"Anyway," Ruby said after they nuzzled some more, "he comes up to me and asks me if I want to get high and, like, would Jamie mind, and I crack up because Jamie is so not my type, except he always has good drugs. And so I say, 'I don't think he'll mind,' and we take a walk to that park in Providence—the one with that big statue of Roger Williams?—where you can look out and see the whole city. The statehouse was all lit up and everything. You know that statehouse has like the third-largest unsupported dome in the whole world? Ben told me that. He should be on *Jeopardy*, honest to God." She beamed at Ben before she continued. "Anyway, it's really beautiful there. And we get high and I make him say all his poems again. And then he asks me if I'll come back with him, to his room, and I say Yeah—"

"You don't have to tell her everything," Ben said.

"Anyway," Ruby said, "that was back in September—"

"The last day of summer," Ben said, locking his fingers into hers.

"And we've been together ever since."

It was not an especially beautiful story; there were the drugs and the fact that Ruby was only fifteen years old. But at the end, Olivia was crying. Because she knew what that felt like, to be together ever since. She believed in so little these days. But she guessed she still believed in this: love that will never end. Such a stupid thing to believe in. But she did.

She was crying and she said, "Okay. Okay. He can stay."

Of course Olivia couldn't sleep.

She gave them her room, her bed, and went into Ruby's room, the nursery. Curled up on the cot there, she heard the murmur of their voices. Then she heard their breathing, heavy, ragged. They were making love. Olivia knew she should cover her ears, but she didn't. She listened. Her own breath caught as theirs escalated. "This is sick," she said out loud. Embarrassed, she went downstairs.

She wrote:

> *Dear Amanda, I hope you are not still on Prozac, because I don't think it's good to stay on it too long. Amanda, I wish you had taken the shortcut, too. You see, he wanted to come back to bed that morning and I was sleepy, so I told him to go jogging instead. So I sent him there, to that road, that curve, but if you had taken the shortcut, he would have come around that corner fine. Amanda, we are both to blame.*

Olivia almost sent that one. But how do you tell a nineteen-year-old girl she really is guilty? Especially when you know who's really to blame.

Without even thinking, she called Winnie in Rhinebeck.

"Insomnia," she said when Winnie sleepily answered.

"I won't even ask what time it is," Winnie said.

Olivia thought of all the things she could say, but only one made sense. "I miss him," Olivia said.

"I know, sweetie."

Olivia was crying again. She wondered if the crying would ever stop. She'd read that a woman was born with all the eggs she'll ever have; maybe the same was true with tears. Maybe she would run out soon.

"I want him back," Olivia finally managed to say.

"Of course you do," Winnie said. "I know you do."

"You're the only one who knows it's my fault—"

"You've got to stop that," Winnie said. "How many times did you send him off and nothing happened? We don't remember those times, though."

"You know what?" Olivia said. "Fuck him for dying. Just fuck him."

"It was so stupid of him to die like that," Winnie said.

"I mean, why didn't he see that one stupid car? All the times he jogged in his life and he saw cars and trucks and dogs and all sorts of dangerous things, right?"

"Right."

"But he doesn't see this one stupid car. And that girl doesn't see him."

"You know," Winnie said, "they say with plane crashes, a series of things have to go wrong. And they do. A whole bunch of things go wrong and the plane crashes. That one in Bosnia? There was bad weather and pilot error and even a broken beacon."

Olivia wondered what series of errors had happened to David. A glare of sunlight, a car going just a little too fast.

"Why didn't he just pay attention?" she said finally. "Or jog a foot closer to the woods? Half a foot?"

"I don't know," Winnie said.

Olivia's crying was slowing down. She thought she could stretch out right there on the kitchen floor and go to sleep. "Just fuck him," she said.

"Yes," Winnie said.

"Oh, Winnie," she said, "why didn't I just let him in bed that morning? Why did I send him away?"

Instead of answering, Winnie said, "I was thinking of coming to visit you."

"Really? But what about Jeff? What about Rhinebeck?"

She heard Winnie take a deep breath.

"Olivia," Winnie said. "I'm going to come for August first."

Olivia moaned. She had not let herself think about it, even though it was less than a month away. She had actually forgotten about her own birthday last October until her parents and Amy showed up with a cake from the supermarket. Such a last-minute cake, she'd thought, imagining them arguing about whether or not to take it to her, then racing to buy one with her name hastily written across the top in pale pink icing, and arguing even as they stood on her doorstep, the cake with its pink rosettes in the box.

But David's birthday, she couldn't forget. She had considered flying out to California to be with his parents, two people she hardly knew; but at least they would be uncertain what to do that day, too. She had considered going away somewhere, someplace far from anything else she and David ever did or dreamed of doing. Peru or Alaska or Vietnam. But now that Winnie said it, Olivia knew that being with Winnie would be the best way to spend that day.

She said, "Yes. Come then. August first."

"I'm a whale. I'm hot and cranky," Winnie said.

"I know."

It wasn't until after she hung up that Olivia realized Ruby would still be there. Two hot and cranky pregnant women, Olivia thought. Maybe Winnie would actually understand. Wasn't she someone whom Olivia could count on?

. . .

Olivia woke to the sound of shouting from outside.

"Her husband is dead, you asshole!" Ruby said.

Olivia went to the window and looked out. Ben stood there, his arms spread like he was about to take flight. And Ruby, her hair wet and her back covered with sand—they'd been to the beach, Olivia guessed—paced back and forth in front of him.

A chill crept up Olivia's arms, sending the hairs there on end.

She could not hear what Ben was saying. Was he trying to take Ruby from her? Or the baby? Or both? Olivia hadn't trusted him, this longhaired poet who claimed to be genetically linked to the introduction of ice cream in America.

"You can't leave like this," Ruby said.

"I can do whatever I want," he said, and he turned from her and headed down the path, toward the road.

Ruby hesitated, then started after him. She ran so awkwardly that Olivia willed her to stop. Olivia remembered how Ben had described her tiny waist, the way he'd shaped such a small circle with his hands.

Both of them disappeared from Olivia's sight.

She stood there, gripping the windowsill for balance. It was another hot, muggy day with air that was too heavy and stagnant. If Ruby came back, they would go to the beach. They would take cold watermelon, a jug of lemonade, a treat from Winnie's food basket. If Ruby came back. Olivia was ready to start bargaining, the way she had when she got the news about David. If you make this go away, she'd said to God or whoever might be listening, I will join the Peace Corps, give away all of my earthly possessions, do anything, *anything.*

What bargain could she make now? she wondered, watching the hydrangeas that bordered the path out. The hydrangeas here grew the most beautiful shade of blue. She tried to remember why. A heavily alkaline soil? Or heavily acid? That was something else David would have known. She tried to name the shade of blue. Periwinkle? Somewhere she had once read that the color of hydrangeas could easily be manipulated by changing the chemical balance of the soil. The ones in her parents' yard were a pale pink.

Olivia sighed.

Still no Ruby.

Only minutes had passed—ten, fifteen? But they seemed endless.

From somewhere toward the beach came the sound of firecrackers. It was the Fourth of July. She had promised Amy that she would go to a barbecue at her condo. She had promised to take potato salad.

Still no Ruby.

David had made the best potato salad. He'd used sour cream and mayonnaise. He'd used fresh dill. Today was the day Olivia and David had planned to have a big party here. The house would be finished. They would have a baby. *What a lovely, lovely life.*

The hydrangeas hung blue and still in the hot summer air.

Olivia imagined the kind of party she and David would have made here. There was room in the yard for a big striped tent. David's specialty was saté, chicken and shrimp, skewers of them with a peanut dipping sauce. They would have grilled corn. They would make drinks in the blender with rum and fruit juice. In a box somewhere Olivia had a collection of brightly colored plastic mermaids and fish that she'd bought at the Sixth Avenue flea market. She saw herself on their lawn, with a baby in her arms, moving through a crowd of their friends, handing out tropical drinks with hot pink mermaids and electric blue dolphins perched on the rims. She was tanned and confident; she was loved. Olivia saw herself there, and almost, *almost*, saw David turning toward her.

Olivia leaned toward the window, as if leaning that way might bring her to him, to that time that would not ever be.

And when she leaned closer, a figure appeared, moved in front of the hydrangeas, came down the path.

Sunburned and crying and pregnant and young: Ruby walked back to Olivia.

Olivia had to take Ruby to Amy's party. The girl had cried on and off nonstop ever since Ben left. "Can't you just say I'm a neighbor's kid? I promise I won't say a word or eat any food or anything. I just don't want to be home alone with my thoughts." She blew her nose loudly for emphasis.

On the ride to Amy's, while Olivia's stomach knotted tighter and tighter—she really had gone mad, taking Ruby along to a family party—Ruby asked, "Which neighbor?" She looked terrible. Her nose was running and her eyes were puffy and her fingers and ankles were swollen.

"They won't ask," Olivia said. "Don't worry."

"You need details to convince them," Ruby mumbled, wiping her nose on the shred of tissue she'd been clutching.

But by the time they pulled into the parking lot at Amy's condo, Ruby was staring sadly out the window and humming an old familiar song softly. "Baby, baby, don't get hooked on me."

She almost smiled when she saw Olivia glancing over at her, frowning.

"B. J. Thomas," Ruby said. "I know so many unimportant things."

For some reason, this started her crying again, and they sat in the car, Olivia ineffectively patting Ruby's arm to console her, when really her mind was trying to sort out if the baby Ruby was setting free was Ben or the real baby. Impulsively, Olivia reached across the stick shift and rested her head lightly on Ruby's stomach. They sat like that, each listening for something different. Ruby's hand settled on Olivia's head, and gently, she stroked her hair, the way a mother would.

. . .

It was a small party because everyone had to fit on Amy's terrace overlooking the scenic route and the grill took up quite a bit of space. Even though Amy kept the condo in her divorce settlement, she took a lot of furniture and household items that worked better in the Victorian in Providence that her ex-husband and his girlfriend still lived in. Like the grill, a gas one with fold-down countertops and areas for warming and smoking.

"This is where I'm staying," Ruby announced, and she flopped into a wing-back chair. "Cool at last."

Olivia's mother came toward them immediately, wearing the frowning, worried expression she had worn since David died. Olivia wondered if her mother ever relaxed her face into its normal shape, or if this was it now: mother of a daughter with a dead husband.

"Honey," she said, taking Olivia's hands and pressing them into her own. "How are you?"

Olivia's mother was small and delicate, with a sweet voice that Amy and Olivia used to love to imitate.

"I'm fine," Olivia said, pulling her hands away.

"Are you?" her mother asked again, her expression deepening.

"Mom," Olivia said too sharply, "David is still dead. This is the best it gets for me. I'm up. I'm here. Now drop it."

She felt dizzy, not from the heat or her mother's strong, sweet lily-scented perfume, but from what she had said. In her mind, Olivia had turned her husband's name over and over. She had felt it on her tongue. But she had not ever said it out loud like that: *David is dead.*

Her mother fluttered around her now, mumbling the weak words of hope and encouragement that she'd been mumbling for ten months. In fact, Olivia realized, they were the same words she'd been hearing from her mother her whole life: "Everything happens for the best. *Que sera sera.* One door closes and another opens. . . ." There was no end to the platitudes of reassurance her mother offered. They were not a family that discussed feelings too closely; they kept emotion at arm's length. Olivia's mother often looked almost frightened at Olivia's mourning—the sobs and screams and wailing that she did at first, the more recent outbursts, which seemed to come without any provocation.

There had been times when her mother's cold comfort actually helped, like a good slap in the face. Other times, the suffocating sympathy from strangers was better for Olivia. People did not know what to give her; they asked again and again: "What can I do? What do you need?" But the truth was, Olivia didn't know, either.

Her mother's fluttering brought her right at Ruby's chair.

"Oh, dear," she said, and looked around nervously.

Olivia came up behind her mother and placed a hand on her small shoulder, causing her mother to jump slightly. Olivia stood a good six inches above her mother, and she could see her pink scalp—Like a baby's, Olivia thought—through her thin hair.

"Mom," Olivia said, "this is the neighbor's daughter. Ruby."

"Oh, dear," her mother said again, staring at Ruby's pregnant belly. Her mother liked to think that there were no drugs or teenage pregnancies or wayward girls. She peered at Ruby and talked in the voice she saved for waitresses and salesclerks, detached and superior. "Which neighbor?" she asked. "In the big house?"

Ruby grinned up at her. "The next one down. Weathered shingles? Blue shutters?"

Olivia was taken aback by the ease of the lie, and by her mother's acceptance.

"Yes," her mother said, nodding. "I know the one."

"They're in the Berkshires for the long weekend and Olivia was nice enough to look after me," Ruby said. She narrowed her eyes at something across the room. "God," she said, getting to her feet—an act that made Olivia hold her breath slightly; it always looked as if Ruby was on the verge of tipping over backward. "Is that shrimp cocktail?" Ruby asked. She must have decided it was, because she was off for the hors d'oeuvres table.

Olivia's mother watched her go.

"My goodness," she said. "She can't be more than seventeen."

"Fifteen, actually," Olivia told her.

Her mother gasped. "How awful. Is there a boy involved somehow?"

"Well, of course there is, Mom. That's how you *get* pregnant."

This was like the conversations Olivia had had with her mother her whole life. "How awful," her mother would say, that some girl's mother was on welfare, or her brother had gone to jail; that such a nice boy would wear a leather jacket or get a tattoo or waste his life in art school. The implication being, How awful that Olivia is with this dreadful person.

"There's no need for sarcasm, Olivia," her mother said. "I just meant, what will this girl do? They don't have those homes anymore, do they? And I've heard"—she lowered her voice, then continued—"that there are girls in New Jersey who actually put their babies in Dumpsters."

"Well," Olivia said, "they do kill them first, Mom."

No sooner had she said it than she wished she hadn't. She wanted nothing more than to tell her mother the truth. That baby is going to be mine, she wanted to shout to her mother, to everyone, to the world. Then she looked at her, the pink rouge settled in the lines on her face, the lipstick bleeding into the corners of her mouth, the resort wear outfit she had carefully chosen for today—white pants, a red sleeveless turtleneck, a blue cotton blazer with big brass buttons, and all the accessories matching—and Olivia knew she could not tell her mother anything at all.

"Newt Gingrich wants to bring those homes back—homes for unwed mothers. And I think he's right. Not that anyone listens to common sense anymore," her mother said, adjusting and readjusting her gold charm bracelet.

"Actually," Olivia said, "she's got an adoption all lined up."

"Well, that's a relief, isn't it?" her mother said. She still watched Ruby greedily eating shrimp. "Such a nice home, too," her mother added.

Amy was slamming bowls and serving spoons around in the kitchen. When she saw Olivia standing in the doorway, she looked relieved.

"Remember the Galápagos Islands?" she said.

"Darwin?"

"No. Edward."

Olivia did remember then: Amy's ex-husband, Edward, wanted to take their son, Matthew, there.

"Or should I say Edward and the bimbo?" Amy continued, sloppily dumping salad into a bowl. "Or should I say Edward and the soon-to-be *Mrs.* Edward. And get this: Matthew wants to go with them. 'Giant turtles,' he said. 'Awesome.' The little traitor. They're getting married and going to the Galápagos Islands to look at turtles for their honeymoon. I mean, we went to Maui for our honeymoon." Amy held up a bowl of Jell-O with bananas and strawberries inside. "And another thing, who brings Jell-O to a party? I mean, it's the nineties. People do not eat Jell-O anymore."

Olivia put her arms around her sister's shoulders. "It's not that bad."

"Sure. It only means he *loves* her, that's all. It only means that my own son loves them both."

"I meant the Jell-O," Olivia said. "The Jell-O isn't so bad."

Amy laughed, but she stayed nestled in Olivia's arms. "It was one thing being left for some kind of crazy affair. It's another thing when your husband actually loves someone. I mean, I know that since that thing happened to you, it's hard to imagine that something like this can be so terrible—"

Olivia turned her sister so that they faced each other.

"Amy," she said, "'that thing' is that David died." She felt less dizzy this time, but her voice dropped to a whisper. "David is dead," she said.

Amy's eyes widened as if she were hearing the news for the first time. "Oh my God, Olivia," she said.

From the doorway, Ruby said, "Great. Jell-O. I love when they put fruit it in."

She came in and took the bowl from Amy, holding it up to the light. "Is it fruit cocktail in there? That's the best. Bananas turn brown. Once my mother called the Jell-O hot line to find out how to keep the bananas from turning brown, but they didn't have any advice, so we just stick to fruit cocktail." Lowering her voice, she added, "Did you know there's like pork in Jell-O? Honest to God. Maybe that's why it's so good."

She grinned and shook Amy's hand with her other hand.

"I'm Ruby. I live in that house next to Olivia's. The weathered shingled one with the blue shutters? My folks are sort of embarrassed to have me with them in this condition, so they went off to the Berkshires, and Olivia is kind of taking care of me."

Amy frowned, and it was as if Olivia were reading right into her brain. Olivia can hardly take care of herself. How is she supposed to look after you?

"They must be pretty hard up for baby-sitters," Amy said.

Ruby slurped down spoonfuls of Jell-O. "Well, actually it's a little late for baby-sitters, you could say, right? But my mother is knitting the baby all of these little tiny sweaters, even though she's like totally mad and upset and everything. She's crazy like that. Isn't she, Olivia?"

Ruby turned her sticky face toward Olivia, who nodded. But

what Olivia was thinking was how good a liar Ruby really was. How very, very good.

Olivia's father was a stiff-upper-lip kind of guy. When his company downsized after thirty-five years there and he was forced into early retirement, he said, "That's the way the ball bounces." Then he took up golf with a vengeance, and now he walked around with madras pants in silly sherbert colors and a lime green cardigan. He liked to brag that he was the first Italian-American to join that country club. "How do you like that?" he'd say smugly.

"Hanging in there?" he said to Olivia. He tapped her lightly on the arm like they were old pals.

"Yup," she said, tapping him back. "Hanging in there."

"Good girl."

Olivia wasn't sure, but she thought those were the exact words he'd said to her when she woke up from an emergency appendectomy when she was eleven. She went out on the terrace, where a crowd of people her own age had gathered. On her way, she grabbed a beer and quickly drank about half of it.

A man wearing an apron that said KISS THE CHEF was grilling sausages. A woman who was either his wife or his date—she hung on to his elbow possessively—told Olivia they were duck, smoked chicken, and garlic and herbs for vegetarians. Inside, she said, there were a variety of condiments, like apple chutney, cranberry relish, and hot mustard. Then she continued talking to another woman.

Olivia looked out, across the road, to the beach. The water was flat and calm; the air hung in a haze above it.

A man smiled right in Olivia's face. He was too cute for Olivia to talk to. Give her Pete Lancelotta and she could handle it. Give her shoulders like this and a pair of blue eyes and surfer-boy blond hair and she was lost.

"Are you going to kiss the chef?" he asked, grinning and pointing with his bottle of Corona to the man at the grill.

"Doubtful," Olivia said in her best leave-me-alone tone of voice. A cute man at a party talked to you and the next thing you knew you had to have drinks with him, exchange phone numbers, all sorts of unpleasant things.

"He's a doctor, too. Can you believe it? A pediatrician. Would you want your kid to be taken care of by a guy who wears an apron like that?"

Olivia gave the cute guy a tight smile.

"Which is my way of asking if you have kids, which is my way of finding out if you are married. Subtle, huh?"

Olivia refused to be charmed by him. "Actually," she said, "no."

A woman came over and linked her arm through the man's. "Hey," she said.

"Obviously," Olivia said, wanting to get him in trouble, "you're here with someone."

Then she recognized the look on the woman's face. She wore the expression that Olivia found too familiar—sympathetic and worried.

"This is Amy's *sister*," she said to the man.

Olivia said what the woman couldn't. "The one whose husband died last year."

"Oh," he said, slightly embarrassed.

"I remember when that happened," the woman told Olivia. "I heard it on the eleven o'clock news and I thought it was one of the most tragic things I had ever heard."

"Me, too," Olivia said. She held up her empty beer bottle as an excuse to leave, then went back inside. Lines like that surfer boy used, and he was here with a date. Who could a person trust these days?

. . .

"That was a good party," Ruby said as they drove back later that night. Ahead of them, the sky was bright with color and smoke from the fireworks show. "I love Jell-O like that. Can you make that? It must be hard. Or maybe not." She shrugged and pointed to the sky. "Pretty," she said.

"I guess," Olivia said.

"You don't like parties, do you?" Ruby said.

Olivia pulled over to the side of the road and got out of the car, leaving the high beams on.

"I want to show you something," she said, motioning for Ruby to follow her.

They stood in the darkness, the two headlights making a funny alien glow. Behind them, crickets chirped so loudly that when Olivia spoke, she had to raise her voice.

"This is where it happened," Olivia said. She pointed to the spot in the road where David's body had flown over that blue Honda Civic.

"No shit," Ruby said, awed.

"Are you going to leave me?" Olivia said. "Are you going to keep that baby? Because if you are, just go now. I cannot do it. I cannot have you promise me this and lie about it."

"I'm not leaving," Ruby said.

"I mean," Olivia said, "you have no idea what I've been through."

"I'm not leaving," Ruby said again.

"Well," Olivia said.

Her heart raced foolishly. She got back in the car. When Ruby slid in beside her, Olivia said, "Well. You'd better not."

The car in the driveway was unfamiliar. So was the woman sitting on the front steps smoking a cigarette.

The woman stood when she saw Olivia and Ruby. She was tall

and slender, blond. She wore khaki trousers and a white scoop-neck sleeveless shirt.

"Finally," she said, looking past Olivia and Ruby, as if someone else should appear.

"Where is he?" she said.

"Who?" Ruby asked her.

The woman threw her hands in the air. "This is so typical," she said. "I wrote him in January and told him I'd be coming through on my way back to New York. I told him to let me know if it would be a big deal for me to stay." She looked behind them again. "Do you know how long it takes to get back from Central America? I'll tell you how long. Forever."

Olivia said, "I'm a little confused. Who are you looking for?"

She imagined it might be Ben. Or maybe the old couple who used to own the place.

"Are you Olivia?" the woman asked.

"Yes."

"I'm Rachel," she said. "The one he was buying the hat for," she added.

"Oh no," Olivia said.

"It is a big deal, right?" Rachel said.

She bent to pick up her duffel bag, but Olivia stopped her.

"It's just so typical of David," Rachel began. "I told him in the letter to leave a message with my service if there was a problem. It's not like you can get messages in Honduras, you know." She shook her head. "That's David for you." Then she noticed Olivia's face. "What?" she said.

"David's dead," Olivia said, and the words, spoken so often to-day, did not come out any easier.

chapter seven

True Colors

Olivia kept refilling Rachel's glass with water, which the woman gulped down noisily. As soon as the glass was empty again, Rachel held it out to Olivia for more.

But finally, Rachel paused and said, "Dead. Jesus." She didn't put the glass down. Instead, she held it in both hands and looked into it as if it might hold some answers.

Olivia wasn't sure what to say, so she gave Rachel the details: jogging, curve, blue Honda Civic. With each detail, Rachel's eyes widened.

"Jesus," she said again, looking up at Olivia. "Death waits at our door, but we don't actually expect it to come inside."

Inside, Olivia cringed. Who actually said things like that?

But clearly, Ruby was impressed. "Wow," she said. "That's heavy. Are you a poet or something?"

Olivia had forgotten Ruby was even there.

Rachel, too, seemed to see Ruby for the first time.

"Is she yours?" she asked Olivia.

"She kind of wandered in one day," Olivia explained, shrugging.

Clearly, that wasn't good enough for Rachel, who sat frowning at Olivia. Olivia considered what she knew about Rachel. She was a mountain climber, a doctor, the woman David had loved before Olivia. She was from the Bay Area, too, had actually gone to Berkeley with David and Rex. In fact, Rachel had moved back to San Francisco. Olivia remembered the computer-made change of address card she'd sent, how she'd cleverly imposed her image on it, her head already in California, her body stretching across the country, her feet still in New York. "Who has time to do things like this?" Olivia had said when she saw it. David had smiled knowingly. "Rachel can do more in a day than anyone I know." And Olivia, already jealous of all the years Rachel had had with David, had muttered, "Well, goody for her."

Now, she was, sitting right across from Olivia, glaring.

"She's a runaway?" Rachel said.

Rachel spoke in the clipped, matter-of-fact voice of someone who was confident and self-assured. Olivia could imagine her giving a fatal diagnosis to someone, delivering bad news.

"Ha!" Ruby said. "I didn't have to run away. My parents kicked me out."

"Because you're pregnant?"

"Duh," Ruby said. "What do *you* think?" She moved closer to Rachel, so close that their knees practically touched. "Where do you live?"

"San Francisco," Rachel said.

"Wow!" Ruby said. "That's incredible. Ben would die if he was here. No kidding. Did you ever hear of Jack Kerouac?"

"I have," Rachel said, obviously touched by the girl's naïveté.

"You have?" Ruby said, grinning. "That is so excellent."

"Everyone's heard of Jack Kerouac," Olivia said sharply.

But Ruby ignored her. "Ben," she told Rachel, "he's the one. You know." She blushed and giggled in her adolescent way, then rolled her eyes.

For the first time, her dramatics annoyed, rather than touched, Olivia.

"He *was* my boyfriend," Ruby continued. "Until this morning."

Rachel frowned even more. "He abandoned you?"

"Basically," Ruby said. "Yeah. I mean, I'm the one who actually has to have the baby, you know? And then give it away after all these months of talking to it and stuff. It can hear and everything. So I try to tell it things. Ben read it 'Howl.' The whole poem. He put his lips right to my stomach and recited the whole thing. But he thinks I'm being so cavalier about it. That's the word he used. I looked it up to be sure I understood. Do you know what the dictionary said? It said 'haughty'! It said 'carefree'! It said 'offhanded,' like I could give up a baby—our baby, no less—all carefree, like nothing mattered."

Olivia tried to stand between the two of them, but she couldn't quite wedge her way in.

"No one's saying that, Ruby," Olivia said, trying to force eye contact with Rachel. They were the adults here, weren't they? Especially Rachel, someone so responsible that she gave up money and time to go to Central America and operate on children with some sort of severe facial deformity; she and David had seen a PBS special on doctors who do that, and he'd told her that Rachel was there, right then.

Rachel didn't give any signal to Olivia at all. Clearly, they weren't on the same wavelength.

"A baby isn't something you discard cavalierly," Rachel said in a voice so soothing that Olivia wanted to scream. "And I know you wouldn't do that."

Ruby was nodding with too much enthusiasm. "Olivia just made it sound so simple, you know? And her husband died and she's all alone."

"Wait one minute," Olivia said.

"Olivia," Rachel said, her voice still all smooth and buttery. "Can I talk to you alone?"

Ruby got to her feet. "That's cool," she said. "I'm going to bed anyway. I can't believe I ever used to stay up all night. I mean, ever since this happened, I like fall asleep at nine o'clock. I never even see *Melrose Place* anymore. I'm totally out of the loop."

Olivia thought of that A&W, those stoned teenagers with their pasty faces and tangled hair.

"Not a bad loop to be out of," she muttered. How had she ended up the outsider here?

Ruby started to walk away, but she twirled around like a ballerina to face Olivia and Rachel again. She laughed. "Oh, yes," she said with mock seriousness, "I'm a wayward teen. A bad seed." She was almost graceful when she skipped away.

Olivia sighed and rolled her eyes. "Kids," she said, aware that she was mimicking Ruby's exaggerated motions. Olivia sat up straighter, cleared her throat, and tried again. "Seriously," she said, "you can't imagine what it has been like since . . ." The words stuck again and Olivia tried to force them out.

But Rachel didn't give her a chance.

"I remember the night David called to tell me he'd gotten married," Rachel said. "I was still reeling from the breakup. Instead of this gorgeous hat, he runs off with the milliner."

"It was one of those things," Olivia said. She could see him in the doorway of her small shop, through the steam from the hats she was blocking.

"I was still at the hospital, and when I heard his voice, I thought something was terribly wrong. Why would he track me down at work? Why not leave a message for me at home? So I immediately imagined that he had some fatal disease." She added quickly, "Not that I had any reason to suspect that, but it seemed so *large*, him calling me there after all those months. I suppose a small part of me thought he wanted to come back."

Olivia considered the word: *large.* That was how her heart had felt when they were first falling in love, as if her ribs, her chest, her body were all too small to contain this thing. That was how her life with David had felt, full and large. That was how losing him felt still.

Rachel was saying, "He told me you were his soul mate. For a time, I had hoped he was mine, I suppose. Funny, I almost envy you, sitting there, the widow."

She looked directly at Olivia. She was a no-nonsense person, in her khaki trousers and sensible haircut and flat walking shoes. David never spoke badly of Rachel. But he had laughed at how organized she was, how practical. She was someone who knew about mulching a garden and how to use vinegar as a cleaning product; someone who put up preserves and knew how to fish and ski and change a flat tire. Rachel was sensible. She was a fourth-generation Californian. Her ancestors had arrived there in wagon trains.

Rachel leaned toward Olivia, her long, tanned arms reaching across the table.

"The thing is," she said, "you can't keep this girl. You have to notify the authorities." She lowered her already-smooth low voice and added, "You're not in any frame of mind to make such big decisions. That's clear."

That was clear? Olivia wondered how she must seem to this self-assured woman, this widow once removed.

"Excuse me?" Olivia said.

"The girl," Rachel said, impatient. "Her parents must be worried sick. And this boy. Ben? He needs to be held accountable."

"Don't you think I've taken care of that?" Olivia said. She had planned to call Ben's parents—or to call John Adams in Bedford Hills, New York. But it was the fucking Fourth of July. Someone named John Adams would be off doing something patriotic.

"It's irresponsible," Rachel said.

And the way she said it, the *largeness* of her words, made Olivia think that Rachel thought all of it was irresponsible—not just Ruby, but David getting hit by that car and dying, and even the meager way that Olivia had carried on since, though of course Rachel had no idea what Olivia had done these months.

"Look," Olivia said, and now it was she who lowered her voice, afraid Ruby would hear what she was about to say. "I've talked to her mother. You have no idea what she's like." She wanted to explain about the ruddy-faced mother—a drinker, maybe—and her willingness to dump Ruby and the baby on Olivia or anyone who might take her in. But she was too worried that Ruby would hear her, so she just shook her head.

"She's just a child," Rachel said, as if Olivia had not told her anything. "Please. And you're promising her solutions that aren't in anyone's best interest."

Olivia was aware of movement somewhere behind her. It was Ruby, of course. She had not gone upstairs at all. Instead, she'd stayed, hidden.

Rachel heard Ruby, too.

The girl's footsteps hurrying up the stairs echoed in the kitchen.

"I think she needs some space to really consider what she's doing. You don't want a young woman out in the world wondering about her choices, regretting a snap decision—"

"It isn't a snap decision!" Olivia said, her own voice anything but calm. "I'm helping her!"

"Then you won't mind if I talk to her?" Rachel said.

"It's a free country," Olivia said, but Rachel was already up, on her way to Ruby.

Olivia waited for Rachel to get upstairs, then quietly followed, hiding in the dark hallway outside Ruby's room. It was her turn to eavesdrop.

"What were you afraid we were going to say?" Rachel asked Ruby, who was pretending to watch television.

Ruby shrugged, kept her eyes focused on the screen.

"May I touch your stomach?" Rachel said. "Just kind of check on the baby?"

Olivia did not hear Ruby's answer, but she watched as Rachel stood and placed her hands on the girl's belly. Olivia was reminded of healers she'd once seen in a documentary, women who used their hands to stop bleeding, heal sores, take away pain.

"I hope it's a boy," Ruby said eagerly. "I would like that. A boy like Ben."

Rachel removed from her neck the thin silver chain with a small cross hanging from it.

"It *feels* like a boy," Rachel said. "Let's see what the universe says."

Olivia fought back a laugh. *The universe?* And here she was, so convinced of Rachel's common sense. But of course, like David, she probably placed a mirror at the front door, refused to put beds against the wall, hung tinkling wind chimes out front, all to keep her environment in harmony. Olivia had relented to David's wishes, and look where it had gotten her. Look where it had gotten him.

Rachel held the cross above Ruby's stomach. Even crouched in the hallway, Olivia could see it sway back and forth, in a straight line.

"Yes," Rachel said. "It's a boy. Girls move in a circle. Like this." She swung the chain in a circular motion. "So they say."

Ruby was grinning. Her hands cupped her stomach; Olivia was always surprised how big she looked lying down.

"Hey, Sage," Ruby cooed. "My man. You almost ready to meet the world?"

This was the first time she'd heard Ruby do this, talk to the baby, sound like a mother.

"Sage?" Rachel said. "What a good name."

"Come on, Sage," Ruby said, her voice lilting like a lullaby. "I'm waiting for you."

"What you do," Rachel was saying when Olivia walked into the kitchen, "is walk up this spiral staircase, and there's a door at the top that leads right to the roof. From there, you can see both bridges—"

"The Golden Gate Bridge? Really?" Ruby said.

"And the Bay Bridge, yes. And you can see Alcatraz and the Bay. Everything really. It's one of the reasons I bought the house. The view." As she talked, Rachel drew on a napkin: long parallel lines for the bridges and a circle for Alcatraz, and little *v*'s for the water.

"You know," Olivia said, sitting across from the two of them, "in the winter, when the trees are bare, you can see the ocean from my bedroom window. Just a sliver of it." She held up two fingers to show how small a piece.

But Ruby and Rachel stared back at her as if she was the intruder here, when really neither of them had been invited guests exactly. Olivia frowned. Even though she was simply across the table from them, she felt as if she were on another planet—a planet somehow spinning away from theirs.

Rachel cleared her throat and began to clear away breakfast

dishes. While she slept, Rachel and Ruby had had a feast, apparently. Food, Olivia knew, was the way to Ruby's heart.

"I was just telling Ruby about my house," Rachel said as she cleared eggy plates, plates with crumbs and smears of red jelly. "It's one of those special places that you find and have to have. Of course, it's funny to be in it alone. It's meant for a family. It's practically screaming for one. I suppose that's partially my fault, the way I painted it and arranged all the rooms."

She glanced around at the disaster—unpainted, hardly any furniture—that was Olivia's house.

"We had big plans for this place," Olivia explained. "We loved it. We really did. And now, well, now I don't know." She felt awkward and embarrassed by the house suddenly, with all its bad memories. Why, she could almost see David walking out this door the day he died, could see the shadow of his back right there in the spot where morning light spilled now. She could remember how the sheets felt when she rolled back into them after pushing him away from her and suggesting he go jogging. If only she had given in to his touch, his searching fingers, his lips. "Good idea," he'd said, disappointed. "Better than a cold shower." And she'd been happy to go back to sleep.

Rachel stopped, a coffee cup in each hand, and said, " 'One does not love a place the less for having suffered in it.' "

"Wow," Ruby said. "Did you just, like, make that up in your head?" She looked at Olivia accusingly. "She's the smartest person I've ever met."

"I can't take credit," Rachel said, returning to her efficient table cleaning, now swiping a damp sponge across the top. "Jane Austen said it first."

"Cool," Ruby said. "I love her. She wrote that movie with Gwyneth Paltrow in it, right?"

Olivia didn't like the way Rachel's mouth turned up at the corners, satisfied. She didn't like the woman's tanned bare legs and khaki wraparound skirt, the way she'd tied her sleeveless white blouse so carelessly around her waist. She tried to imagine her with David. She'd seen pictures, the two of them always frozen in some athletic moment: in skis or on bikes, triumphant on top of mountains, both of them sturdy and sure, wrapped in fleece or Gore-Tex or down.

Her David, Olivia thought, had let her try new hat designs on him, sat in bubble baths until his fingers and toes grew raisinlike, ate in bed and slept late. This woman isn't even mourning the right guy, Olivia thought angrily.

"I brought coffee from Guatemala. There's a fresh pot," Rachel said. She inhaled sharply, then blew it out in a fast exhale. "I know how much David liked his coffee. Do you know that he never went camping without Peet's coffee and a Melitta one-cup?" She pressed on her temples. "Jesus," she said.

"We didn't do much camping," Olivia said. "It's hard to pitch your tent in Washington Square Park." She had meant it as a joke, but it came out flat. All right, she admitted, Rachel had had him longer. But she hadn't had him better.

"I think," Rachel said evenly, "it's time for me to leave."

Later, after Rachel had cleaned the counters and scrubbed the sink with Ajax, after she had put the Guatemalan coffee in an airtight container, after she'd gotten in her rented Geo and driven away, and the day grew hot and muggy and long, Olivia could only wonder why Ruby would not let go of that stupid napkin with the childish drawing of a floor plan and a view from a place she would never go.

When Ruby had wandered outside, waving good-bye to Rachel like an idiot, like an old friend, Olivia had thrown the coffee grounds onto the wall, where they scattered and settled like a colony of ants.

She made sure Ruby was still outside; then she called information in Westchester.

There was no John Adams in Bedford Hills, New York.

For days after Rachel left, Ruby ignored Olivia. If Olivia walked in on her in bed while Ruby was playing music on her Walkman, the headphones on her stomach, Ruby pretended not to notice her standing there. Another time, Olivia heard her in the bathtub, the water sloshing and Ruby whispering, "Sage, Sage, can you hear me?" "I can hear you," Olivia shouted through the locked door. Then the bathroom grew silent.

On Thursday afternoon, Olivia chopped plum tomatoes and fresh basil, boiled water for pasta. She hummed, then stopped. The basil was bright green, pungent. The tomatoes spilled seeds across the counter. She had been humming a Beatles song, "Eight Days a Week." Olivia took all of this in: the food, the song she'd been humming, the stillness of the midsummer-afternoon air, the hushed sound of water boiling on the stove.

She stood there like that for what seemed like a long time. Then she went back to cooking, to humming.

At four o'clock, Olivia took a glass of lemonade out to Ruby, who was in her usual spot on a chaise longue in the far corner of the yard. She opened her eyes when Olivia's shadow fell across her face.

"You're blocking my sun," Ruby said.

Olivia didn't move. She held out the glass of lemonade, which Ruby took, reluctantly.

"Excuse me for asking," Olivia said. "But what's going on here?"

"Rachel says it's unethical, what you're doing," Ruby said.

"Rachel says? What does she know about anything?"

"She's totally cool," Ruby said. "She says I can come and live in San Francisco if I want. She says I can bring Sage. We can *both* live there. We can be a family, a real family. You know, someone walking by, some kid, could look in at us and see a mother and a baby. They could see them together and think, I wish I had what they have."

Olivia swallowed hard, but the lump of anger in her throat stayed put.

"You know what's in San Francisco?" Ruby asked, as if it was a demand.

She sat up, spreading her legs to make a place for her belly to rest.

"The Gap is in San Francisco," Ruby said.

"The Gap?"

Ruby nodded. "That's right. I can get a job there. In corporate headquarters. I could invent colors or something. Like they don't have red; they have mango. You know what flax is?"

Before Olivia could answer, Ruby said, "It's beige! I've already got a whole bunch thought up."

"Wait a minute," Olivia said. "The Gap is not going to hire a fifteen-year-old high school dropout to name their colors. Did Rachel say that? Because it's preposterous."

"Rachel said I could go to a special school they've got in San Francisco that lets teenaged mothers get their high school diplomas at night and weekends, so I *could* work at the Gap and do something really interesting."

"Like name colors? That's not even a job," Olivia said. Damn Rachel. Damn that do-gooder, that meddler, that asshole.

"It is too a job," Ruby said, her face red from sun and anger. "They have a bazillion jobs that are totally cool. Like I could think up baby-clothes ideas. I'll have a baby, right?"

At this, Olivia's heart lurched. She sat down on the scratchy grass to try to stay on balance.

"So I could think of ways to make baby clothes easier. Or hipper. Like already I was thinking how you never see babies in black. Black is the coolest color, and they always put babies in like pink or yellow or something. I already have ideas for a whole line of black baby clothes."

"Tons of babies wear black, Ruby," Olivia said.

"Like who?"

"Like every baby in New York City, for starters."

Ruby rolled her eyes in that annoying adolescent way of hers. "That's not even the point. The point is, I have all these options. You never gave me any options. It was just like, I'll feed you and take you to the doctor and you give me your baby. Plain and simple. But it isn't so simple, you know. Giving up something like a baby. I mean, this kid is inside my stomach. He's part of me. Rachel sent me this book that has all these pictures from like when it's just a fertilized egg, and how it changes into a person. I mean," Ruby said, "it's a fucking miracle."

"What about Ben?" Olivia said, desperate. She wished she could shake Rachel, hard. "What about Bali?"

"Ben is like totally pissed off because I was so willing to throw our baby away—"

"Throw it away?" Olivia said, too loudly. "I want this baby. Giving it to me is not throwing it away."

Ruby jumped up and hovered over Olivia, her belly large and intimidating, ugly blue veins crisscrossing her legs like a map of back roads.

"Stop calling my baby 'it'! This is a person, not an it!" Ruby shouted. "Call him Sage," Ruby said, her voice softer.

She sunk down beside Olivia.

"You don't understand," Olivia said. "I would make a family

for your baby. I would. And someone looking in the window at us would pause and smile and think we were happy."

"You don't give a shit about me," Ruby said. "You're using me."

"You robbed me," Olivia said, "and I took you in again. You had nowhere to go."

"You cut a deal with my mother," Ruby said, actually pointing a nail-bitten finger at Olivia. "I heard you tell Rachel you went and talked to them, so don't deny it."

She had heard. Olivia tried to catch her breath, but she only made pathetic little gasping noises.

"I didn't cut a deal—" she began.

"She probably paid you to take the baby so she and Mr. Wonderful can live in peace."

"Ruby," Olivia said helplessly.

"Do you know what he does for a job?" Ruby was saying. "He works at EB. He builds nuclear submarines." Then she added, "He hates me."

Olivia took Ruby by the shoulders, her skin slippery with sweat beneath Olivia's hands. "Listen," Olivia said. "I didn't cut a deal with them. I should have told you I talked to her. Okay? But I didn't get money from them. The only person I cut a deal with is you." Olivia waited for Ruby to consider this. "I had to be sure," Olivia said. "I had to."

Ruby slid out from under Olivia's grasp.

"Maybe I can win Ben back," she said. "Rachel says if I go there and go to that special school and work for the Gap and take good care of Sage, Ben will see what kind of person I am. He'll see how desperate I was to almost give away our baby. He'll love me again. He'll know I wasn't what he said. Cavalier."

"Fine," Olivia said, standing. Now she loomed over Ruby. She felt tall and thin and wise and lovely. "Go to San Francisco. But I can tell you something that Rachel neglected to tell you. You're not going to be thinking about cute ideas for baby clothes or quirky names for colors. You're going to be folding thousands of pairs of jeans. You're going to be hanging up shirts and waiting on customers and cleaning out dressing rooms. Then you're going to go home and clean shitty diapers and make bottles of formula and stay up all night with a crying baby. This isn't a game, Ruby. This is life. And Doctor Rachel works fourteen, fifteen hours a day. She's not going to be there holding your feet and giving you aromatherapy."

"Fuck you," Ruby said. She was too ungainly to get to her feet. Olivia had the advantage. "Just fuck you," Ruby said again.

Even though the book they had read and discussed was *The Beauty Myth*, all of the women—except Mimi, who was away at Club Med—were in the bathroom, positioned around Olivia, who sat facing the mirror, a towel around her shoulders, her hair damp; they were trying to agree on a good haircut for her. Amy thought she should lose a good four inches and get a simple blunt cut; Jill, whose own sexy shag gave her a good deal of credibility, thought she should lose only an inch or two and layer the front; and Pam, whose Snow White hairstyle made Olivia afraid she might end up looking like a cartoon character, too—the Little Mermaid, the Wicked Stepmother?—was talking about bobs.

Olivia looked at herself, at her cheekbones and at her eyebrows, which were in need of a good waxing, and remembered the days she'd take a taxi to her hair salon on Madison Avenue and give herself over to first her colorist, Courtney, and then her hairstylist, Robert, and then to a woman named Iliana, who waxed her facial hair and popped her blackheads and dyed her eyelashes with a vegetable dye. It was another lifetime when Olivia would go there for all those hours and emerge so self-assured, all smooth-skinned and with blow-dried hair. She would step off the curb and raise her arm to stop a taxi, certain that she looked good; that when she got the food from the Chinese delivery boy that night, he would smile at her; that if she saw Winnie, her friend would tell her how great her haircut was; that David would want to go to bed early and make love.

"I'm a mess," Olivia said. She said it without any self-pity; it was true.

"When's the last time you got your hair cut?" Jill asked her, lifting the heavy ends, then shaking her head before she let them fall.

"I don't even know," Olivia said.

"You need some good layers around your face," Jill said.

"Layers are so eighties," Amy said. "I mean, they look good on you. But in general, they don't work anymore."

Pam shook her head. "Bobs are in now."

"I know exactly what she needs."

Olivia recognized Ruby's voice before she saw her face in the mirror.

"Something hip," Ruby continued. "The thing about Olivia is, she's a lot hipper than her grieving-widow look lets on."

The others stepped aside to make room for her. Olivia saw them exchange surprised looks.

Ruby ran her fingers through Olivia's hair, untangling, smoothing.

"Something very Cheryl Tiegs. Very late sixties. To here, maybe," she said, sweeping Olivia's collarbone with her fingertips. "You want to flip it up, like Marlo Thomas's hair in *That Girl*. Bangs are good. Long bangs." She looked at the women. "Don't you guys read *You!*?"

She took the scissors from Pam, then smiled broadly at them all in the mirror.

"I'm the neighbor's wayward kid," Ruby announced. "Knocked up and kicked out. Can't go home until the baby's been adopted and I'm skinny again. Olivia's baby-sitting me."

"Ruby's moving to San Francisco," Olivia said, staring in the mirror right at Ruby. "She's got a future working at the Gap."

"Their stocks are doing great," Jill said, shrugging. "Maybe it's a good place to go."

"Do you guys all have kids?" Ruby asked. She kept running her fingers through Olivia's hair. Even though they all nodded, she didn't really pay attention. "I mean, once you've done this, had a baby inside you, moving around and stuff, you're a changed person. You can't even go back to your old self. You try to imagine your life the way it used to be before the baby. You were like a hundred pounds lighter and you got stoned all the time and stayed up all night and didn't think about things, except in a kind of vague way, you know? Well, you can't be that way anymore, so you imagine what your life will be like with a baby. Maybe you'll live someplace different. Maybe you'll get a cool job at the Gap. And your kid will wear funky hats and learn how to surf and not have to go to school or anything. But then you wonder if you can be a person like that. Or do you have to just reinvent yourself? Maybe you can't go back to your old self and maybe you can't keep the kid alone, so you have to become a person who had a baby and gave it away. Maybe you don't know who to trust." Ruby sighed. "Maybe you spent your whole life wanting a family and then when it was your turn to make one, you blew it. You acted cavalier."

They all watched her as she talked and played with Olivia's hair. It was as if they were all holding their breath, waiting to see where she would end up.

Ruby took a breath, then said, "I am so good at this. Cutting hair. I used to always cut my friend Betsy's hair. Once I shaved both our heads. Bald. And my mother got so pissed off. She's like, 'There are women who have lost their hair from chemotherapy and you are mocking them.' But we weren't. It was just cool, you know?"

She started cutting, holding the ends out toward Olivia's chin like a professional, the way Robert did at the Madison Avenue salon where Olivia paid over a hundred dollars for a haircut.

"The other thing I'm really good at is piercing," Ruby said. "I used to, like, sit on the phone and just put needles through my ears." She stopped long enough to show her array of earrings. "I didn't do my nose myself, though. I had that done. And after I have the baby, I'm getting my navel pierced. My friend Betsy got hers done and it got all infected and stuff, so I figured maybe that wasn't good for the baby, you know, so I waited. But in another month or so, I'll be able to get my navel pierced and dye my hair some good color, maybe like platinum blond."

Ruby stopped cutting long enough to meet their shocked stares. She smiled and started cutting again.

"Hair dye can make your baby like stupid or deformed or something, because, I mean, it goes right in your brain, through your scalp, your follicles, and all those chemicals are so toxic."

Ruby looked right at Olivia.

"No one would adopt it then, right? If it was stupid or deformed?" she said.

"But your baby is perfect," Olivia said. "Don't worry."

"So even if its mother acted stupid and like got all carried away with some fantasy about making a family when really she knew she couldn't, she didn't have the skills or the maturity or whatever, someone would still adopt the baby? Someone who had all those things, the skills and like, the desire and the love and stuff, maybe? Like they wouldn't worry about stupid genes or anything?"

Olivia had won. She closed her eyes and let the pieces of her hair fall around her, let this girl cut and shape it for her.

"They wouldn't worry about any of that," Olivia said. "Someone will adopt your baby."

chapter eight

Babies and Mariachi

Olivia waited in the offices of Kurz and Beekman to see Ellen, the lawyer. The cool air-conditioned air felt so good that Olivia regretted not having brought Ruby. The girl had wanted to come, but Olivia thought she should do this herself, get her own information and ask her own questions.

An office door opened, and a man called Olivia's name, pronouncing the Bertolucci perfectly.

When she stood, they looked at each other in surprise. It was the surfer boy from Amy's party. The *sleazy* surfer boy, Olivia reminded herself.

"Well, well," he said, shaking her hand firmly. He smiled a broad white-toothed smile and showed her into his office.

"I was supposed to see Ellen," Olivia said.

"She's on vacation. Cancún, if you can believe it. It's probably a hundred degrees in the shade."

He bothered her—the crinkly laugh lines at his eyes and those shoulders that hardly seemed contained under his suit jacket.

"You're frowning," he said. "Maybe you like Cancún in July?"

"No. I don't know. It's not Cancún—"

He raised one eyebrow. "No?"

"It's that I can't believe you're a lawyer," Olivia said. He should be a construction worker on a television commercial, a glamorized version of a working-class guy, she thought.

"That's because you think of me as some idiot who came up to you with a bad line at a party," he said. "Or worse, you think of me as a guy who hits on women at parties when he's actually with someone. But I can explain. I tried to find you and do that then, but it seems you had already left."

"Actually," Olivia told him, "I don't think of you at all."

She shifted her weight uncomfortably. The truth was, Olivia *had* thought of this surfer boy. Up in her hot, airless bedroom, trying to sleep, he'd popped into her mind, dressed in the ridiculous Jams he'd had on and the brightly colored T-shirt. After that night she'd heard Ruby and Ben, Olivia had ached for someone to moan with. She'd tried to conjure David, but somehow the sex with him felt distant and meager compared to how much more of him she missed. No. What she longed for at night was simply fucking. And she was embarrassed, confronted with him now, that this surfer boy had been the focus of her fantasies lately. Touching herself so frantically, so desperately, burying her face in her pillow so that Ruby wouldn't hear. Then feeling guilty afterward, and unsatisfied.

She shifted again, watched him shuffle some papers, his head bent in such a way that his profile looked almost appealing. All right, Olivia admitted. From this angle, he did seem harmless, like a guy you could have a beer with. Then her brain darted past a simple beer and again she imagined it: fucking him. She let out a weird little noise, like a seal barking.

Even now, as he looked up from his papers, puzzled, the guy made her irritable.

"Do you need some water?" he asked.

"Why would I need water?" Olivia asked crossly.

"Well, you barked or something," he said.

"I'm perfectly fine." She held her purse in her lap, the way her grandmother used to, as if someone might rush in and try to take it from her. Awkwardly, she set it on the floor.

"Well," Jake said. He used the word *well* too much—a verbal tic, like saying *uh*, or *like*. "You'll be happy to know that I'm just helping Ellen out while she's away. You don't need my type of lawyering."

Relieved, Olivia relaxed a bit.

"I'm sure you're very good," she said, reading the framed diplomas behind him. Did that say *Yale*? She leaned forward for a better look. It did. Yale.

"I am very good," Jake said, following her gaze. "These really are mine."

Olivia blushed. "Anyway, Ellen is the one I need to see. When is she coming back, exactly?"

"Well," Jake said, and Olivia wondered how he got through Yale Law School saying *well* all the time. "Ellen's getting back in two weeks and she can handle all of your estate issues. I do family law. Like Amy's divorce."

"You do family law? But I spoke with Ellen on the phone!"

Jake shrugged. "She might have been covering for me."

"Shit," Olivia muttered, "I need to see you."

"Family law? You have kids?"

She shook her head. "I want to adopt a baby. A particular baby."

"Whose?"

"The mother is fifteen. Alone. She wants me to adopt the baby." Remembering Rachel's attitude, how inept she had made Olivia feel, Olivia added, almost defensively, "Of course, I've already talked to someone at Social Services—"

"What about the father?" Jake said, taking notes.

"Gone," Olivia told him.

"But he'll sign away his paternal rights?"

Another obstacle, Olivia thought, imagining Ben refusing to do it. Hadn't Ruby said their fight was over this very thing? She swallowed hard.

"Olivia?" Jake said.

"I think I need a parental consent form or something. Then I can go." She half-rose from her chair, looking around as if there might be stacks of these forms lying around, the way the IRS kept piles of tax forms.

"Whoa," Jake said. "Can you bring the mother in here? And the father?"

Olivia sank back into her chair and, from seemingly nowhere, began to cry.

"Don't badger me," she said, though he wasn't badgering her, of course.

Now Jake was hovering around her, clearly uncomfortable with a crying woman in his office.

"What did I say?" he asked nervously.

Olivia shook her head. How would she ever handle a baby? Babies had things like colic, cradle cap, clubfoot, lazy eyes. Babies shit all over themselves and cried all night. What had she been thinking?

"I must be crazy," she finally managed to say.

Jake was kneeling beside her now.

"I do this, too, you know," he told her. "Lose it, I mean. I never lost someone the way you did. But my ex-wife and my daughter moved to Australia. Can you believe that? I think it's the farthest place they could have moved to. But my ex-wife married an Australian doctor and they moved to Perth. When it snows here, they're at the beach. Do you know that their Santa's sleigh is pulled by kangaroos? They might as well have moved to Mars."

Something in what he said—or maybe it was how he said it—told Olivia that he understood, that perhaps he was the first person who did.

"When they first moved," Jake said, "I immediately told my girlfriend that I wanted to get married and have a baby. 'Why wait?' I said. But it was just to have something. A replacement family, I guess. By that time, we'd been divorced several years, but we had joint custody. I mean, Gillian was with me three nights a week. How do you continue that when she's halfway around the world?"

"Did you do it?" Olivia asked him.

"Have another baby?" He shook his head. "Thank God. We actually tried. What I had instead was a total breakdown. I flew out there, to Perth, and tried to live there. I even tried to win my ex-wife back. What a disaster. Look," he said, "all I'm saying is that maybe, just maybe, adopting this baby isn't what you think."

"I'm thirty-seven years old," Olivia said, "and the love of my life is dead, and who knows when or if I'll get married again. Who knows what my life is going to be like from now on."

"No one," Jake said.

"This girl," Olivia told him, "I think someone sent her to me."

"Who sent her?" he asked gently.

But Olivia only shrugged and looked down at the floor.

Jake stood, handed her a box of Kleenex. "Bring her in. I'll get the forms ready. Make sure the father isn't going to stake some kind of paternal claim."

For the rest of the day, she wondered why what stuck in her mind the most about him was the word *girlfriend*, the way Jake had said it.

When Olivia saw Winnie step off the train, her heart lurched as if she'd spotted a lover. There was her friend, dressed in black Capri pants and a scoop-neck black shirt, and underneath it a little watermelon of a baby, tight and round and perfect. She was wearing one of Olivia's hats: Columbine. She walked like a New Yorker, arrogant, sure, fast.

Olivia ran to her, forgetting to close the car door behind her.

"You look wonderful," Olivia said after they'd hugged and examined each other.

"*I* look like hell," Winnie said. She ran her fingers through her hair, even though it was cut short, just the way Olivia always imagined her doing when they were on the phone. "The sleek profile for fall," Winnie explained. "Of course, it means paying extra close attention to other details—the tweezed eyebrows, the straight eyeliner. Does it sound like copy from *You!*?"

"Naturally," Olivia said.

Winnie spun around. "Twenty-three pounds and counting. But the thing to do, afterward, is Pilates. We just did this whole piece on it. The equipment looks like some form of medieval torture, but if you need toning, it's the only way to go. Meanwhile," Winnie said, peering closely into Olivia's face, "you look incredible. Or at least good. Which is a step up from the last time I saw you. Several steps up. I would almost accuse you of being in love, if I didn't know better."

"What does love get you? A house in Rhinebeck?" Olivia said, guiding her toward the car, unwilling to let go of her arm. "I could have warned you. You fall in love and you do crazy things."

"I actually make recipes from Laurel's Kitchen. Can you believe it? That's another thing. Jeff's a vegetarian." Winnie sighed. "A vegetarian investment banker. Isn't that incredibly oxymoronic?"

They stopped in front of Olivia's car. "Wonderfully oxymoronic," Olivia said as Winnie patted the hood of the car affectionately. She didn't hate Winnie at all. She adored her.

"It still runs?" Winnie was saying. "What does it have, a million miles?"

"One hundred and eighty-seven thousand," Olivia said.

"And you can just leave your car door open around here and no one takes it?"

"I don't know about that," Olivia said, sliding into the car.

When Winnie finally got herself arranged inside, Olivia sat without moving, taking in her friend's smells, her presence.

"God," Olivia said finally. "You're really here."

"I've been a total shit, haven't I?" Winnie said. "Not coming for so long. Me, me, me, me."

"I hated you for being happy."

"I hated me. But I couldn't stop. I wanted you to be with me all the way."

"Look at you," Olivia said. She reached over and rested her hand on her friend's taut belly.

"We didn't even think, you know?" Winnie said, her voice hushed. "We just had sex like teenagers, thoughtless, reckless sex. Too many margaritas. Too much mariachi. Sex on the beach, on our little balcony, even on the plane on the way home. I guess we're members of that stupid club. What's it called?"

"Mile High?"

Winnie rolled her eyes. "Not worth it. Too cramped. And now I've got a vegetarian husband and a country house and a basketball for a stomach." She paused and pointed one finger and thumb at Olivia, a gun aimed right at her heart. "You wait, Olivia. It's going to happen for you, too."

"Don't," Olivia said.

"It *will* happen again. Someday you will look back and wonder how you got from here to there. Babies and mariachi. The works."

"Okay," Olivia said.

"And now let's go home, because I fall asleep so early, and I brought pictures to show you."

"We can't go home," Olivia said. "Not until we've talked.

"Don't tell me you have a boarder or something? Or wait. A lover?" Winnie grabbed Olivia's arm too urgently. "Do you?"

Olivia started the car. "No. But I did let Janice fix me up."

"Janice." Winnie groaned. "Has it been that bad up here? Not with one of Carl's friends, I hope."

"Poor guy. Poor nice guy," Olivia said.

Winnie let her hand stay on Olivia's arm. "You can have a lover and still not love him. It could be purely physical, the way it was in the good old days. You could just take this poor nice guy, friend of Carl, and fuck his lights out. Orgasms are therapeutic. Good for the skin."

The surfer boy flashed through Olivia's mind and she couldn't shake him. He had full lips and a good chin. He had, she'd noticed in his office, one pierced ear, and she had found it sexy.

"Remember how when you and Josh broke up I talked you into going out on a date with the guy from the farmers' market? The one with the good lettuce?"

"He said Feb-*u*-ary," Olivia said.

"Remember how I thought he might be Amish? And I had you all set to go and live on a big farm in Pennsylvania, to swear off buttons and cars and live a simple life?"

"He said li-*berry*," Olivia said.

"My point is . . . " Winnie began.

But Olivia stopped listening. She knew Winnie's point. That

farmer, Olivia remembered, had had the softest hands. He used to rub beeswax on them every morning. Instead of a bottle of wine, he'd brought her two big jars of amber-colored honey and a pattypan squash. She had slept with him, too, and Winnie had been right—she had felt better about things. But Josh hadn't been dead. And Olivia hadn't been about to make changes on her own, at least nothing like adopting a baby.

"Hello?" Winnie said. "If you're not going to listen to my good advice, then you at least have to let me pee. Hello?"

"I'm here," Olivia said.

Winnie squeezed her arm. "I'm here, too."

On summer nights, the Coast Guard House restaurant opened their deck and people sat at tables overlooking the ocean. Olivia ordered a margarita with extra salt and Winnie ordered warm water with lemon.

"See the light from the lighthouse," Olivia said. "Wait. It'll sweep across in a minute."

"Why do I keep expecting you to tell me something big?"

"I do have to tell you something," Olivia said. "Big."

"My God." Winnie laughed. "I just had the weirdest feeling. Like you were going to tell me you were pregnant or something."

"I guess I should just say it," Olivia said. She laughed, too, because she was so nervous.

"You aren't pregnant, are you?" Winnie's voice turned suddenly very serious. "You didn't do the turkey-baster thing, did you? Or Carl's friend?"

"Not exactly."

Now Winnie was frowning. "Olivia?"

"Did I tell you I started jogging? It's strange, I know, but I started, and one day I came home and this girl, this teenager, was in my house—"

"Robbing you?"

"No. Not exactly. Not then anyway."

"Stop saying 'not exactly,'" Winnie said. "You're making me nervous."

"The thing is," Olivia said, "*she's* pregnant. Pregnant like you."

"The girl?"

Olivia nodded. "Ruby. And she's living with me now."

Winnie was still frowning. "Living with you?"

"The thing is," Olivia said again, "she's giving me the baby."

Winnie could be counted on to tell Olivia she was crazy. To remind her that she was still in mourning, that she hadn't even taken the step of sleeping with someone again, never mind adopting a baby. Winnie could be counted on to tell Olivia that their babies would be best friends. Little city babies, little New Yorkers. She could be counted on to say that no matter how it turned out—the kid could change her mind; Olivia could change *her* mind—no matter, it would be the absolutely right thing. By the time they were back in the car, headed home, Winnie was repeating all the fun baby things they would do together. The park on Bleecker Street, little high-tops in size zero.

When they pulled into the driveway, Winnie said, "Now we can do things like go to watch them light the Christmas tree at Rockefeller Center and go to musicals. We'll have a reason."

Olivia was that much closer to getting this baby: Winnie understood. Winnie would help.

But they didn't talk about the baby with Ruby. Instead, Winnie took a mango and kiwi tart from her big straw bag, and a pound of macadamia nuts, and they sat on the living room rug—Winnie, Olivia, and Ruby—and they ate until Winnie said, "It's time." Then she took a fat brown photo album from her big straw bag.

"The husband," Olivia said. "The house in Rhinebeck."

"What's Rhinebeck?" Ruby said.

Winnie took Olivia's hand. "I made this for you," she said. "These are all the pictures I had of you guys. It's a good thing, I think—to remember the way it was."

"You think I don't remember?" Olivia said, but she stared hard at that brown album.

"I know it's totally different," Ruby said, "but it's like my old dog, Rover. He got hit by a car, and for the longest time I slept with his little toys and stuff, and I wouldn't let my mother throw away his dog dish because I had made it in school, in art class. And then one day, I like took out this picture of Rover and me, when he was new, just a little puppy, and it broke my heart, seeing him so little, and I kept thinking he only had like five years to live and he was so dumb and happy. But then I kept that picture on my bureau. You know, like in the corner of my mirror? And after a while, it didn't make me sad. It even made me kind of happy." Ruby considered this, then added quickly, "I mean, it's like totally different, but you know." Then she smiled, pleased with herself.

Olivia picked up the album and fingered it the way she used to touch that minicassette that held David's voice. The power we give objects, she thought. What are pictures, after all? Flat. One-dimensional. Not even true representations of the thing itself. Tricks of light can blur faces or send red dots into people's eyes.

Ruby's voice rose above Olivia. She said, "I imagine him to be very handsome. Mysterious, even. Like Omar Sharif."

"How would you know Omar Sharif?" Winnie said. "You're too young to know Omar Sharif."

"Oh please," Ruby groaned. "That's like saying I shouldn't know about the Civil War, or Julius Caesar, or anything that happened before 1982."

"Jesus Christ," Winnie said, "don't even tell me you were born in 1982. That is too depressing. Jesus."

Olivia looked at the two of them. "He wasn't particularly handsome," she said. "Not really."

"He wasn't *not* handsome," Winnie said. "All of his parts fit together nicely."

"Not dark and mysterious?" Ruby asked, disappointed. "But he has to be. With a little mustache and piercing eyes."

Olivia opened the photo album. "See for yourself," she said to Ruby, but it was really a directive to herself.

At first, she couldn't focus. But slowly, the faces and images became clear and Olivia realized she was looking at her own wedding. The silly Polaroids that Rex had taken that day.

"Wow," Ruby said, "you look beautiful."

She was right, Olivia *did* look beautiful in her wedding hat, her face so happy beneath it. There she was, smiling up at David, who looked right at the camera.

Olivia let her fingers drop to his face. She touched the flat laminated surface of his cheeks. So alive was he in this picture, she imagined her touch would settle on real warm flesh. But of course it was just plastic over paper.

"When I went to the hospital," Olivia said, "I didn't really look at him. I glanced. To be sure, you know. And even then he was clearly so dead. So not there."

"You had to identify the body? Like on TV cop shows?" Ruby said, impressed.

Olivia nodded, keeping her fingers on *this* David, thinking how that other one, laid out in a cold room on a metal table, was just that: *the body.*

Winnie began to turn the pages, to narrate what lay before them. There were other pieces of their lives: a New Year's Eve party, the two of them walking through Washington Square Park, smiling over a pan of lasagna, nestled on their couch in their apartment on Bethune Street, and finally the two of them here, in Rhode Island, dramatically posed in each room like Disneyland tour guides.

"It's hard to believe he died the day after this," Olivia said, looking down at a picture of David in khaki shorts, shirtless, standing in front of the house.

She touched that picture, too, her fingers remembering the feel of his ribs and skin and muscle, the way his hair grew coarser as it crept down his belly. And then she remembered all of it: the citrus smell he seemed to carry on him, the dimple in his chin, the lightning bolt–shaped scar that ran across one knee. If only she could remember the exact pitch of his voice, the rise and fall of his laugh, she would have him back again, even for this small moment.

"Olivia?" Winnie said, her voice soft.

Olivia closed her eyes, lost herself in these sensual memories. She ached for him, all of her, the way a person who has lost an arm or leg claims they feel pain in that missing limb. She imagined—no, she actually felt—the particular way it was to be in his arms, how her head settled in the crook between his shoulder and chest, that smell—limes, or orange blossoms?

"Olivia?" Winnie said again, louder.

Olivia wasn't crying, but she trembled; all of her was trembling.

"Good idea," he'd said. But it had been the worst idea she'd ever had.

Winnie and Ruby wrapped their arms around her, held her as close as they could. But she did not fit against them the way she had with David. She could not stop trembling for a very long time.

There was a storm that night.

Olivia listened to the trees scrape the windows, to the waves pounding the beach, to the wind howling. Beside her, Winnie slept, curled up in a tight ball, snoring. She heard Ruby snoring across the hall.

When lightning scratched the sky, Olivia got up. She was sore, as if she had been hurt somehow, bruised. Barefoot, she walked around the house, pacing, searching for something that she could not possibly find. Then more lightning flashes, and she saw all of her hats, left on the lawn to dry, sitting there, soaked.

Olivia ran outside, into the rain, and picked them up, crushing them to her.

"Happy birthday, man," said a voice from the driveway.

It had that California accent that Olivia loved so much. She ran toward it.

"Oh, darling. I'm drunk and wet and lost without him," Rex said, swaying before her in his leather jacket and faded jeans. "But I had to come. Took a bus all the way from Boston. Left the lighting to my assistant and drank an entire bottle of tequila. Well," he said, rain dripping from his chin, "not quite an entire bottle."

He held up what was left and Olivia took it from him.

"Have I ever been so glad to see you, Rex?" Olivia said.

She put the hats in her car and then sat on the wet grass in the rain with David's best friend and drank a hot, heavy swallow, then another.

"Remember your cat? Arthur?" Rex said. He draped one arm over Olivia's shoulder. "Now that was a cat."

Olivia raised the bottle. "To Arthur," she said.

Except for Winnie, there was no one she would like to be here with more than Rex. Happy, on her way to drunk, she sighed and leaned against him.

"To David," Rex said.

They both took a drink and then sat watching the storm recede.

"I kept telling myself that when I got here, he'd be waiting. That all of this dead stuff was a joke," Rex said.

"Don't make me cry, okay? Promise me?" Olivia said.

"Shit, honey, I can't promise you that."

"Then let's go walk on the beach."

"A plan!" Rex said. "I always liked that about you."

He pulled another bottle of tequila from his duffel bag and they walked arm in arm down the grassy slope to the beach. But they couldn't get too far; they were too tired, too drunk. So they sat and watched the waves, not talking. Later, Olivia wondered if she had been surprised when Rex leaned over and kissed her or if she had known as soon as she saw him standing on her lawn that they would get to that point.

His face was scratchy from needing a shave. He tasted sour. But his kisses felt good, almost familiar, and she let him kiss her for what seemed a long time. She let him kiss her until she knew that if they didn't stop, they would make love on this beach, both searching for David in the other. She knew that they wouldn't find him.

Olivia pulled back and said, "Now I know."

"Do you?"

"I know what it's like to kiss my husband's best friend."

"Oh, honey," Rex said, "I'm drunk and sad."

Olivia stood and took off her wet shirt and shorts, pulling Rex to his drunken feet.

"Last one in is a rotten egg," she said, and ran naked into the cold ocean. She heard the thump of Rex's footsteps as he ran behind her, but she didn't turn around or wait. Instead, she plunged in, headfirst, into the first wave that swept above her. She rode it into shore, until she felt sand in her mouth. David would be laughing to think she and Rex had made out, drunk on tequila, on the beach.

Floating, letting the waves carry her, Olivia stared hard at the starless sky; storm clouds still hung there, blue-black above her.

"Happy birthday," she said into the salt air.

Somewhere beside her, she heard Rex say the same thing.

It was Winnie who insisted on taking Ruby with them to dinner. The three of them went to Providence, to the Pot au Feu, where Amy insisted Julia Child liked to eat. Winnie did bring a short black dress and high-heeled Mary Janes for Olivia. She even remembered the black panty hose. "God knows, I can't wear them," she said, tossing everything at Olivia. They sprayed themselves with Winnie's too-expensive perfume and lathered pale lipstick on their lips.

So that by the time they arrived, and climbed the steps past the happily noisy bistro to the more expensive upstairs salon—"Go upstairs," Amy had told Olivia. "Treat yourself"—Olivia felt like a new version of her old self. I am a person who can still look sexy, she thought. I am a person who carries sadness inside. Rex was gone before any of them woke up, and in a way it felt like a dream to Olivia that he had been there at all.

But those few kisses had awakened something in her. She surprised herself by smiling back at a middle-aged businessman who had smiled at her approvingly when she walked in.

Over salad Ruby said, "I don't think I've ever eaten in such a fancy place." Her voice was hushed, as if she were in church.

In this low lighting, her face looked less bloated and blotchy and more radiant, the way women wore pregnancy in movies. The way Winnie wore it. Ruby had borrowed Winnie's black Capri pants, the waistband under her large belly, and one of David's shirts. With her hair in a rhinestone barrette—also Winnie's—and the pale lipstick, it was obvious to Olivia the pretty girl Ruby had been when Ben first saw her. The pretty girl she would be again in just a few weeks.

"Do you think David knows we're here?" Olivia asked, her voice as hushed and reverent as Ruby's. "Do you think he knows we're celebrating his birthday?"

"Absolutely," Ruby said. "No question. I think he's like this big thing—a soul or whatever—and that he's all around us, watching and grinning. Like a blob of positive energy."

"That sounds like something David might have said," Olivia said.

"You know what Ben says, the asshole?" Ruby said. "He says people are made of dreams and bones. Of course, he's an Aquarius," she added, as if that explained everything.

"No offense," Winnie told her, "but that's from a song. A kid's song about planting a garden."

Ruby blinked, startled. "You're kidding. He stole that? From a kid's song?"

"Well," Winnie said. "It is in a song."

"Maybe he never heard the song," Ruby said hopefully.

After their dinners arrived, after Ruby gasped at how beautiful it all was and said that she had never tasted anything so spectacular, after Ruby made Olivia promise that she would bring Sage here, too—"You'll come to the beach house weekends and bring him here for special occasions, right?" she said, dreamy-eyed, and Olivia said, "Even for not so special occasions"—after they'd eaten and ordered creme brûlée because it was David's favorite dessert, Winnie said: "I think he's up there celebrating his birthday, too." She pointed to the ceiling and beyond. "What was David's favorite thing in the whole world?" she asked. "That's what you get to do in heaven on your birthday, I think. Your most favorite thing."

Olivia smiled and sipped her wine. Then he is here, she thought, raising her wineglass slightly, because what she knew was that David's most favorite thing was her.

chapter nine

Milagros

Olivia looked at the room full of pregnant women, all clutching their partners' hands, and was relieved that she and Ruby were not the only pair of women. In fact, of the ten pregnant women, four of them had female partners. She took comfort in this, as if she was part of a club of sorts. She took comfort, too, in the way that Ruby clutched her hand.

"This makes it so real," Ruby said to her.

Ruby was wide-eyed, staring openly at the other bulging stomachs, the odd shapes they took. Olivia noticed, too. When her sister, Amy, was pregnant with Matthew, their mother used to point out pregnant women in stores and restaurants and describe how they were carrying: "all in the front," she'd say, or "low around the hips." Olivia had not really paid attention then, but now she saw what her mother meant. Right across from her was a woman shaped like a barrel, then another who appeared to be straining over her high breasts and belly.

Although all of the pregnant women had attempted to look cute, with wide sleeveless blouses or maternity T-shirts, everything in baby colors—mint green or pale pink—and baby designs—rocking horses and bunny rabbits—they still looked hot and uncomfortable and too big for their bodies. Olivia peeked at Ruby, who was still carefully checking out the others, even muttering under her breath. At least in David's black T-shirt and the stretch pants Winnie had left behind for her, Ruby looked less ridiculous than some of these women, even though her belly sometimes poked out, revealing a band of stretched flesh. Olivia was proud of her, and she gave Ruby's sweaty hand a little squeeze.

The class that was about to begin, the one they were all waiting for so nervously, was named the Planned-Birth Class, which sounded ridiculous, especially considering that Ruby's pregnancy, at least, was so unplanned. From the looks of the other young girl who sat in the corner chewing a hunk of hair and gripping her mother's hand tightly enough to leave marks, there were other people here with equally unplanned pregnancies.

When the instructor arrived, everybody gasped a little. Maybe they, like she and Ruby, had expected an Earth Mother type, someone with long, unruly hair, unshaved legs, a gypsy skirt. Someone who looked like she'd had several babies at home in Oregon or Vermont, who would share a chant or odd birthing position that would make all of this easier. "Her name," Ruby had said on the ride over, "will be Sarah—with an *h*. Or something else biblical. Naomi, maybe."

Instead, the instructor was tall and thin—the word *lithe* came to mind—with stylishly short blond hair, a deep tan, and bright blue eyes. She had on a hot-pink Lycra minidress and high-heeled sandals.

"Hi," she said, in such a bubbly voice that everyone eyed one another. They were big and hot and uncomfortable, these women. She sounded more like a flight attendant than a birthing teacher. "I'm Nikki, the instructor. It looks like you're all in the right place."

Even though everyone laughed politely, there was hostility in the air.

Nikki took off her sandals and sat down on one of the soft sofas. All of the pregnant women had rejected them. "Too hard to get out of," Ruby had explained.

Ruby narrowed her eyes suspiciously at Nikki, who seemed to bounce into and out of the sofa with great ease before finally settling in its center.

"Okay," Nikki said in her perky voice, "So who am I? I've taught this class for three years." Then she added, "I'm an R.N. Studying to be a midwife."

"Excuse me," said a woman who looked older than Olivia. She had wiry salt-and-pepper hair, oversized glasses, and a stomach that was so oblong, it looked as if her baby were actually lying sideways. "I would feel more comfortable with someone who's had real experience."

Nikki kept grinning. "I've taught this very class for three years."

"No," the woman insisted, "I mean someone who has gone through this herself. Someone who's had children."

"Yes!" said another woman, this one as short and square as a Jeep. "Me, too." Her husband had grease under his nails and in the lines of his hands, a mechanic's hands.

Nikki smiled broadly, showing all of her dazzling white teeth. "Believe me," she said, "I've been through this, too. I have three children, all delivered without any pain medication at all."

As a group, everyone looked at her tiny body and then down at their own, miserably.

"Of course, you can get pain medication if you choose," Nikki was saying. "But I think we can work on ways that will make that unnecessary. Breathing. Creative visualization. But I'm getting ahead of myself."

No one was really paying attention. The hostility in the air thickened. They all hated Nikki, that was for certain.

"I want my Sarah," Ruby told Olivia as they filled out information cards. "Not Pamela Lee."

"In a way, this is good," Olivia said. "She represents something to look forward to."

"I never looked like that before I got knocked up," Ruby blurted, and across the room someone snickered.

Then Ruby added, "I think she's lying. I don't think she's ever had a kid."

"That would be unethical," Olivia whispered.

"Ha!" Ruby said. "You think people aren't unethical."

They both watched Nikki leave the room to get a VCR; they were going to watch a film of real births.

"Maybe she's all they could get," Ruby said, worried. "I don't even think she's a nurse. Not a real one. She's probably a nurse like my mother. An L.P.N." Then she added, "A bedpan cleaner."

Olivia had been so willing to accept Nikki's credentials. Why would Ruby doubt the woman?

"I'm sure she's fine," Olivia said. But now Ruby had caused her to doubt this. How do you get to be fifteen and so wary of everything, of everyone? Olivia wondered.

Nikki returned, easily rolling in video equipment that the tech boys in high school would have struggled with.

"Everybody done?" she asked, and they all silently, angrily almost, handed her their cards.

"So," Nikki said, sitting again on the soft couch, "I thought we'd introduce ourselves. Tell one another our names and who our partner is and our due dates and any other pertinent information you want to share. Okay?"

Everyone glowered.

"Good. Let's start with you two," Nikki said, and pointed right at Olivia.

Olivia had expected Nikki would begin to her left, with the Jeep-shaped woman and her mechanic husband. She had no idea what she and Ruby would say. Even in the air-conditioned room, Olivia felt a trickle of sweat creep down her arm as everyone turned to look at her.

But Ruby didn't hesitate.

"My name is Ruby," she said.

"I love that name," Nikki gushed. "My youngest is named Scarlet."

Ruby frowned. "*Anyway*," she continued, "I'm Ruby and my due date is Labor Day. I guess I'm probably the youngest person here." She lowered her voice. "I'm a pregnant teen. You know, unwed. The kind they do television specials about. And this is Olivia. She's going to adopt my baby. It's like one of those—what do they call them? Open adoptions? Where she like pays for everything, doctors and vitamins and stuff, and then she gets the baby. They put an ad in the paper. You know, 'Couple seeking baby.' That kind of thing."

Olivia stared down at her toes, trying not to listen, thinking about how soon, when this was over, she was going to make an appointment for a pedicure.

"Wasn't there a movie about that?" Ruby said, showing no indicating of shutting up anytime soon. "With like Glenn Close and one of those actresses with the three names. I always get them confused. Mary Jessica somebody?"

Olivia decided she would get one of those colors they were showing in *You!* A sparkly blue or green.

"Of course," Nikki said, and Olivia felt the woman looking at her, "I usually get both partners in with the mother in cases like this."

Olivia looked and saw not just Nikki and Ruby but everyone watching her.

"Will your husband be joining us?" Nikki said. "Maybe next week?"

Ruby didn't miss a beat. "He travels so much, you know?" She pointed upward. "He's a pilot. Always has his head in the clouds."

"Isn't that exciting?" Nikki said.

Olivia swallowed hard, nodded.

The next couple was talking now, all giggly and excited. When Olivia met Ruby's eyes, the girl grinned and gave Olivia a big wink.

It was the heat.

It was those stupid drunken kisses with Rex.

It was loneliness.

It was neediness.

Olivia didn't even care what it was. She was so hot and the air was so thick that she couldn't breathe or think clearly. She dressed—a tank top and cutoffs, her old Jack Purcell's, one of her new hats: Hyannis—and she drove straight to the surfer boy's house. "Get it over with," Winnie had advised her before she left. "It's a hurdle. It's nothing. It's sex."

She rang the doorbell and hoped he wasn't home.

She held her breath, waiting. It was the middle of the night. He had a girlfriend. This last thought pleased her. The surfer boy, though disarming, was safe. He was not going to want a relationship or a commitment. He would go away.

When he opened the door—shirtless, also in cutoffs, tanned bare feet—he looked very awake.

"Well, hello," he said.

That word *well* again.

Good. She didn't even like him. This gave her confidence.

"Are you alone?" she said. "Which is my way of saying, Is your girlfriend here?"

"I don't have a girlfriend," he said, disappointing her. "Come on in."

She wanted to question him about this discrepancy, but she was afraid she'd lose her nerve if there was too much conversation.

"Okay," she said. "So. My husband died a year ago and I just sort of figured out that he's not coming back. And my best friend, Winnie, when I told her about how at night sometimes when I can't sleep, for some reason I see your stupid face, she said, 'Go tell him.' "

"What part of this is supposed to win me over?" he said. "The 'stupid face' part?"

"Yeah. No. I mean, I want to kiss you."

He cupped her face in his hands—big hands, she noticed—and said, "I have wanted to kiss you since the minute I saw you at that party."

He did. He kissed her and she liked it too much.

"Actually," he said, "my intentions are bad. I've wanted to do a hell of a lot more than just kiss you. That day in my office, I thought I would go crazy not touching you."

This is just sex, Olivia told herself. This is a good thing.

"Why are you wearing a hat?" he whispered as he kissed her throat.

"I'm a milliner," she whispered back.

He knew nothing about her. She was a blank to him. So she lifted her shirt over her head and let him take one of her breasts in his mouth. Damn. It did feel good.

All of it felt good.

Until he said, "I was so crazy about you and I didn't know you were a milliner or that you have a friend named Winnie or anything. I don't know anything."

"There's nothing to know," she told him.

Afterward, she felt good and not guilty at all. This was just sex. She'd had fun, more fun than she'd had in a long time. But she wanted nothing else from this surfer boy. You open yourself to someone and anything could happen. They could go out for a jog and get hit by a Honda Civic.

This was better. He knew how she liked to be touched, the way her skin felt under those big hands of his, the sound of her sighs and moans and breathing during sex. That was plenty. Olivia did not sit up and watch him sleep, the way she used to watch David.

Instead, she left. She made her way quietly out of his bed, out of his room, down the stairs, and outside, where the hot air felt good for a change with its suffocating intensity. Funny, Olivia thought, I can breathe better out here than in the cool bed beside Jake. Before she got in her car, she made sure she had remembered everything so that there would be no need to go back. She had her shoes in one hand, her hat in the other. And she had remembered to go without bothering to say good-bye.

At the outdoor art fair in town, Ruby liked all the bad paintings—the too-bright oils of turbulent oceans, the watercolors of lighthouses. She was eating her third cotton candy and pink sugar stuck to her chin. Olivia reached over and tried to wipe it off, but it was stubborn. She licked her finger to clean Ruby's chin with her spit, the way a mother would. But Olivia stopped herself, her finger in midair until she jammed her hand into her pocket. Like a mother, she thought, pleased.

"You'll do it, right?" Ruby was saying. She stared longingly at a painting of a purplish-blue ocean and a pink-and-yellow sunset. "You'll teach Sage about art. And music, too. Mozart and all those guys?"

Walking straight toward them was Amy. After the book-club meeting, she had called Olivia and said, "I know what you're thinking, and you're crazy. You should not adopt that girl's baby."

"Who said anything about adopting her baby?" Olivia had said angrily. Amy's ability to see through every situation unnerved Olivia. She wondered how her sister had missed the fact that her husband had been having an affair.

Olivia returned Amy's wave halfheartedly.

"Well," Amy said right away, "he's off."

"Who?"

"Matthew. He went to the Galápagos Islands with Edward and the bimbo. Soon to be the next Mrs. Robbins, thank you very much."

"Amy," Olivia said, "she is a full professor of anthropology at Brown. She is not a bimbo."

"What do you know about it? She has the fakest blond hair you've ever seen and I have it on good authority that she had a nose job."

"The Galápagos Islands?" Ruby said. "That is so totally awesome. Didn't like evolution get discovered there or something?"

Amy glared at her.

"Remember me?" Ruby said. "The pregnant teenager from next door? I cut Olivia's hair? It still looks good, doesn't it? Or do you think she could use some more pieces?" She touched Olivia's hair in a familiar way. "Like here? *You!* says the chopped bob is in for fall."

"I remember you," Amy said, still glowering. "Haven't you had that baby yet?"

"Tell me about it. I swear I'm going to burst. Like it could pop right out of my skin. I think that happened in a movie." Ruby's eyes settled somewhere beyond Amy's head. "Hey," she said, "look. That guy does the scribble painting I like. I'm going to go see." She smiled at Amy. "Good to see you again."

"Yes," Amy said. "Great." Under her breath she said, "I don't like that kid, Olivia."

Ruby turned around. "By the way," she said, "did Olivia tell you? She's my birthing partner."

They both watched her make her way through the crowd.

"That's an interesting turn of events, considering you have absolutely no interest in that baby," Amy said in a flat voice, still watching Ruby.

"She's all alone," Olivia said.

"She does have parents, though, right? In the house next door?"

Amy looked at Olivia now, waiting.

"All right," she said. "I'm thinking that I might maybe—"

"I knew it," Amy said, grabbing her arm. "You can't, Olivia. Think about what you're doing."

"I have thought about it," Olivia said, shaking free of her sister's grasp.

"Look at her. Do you want a kid with those genes? And she's probably been stoned for half this pregnancy. Have you done drug testing? Genetic testing? For all you know, strange things run in her family. Have you thought about anything?

Beyond Amy, in the distance, Olivia watched Ruby, who was sitting beside the young man painting.

"I want that baby," Olivia said, keeping her eyes fixed on Ruby.

"I think you've lost it, Olivia," Amy said. "I really think you've lost it."

Ruby saw Olivia watching her, and she waved. Something filled Olivia. She wanted to jump up and down, foolishly. She wanted to run through this crowd, across the street, to the beach, and jump into the water. Maybe Amy was right. Maybe she had lost it. But the girl was important to her. She was changing Olivia's life.

Olivia lifted her arm and returned Ruby's wave with a large sweeping one of her own.

"And another thing," Amy was saying. "Why won't you return Jake Maxwell's calls? He's driving me crazy asking about you."

"What do you know about that?" Olivia asked sharply.

Surprised, Amy took a step back. "You didn't."

"You seem to be forgetting," Olivia said, "that I'm the big sister. I ask you questions. I give you advice."

"He's a nice guy, Olivia. And you are irrational."

The nice guy was walking toward them. Shit, Olivia thought. Shit, shit, shit. She hated these little towns where you so easily walked into your indiscretions. In New York, she would never have to see Jake Maxwell again.

"If it isn't the elusive milliner," Jake said. His jaw muscles twitched from being clenched so tightly. Possessive.

Amy put her hand on Jake's arm. "Stay away from her. She's acting irrational."

Jake raised his eyebrows. "Is that right?"

Olivia adjusted her hat. It was an old one, a favorite, from the series she'd named after old movie stars. This one was Gene Tierney.

"Doing crazy things, huh?" he said. "Like sleepwalking?"

"I've got to be somewhere," Olivia said.

She didn't like the way Jake Maxwell made her feel: she wanted him to shut up and undress. She wanted to climb on top of him the way she had that night. She wanted too much from him.

"I think we have some unfinished business," Jake said.

Olivia cleared her throat. "I think we're finished," she said. "In fact, I'm certain of it. Positive."

"Those papers?"

"Oh. The papers. Right," Olivia said. "I'll call you. I'll make an appointment."

She walked away fast, bumping into a table that held small models of lighthouses. She heard Amy saying, "Someone's got to help that girl."

Olivia made the appointment through Jake's secretary and showed up exactly on time with Ruby.

"I don't know why," Ruby said as they waited in the waiting room, "but every time you mention this guy, your voice gets funny."

"I doubt it," Olivia said.

Jake opened the door to his office and motioned them inside. He had on khaki pants, a blue-and-white pinstriped shirt, and a Nicole Miller tie of various animals running.

Good, Olivia thought, studying all the rats and rabbits racing diagonally across the tie, he's probably in PETA or something. A radical. An asshole.

"Now I know why," Ruby whispered. "He's cute."

"Really?" Olivia said. "Not my type."

"No whispering," Jake told them, closing the door. He got them chairs, offered coffee, water, iced tea. Then finally, he sat at his desk and opened a folder.

"Well," he said, and Olivia smiled—that awful tic: *well, well, well.*

"Nice tie," Ruby told him. "Does it mean something?"

Jake shrugged. "A gift," he said, and Olivia felt as if he was saying it directly to her.

"Oh," Ruby said, "a gift. You've got a girlfriend."

"One of those on-again, off-again girlfriends," he said, looking at Olivia. "Which isn't to my liking. I much prefer monogamy. I like to get to know someone, spend time with her. Call me crazy, but I'm not really into one-night stands. Or playing games. Or bullshit."

"Jeez," Ruby muttered. "I only asked about the tie.

"I think we're here to settle that unfinished business?" Olivia said. Despite the air conditioning, she was hot and sweating.

"You're exactly right," Jake said. He pushed some papers across the desk to Ruby. "Basically, these are parental consent forms that say you, as the mother, are willing to give your baby to Olivia." As he talked, Jake pointed to the paragraphs that illustrated, in legalese, what he was explaining. "That you're not being paid to do this, or blackmailed, or otherwise coerced, but that you're doing this of your own free will."

Ruby nodded. Olivia had never seen her face so serious. Olivia felt it, too, the importance of these papers, of this moment. She looked from Ruby's face down to her stomach. Ruby's hands were folded over her belly. In there, Olivia thought, is my baby. It was fully formed by now, perfect. Together, Ruby and Olivia had studied the book Rachel had sent. They watched as the fetuses in the photographs grew larger and clearer, how the ears and the fingers and the toes all took shape. "This is freaking me out," Ruby had said, but Olivia could only trace the shape of that baby in the picture and marvel at its development.

"And this section is for the father to sign, agreeing to all the same things," Jake was saying. "I need to ask you if you know who the father is."

Ruby nodded solemnly.

"Does he admit he's the father?" Jake asked.

Ruby nodded again.

"Okay. Good. Well, he needs to sign right here. And then you get the whole thing notarized, and then you have your baby and hand it over legally to Olivia." Jake turned his attention to Olivia.

. . .

"I have adoption papers being drawn up for you. It's all routine really."

Olivia nodded, too. It was as if some force greater than she or Ruby had taken their voices. In no time, she would have this baby with her. She would hold it, swaddle it, take it home with her to New York. She and Winnie would push their strollers side by side through the Village. Go to story hour at Tootsie's and buy baby ice cream cones at Moon Doggie's.

"You should read this yourself," Jake told Ruby.

"No," she said in a quavering voice that Olivia did not recognize. "I believe you."

He slid the papers across his desk, toward Ruby. "I've marked where you need to sign," he said, and placed a pen on top of the papers.

Ruby's lips moved as if she were talking. Talking herself into this? Olivia wondered. Or out of it? Ruby picked up the pen, hesitated, then put it back down.

"There's a provision here," Jake said, pointing with his pen, "that gives you the right to change your mind within sixty days."

Olivia looked at him, startled. How could he have left out such an important detail? Hadn't he said this was pretty routine? Hadn't he made it sound practically finished?

"You mean I can take the baby back?" Ruby asked him.

"You have sixty days," Jake said. "But it's highly unusual." This last, he seemed to add for Olivia's sake.

"I want to talk to Ben first," Ruby said, getting up. "I need to talk to him."

"Ben?" Jake said.

"The father," Olivia said miserably.

"I'm afraid he won't sign," Ruby said.

Olivia looked at Jake, desperate, as if to say, She has to sign. "Well," Jake said, "can we call him in here now?"

Ruby shook her head. "He's in New York." She grabbed

Olivia's hand and held on tight. "I just want this over with," she said, and Olivia was relieved.

The other teenager in childbirth class had her baby, a girl, six pounds, twelve ounces.

"Hillary Jane," Nikki announced. "Isn't that pretty? Everything went smooth as pumpkin pie. No drugs!"

They all groaned. The pressure was on for a smooth, drug-free delivery.

Ruby whispered to Olivia, "I want drugs. I'm telling you right now. I don't want to remember any of it, and I just want to hand you the baby and go home."

It was time for creative visualization. The pregnant women lay down, with their heads on fat red pillows, their partners kneeling beside them. Ruby and Olivia had problems with getting the breathing right, when simply to pant, when to *hee-hee-hoo.* Hopefully, they would do better at this.

"I mean it," Ruby said. "Tons of drugs. Whatever they've got."

"Okay," Olivia said. But she couldn't shake something Ruby had just told her: She wanted to go home. Where did she mean? The girl had no one, no place to go. Olivia thought of that small house on Strawberry Field Lane, of the red-faced mother—"A bedpan cleaner," Ruby had said. And what lay beyond that door that the woman had held so protectively closed? Olivia imagined scenes from B movies, from cheap novels. But perhaps those scenes were really Ruby's life, her home. Somehow, Olivia hadn't thought past getting this baby. But now she wanted Ruby to have something better, too. Something good. What would happen to Ruby?

Nikki was telling the mothers to close their eyes and imagine something peaceful. Olivia tried to do the same, but she kept getting ugly pictures instead, images of Ruby alone in that fraternity basement, in that A&W parking lot, on the street somewhere.

"The most peaceful thing you know," she said in a hypnotic voice.

"A handful of Quaaludes and a big fat joint," Ruby whispered to Olivia. "That's what I intend to do."

"Sssshhhh," Olivia said. "Close your eyes." But she took hold of Ruby's hand and held on tight.

"Hey," Ruby said, "lighten up."

Nikki stood over them.

"What are you imagining?" she asked Ruby.

Why did they always have to go first? But of course Ruby had already come up with a lie.

"The beach at sunrise," she said. "Before it gets crowded, you know? It smells like seaweed, but not in a bad way. And like salt. I like that part of the morning."

It sounded convincing enough for Nikki to coo, "Wonderful."

Someone else thought of a forest; another person chose a meadow. Olivia closed her own eyes, willing to let a peaceful image in. But it was that damn Jake Maxwell who worked his way inside her head, pressing against her eyelids. Jake Maxwell shirtless, in cutoffs, standing at his door and letting her in. She opened her eyes and Ruby was staring at her all funny.

"What?" Olivia said. But Ruby shook her head, closed her eyes again, and went back to her beach.

Before they left, they were asked to choose a focal point, something to take with them to the hospital and stare at when things got rough.

"Something," Nikki explained, "that will keep you focused."

The others chose quilts and sonogram pictures and a wedding photograph.

Ruby took Olivia's hand and whispered, "I choose you. When I start to lose it, before the drugs kick in, I'll just look at your face and that will get me through."

. . .

When they got home, Ruby announced that she needed to be alone. She had to call Ben and get him to agree to sign the parental consent form. "Then we'll fax it to him and everything will be settled," she said. Her voice had taken on a weary seriousness.

Satisfied, Olivia decided that Ruby was determined to do it. She drove to Mia Bambina, the specialty baby store in town. There, she turned herself over to a woman named Mara, who assured her that they carried everything she would need for the first few months of her baby's life.

Mara helped her choose blankets, tiny things called "onesies," baby bottles with balloons and the ABCs on them, a black-and-white mobile, booties and hats and a hand-knit sweater, and all of the Winnie-the-Pooh characters in miniature soft stuffed animals sitting in a plush blue honey jar.

"If you have any black baby clothes," Olivia said, grinning, thinking of how pleased Ruby would be, "I'll take them."

Mara added those to the pile, too: tiny black leggings and high-tops and turtlenecks.

"It's really wonderful, isn't it?" Mara said as she wrapped all of the items in tissue paper. "We get a lot of people in here preparing for an adoption." She smiled warmly at Olivia. "You and your husband must be pretty excited."

"Thank God for adoption," Olivia told Mara, because that was exactly what she felt. Thank God for adoption and thank God for Ruby.

The colorful bags with Mia Bambina emblazoned across the front filled the trunk. Olivia stopped at the A&P and bought two cases of formula and a case of Pampers. When she got in her car to drive back home, the faint sweet smell of babies filled the air.

The sun was bright and hot, and Olivia began to hum an old Jackson Browne song as her car hugged the curves on the windy scenic route. Her hands beat out the rhythm on the steering wheel. No lullabies for her baby, she decided. She would hum him Beatles songs, and Simon and Garfunkel, and all of those Jackson Browne, Van Morrison, and Bruce Springsteen tunes from her college days. She would teach him to dance the twist, the swim, the monkey. Olivia saw herself with a little boy who looked like David, the same curly brown hair and straight nose, the two of them twisting across the hardwood floors of her apartment on Bethune Street, with the stereo turned up too loud, and both of them grinning and sweaty.

Around the next curve, the sun was so bright that she was blinded for an instant; and in that instant, she heard a small thump beneath her car. She had run over something. Olivia pulled over, beyond the shoulder, onto the scratchy grass that grew there. Trembling, she got out of the car.

It's just a paper bag, she told herself. A bag with empty beer cans in it.

She saw those all the time, tossed from car windows onto the side of the road.

Whatever it was had been thrown by the impact, and Olivia had to walk several yards to find it, thinking the whole time of David, of how he'd hit that Honda Civic and was airborne for an instant before he landed with a sound that the girl—Amanda—had described as "sickening." She thought of all the details she had tried to forget: how his sneakers had been knocked from his feet, how they'd recovered only one. She thought of the way the policeman held the few things David had carried in his pocket: his house key, a five-dollar bill, and a scrap of paper with her name written on it and their phone number below that. By the time she saw it, she was crying. It was a cat, and it was very dead, eyes opened in horror, guts spilling onto the road.

Her own stomach flip-flopped as she bent toward the cat, a fat orange one with a red collar with a charm hanging from it. Olivia recognized the charm as a *milagro*, a good-luck charm from Mexico, this one a hand with a heart on its palm. There was no tag, though, no owner to call. In a way, Olivia was relieved; she didn't want to knock on someone's door and deliver such news.

Olivia got the blanket from her trunk and used it to drag the cat off the road to the grass. She could not stop thinking of the policeman who had come to her door that warm Tuesday morning last September, grim-faced and nervous. "Mrs. Henderson?" he had asked, sweating, almost ashamed. In that instant, Olivia had known why he was there—a little earlier, she had heard the wail of sirens close to home—and, not wanting to hear the news, she had shut the door on him, leaned against it, shaking, muttering, *"No, no, no, no."*

What would these people think of a crying woman coming to their door with a bundle wrapped in a sandy beach blanket? This way, she thought, leaving the cat in the blanket beneath a row of beach roses and sea lavender, they might think the cat had simply wandered off. They might remain hopeful that it would return. They might imagine it with another family, happy somewhere else, loved. It was what she imagined Arthur doing. Though of course she knew how unlikely that was.

That *milagro* was what she thought about for the rest of the ride home. Someone's hope that death could be held at bay by a foolish charm. But once home, she wished she had taken it from the cat's collar. Maybe it was meant to do some other magic—to make good things happen. Olivia even considered driving back and retrieving it.

But then Ruby came outside. She had been crying; Olivia recognized the red blotches that crying always left on her face.

Olivia stepped out of the car, but she couldn't seem to move closer to Ruby, who stood at the front door. Behind her, the house looked more run-down than ever, the purple paint blistered in the heat, the roof sagging a little in the middle.

"You talked to him?" Olivia said. Her knees were weak; that cat with his guts spilling onto the street, the thump, the small *milagro* around his neck.

"He says okay," Ruby told her. "He says he'll sign."

Relief so strong washed over Olivia that she feared she might fall over. When she opened her hands to welcome Ruby into a hug, there were cuts on her palms from her nails digging in, small half-moons of hope.

chapter 10

Still, I'm Going to Miss You

Olivia was ready.

She spent each night in a half sleep, listening for sounds from Ruby's room: a gasp at her water breaking, a groan from the first twinges of labor, the creak of bedsprings as Ruby got up to tell Olivia it was time.

In their childbirth class, half the women had already had their babies, all of them early. Each week, there were fewer pairs there, more reports of babies born, labors induced. As Olivia listened to the women's stories, to the names of these new lives, she rocked in her seat, gently, back and forth, as if she already had a baby to soothe. Sometimes, she left the class angry at Ruby for taking so long.

"Jeez," Ruby told her, "it's still early. Give me a break."

But Olivia was anxious. She paced and prodded Ruby with questions. Was there any sign of labor? Anything at all?

"It's easy for you to want labor to start," Ruby said. "But I'm the one who's got to go through it. Right now, I feel like it would be okay just to stay like this. You and me living here, thinking about the baby and stuff. In limbo, you know?"

But Olivia couldn't imagine anything worse. Get on with it, she willed the girl. Get on with it already.

One morning, sounding young and frightened, Ruby described how the baby's head was lodged in the birth canal.

"It's like so low, I feel it could drop right out. I mean, I keep feeling like I have to pee, but then I don't; it's just the baby. And you know, I was thinking, If it's so low already, maybe it won't hurt so much. It doesn't have that far to go to get out, right?"

It was easy for Olivia to forget that Ruby was a child herself really. Especially lately, with the baby so close to being hers that Olivia could think of nothing else. But she saw how scared Ruby was, and she drew the girl close to her. Ruby smelled of strawberry shampoo and sea air.

"Think of all the people from class who've done it now," Olivia said. "It's all over and they have their babies."

The girl stiffened in Olivia's arms. "Yeah. Right. But I'll go through it, the water breaking and the pain and the pushing. But in the end, I won't even have the baby. I won't have anything."

"Of course you will," Olivia said guiltily, because for the life of her, she could not think of one thing that Ruby would have. Not one.

There was no relief in the heat, and Ruby stayed inside in her underwear, in front of a fan, miserable and uncomfortable, cranky.

"I can't breathe," she moaned, trying to adjust the baby inside her, to move it out from under her rib cage with her fingers.

She pushed away all food except for Ben & Jerry's ice cream, the smooth variety.

"There's no room in here for anything else," Ruby said.

But Olivia made her red currant iced tea and tortellini with pesto sauce, Nikki's suggestions for natural ways to induce labor.

"I can't," Ruby said, and pushed away the food, the tea.

Sometimes, Olivia came home from her morning jog and found Ruby in a bathtub of cold water, the skin of her stomach so stretched that Olivia saw whorls and patterns on it, like blown-up fingerprints, like the blots on Rorschach tests. Ruby's breasts drooped the way Olivia remembered her grandmother's doing, resting ugly on her belly, the nipples dark brown and swollen, the breasts themselves covered with puffy blue veins. They leaked, too, a thin, clear liquid, like tears.

"No wonder Ben doesn't love me anymore," Ruby said one morning when Olivia came home sweaty and aching, to find her in the tub, crying. "Look at me. I'm so disgusting."

"You're not," Olivia said, kneeling beside the bathtub. She thought, Only two more days. Only two more days of this.

"Oh please. I look down and I get so freaked out," Ruby said, lifting her arms to indicate her body, all of it. "Once I broke my leg. I was in fifth grade and I fell down our front steps. Just stumbled really. And my leg broke. It was so weird. I had to wear a cast up to here"—she indicated somewhere under the water—"for like seven weeks. About halfway through, it got really itchy. I thought I was going to lose my mind, you know? And then it even started to smell kind of funky. I kept pretending it was happening to somebody else, all that pain and the itching and the smell. But this is even worse. And I can't escape it. I mean, I can't breathe, I can't sleep. And it's so hot."

"I know," Olivia said.

She thought of herself this way—pregnant and uncomfortable. What would David do? she wondered. He would wash her hair and rub her back and give her ice cubes to rub on her neck. So that was what she did. Olivia washed Ruby's hair with the shampoo that smelled like rum. She put ice cubes in the bathtub. She read *Green Eggs and Ham* out loud to Ruby, because Winnie said that hearing rhymes made babies smarter. For a little while, Ruby felt better.

Olivia agreed to go out to dinner with her parents and her sister. They wanted to talk her out of this. She wanted them to be ready for the baby. She left the number of the restaurant all over the house—by the telephone, beside the bathtub, next to Ruby's bed. Then she put on a new dress, a long flowered one with buttons down the front, and met her family at the Spanish restaurant on the ocean.

They ordered calamari as an appetizer, and before it came, Amy began to talk.

"I see a pattern of irrational behavior," she said. "This is just one more thing."

"What irrational behavior?" Olivia said. "I didn't kill my husband. He just died. And that is the only irrational thing I can think of in my life."

"How about eloping with someone you hardly knew?" Amy said. "How about dressing your cat up in doll clothes? How about a million nutty things you did your whole life?"

"I'm finally taking charge of my life again," Olivia said, her head reeling from Amy's accusations. How could her sister see marrying David as foolish when it had been the smartest thing Olivia had done? "I finally see a future for myself," Olivia added.

Amy lowered her voice. "Is that what sleeping with Jake was all about? Taking charge?"

"Did he tell you that?" Olivia said.

"He didn't have to," Amy said. "It's so obvious."

Their mother interrupted. "Girls! I don't want to hear this kind of talk. Olivia, I can't believe that you are having sex with men at this point in your life. You are supposedly grief-stricken."

"Supposedly!" Olivia said.

But her mother waved her hands dismissively. "I don't want to discuss morals with my thirty-seven-year-old daughter. The point is that you shouldn't make any big decisions for a while yet. If in six months or a year you still feel like you want a baby, adopt one then. It hasn't even been a year, Olivia."

Olivia recognized this advice from the articles her mother clipped from magazines for her.

"It will be a year," Olivia said. "In one week."

"The point is, you need to get past each season without him," her mother continued. "Every landmark. Christmas and anniversaries and birthdays."

"We're past all that," Olivia said, weary. "Where have you been?"

Olivia's mother was wearing a ridiculous hat, a bronze thing with a dark brown band. It wasn't one of Olivia's, even though Olivia sent her a hat every Mother's Day. Hats that she never wore, that sat in her closet getting dusty and misshapen. Why do I even bother? Olivia thought. Her mother's gold seashell earrings looked like bugs. And her lipstick made her seem almost ghoulish. Her father sat, looking out the window, though it was too dark to see the ocean lying beyond it. These people could not possibly understand why she was doing this.

"You're just being unrealistic. As usual," Amy added.

She was pouting, the way she used to when she was a child and didn't get her way. She had on a cropped black sweater that showed her flat tanned belly. Olivia saw that and thought of Ruby's stretched, full stomach. What am I even doing here with them when Ruby might need me? Olivia thought.

"I'm going home," she announced.

"But you ordered paella to split with Amy," her mother said in her fluttering voice.

"Sit right down and eat with us," her father said. "By God, there's been enough talk."

But of course, as usual, there hadn't been nearly enough.

"Any day now, I'm going to have a baby," Olivia said. "I'll call you before we go back to New York."

A woman at the next table looked up at her, frowning.

But Olivia didn't care; saying *we* felt wonderful, like the right pronoun, at last.

Ruby was sitting at the kitchen table when Olivia got home. She had put the fan right in front of her, and her face was lifted into the air the fan spit out. But the only thing Olivia could focus on were the papers on the kitchen table, all with Ben's signature in the right spots, in triplicate and notarized.

"It's so fucking hot," Ruby said.

"Any pains?" Olivia asked her. "Twitches? Twinges? Cramps?"

The papers lay between them, Ben's signature a model of good penmanship.

"Just those stupid Braxton-Hicks," Ruby said, locking her gaze on Olivia.

Olivia waited for more; Ruby always had more to say. But the girl was quiet.

When Olivia moved toward the steps, and bed, Ruby spoke.

"You never told me," she said. "What names you picked out."

"Nell for a girl," Olivia said. "Thomas for a boy."

"Thomas!" Ruby said. "But that's awful."

"It was David's father's name," Olivia said.

They had thought it a name filled with historical significance—like Thomas Jefferson—and fictional integrity—Tom Sawyer.

"I don't like Nell, either," Ruby said. "It's a stupid name. An old-lady name."

Olivia thought of those papers, signed and notarized.

"I told you I'd name him Sage, didn't I?"

"I don't care what you name him. But those names are terrible. I'm just saying."

Olivia went over to Ruby. "Are you okay?" she asked her.

There were tears in Ruby's eyes, but they seemed frozen there, as if the girl was actually unwilling to let herself cry this time.

"Of course I'm not okay. This is going to hurt like hell and Ben doesn't love me and you want to name my baby stupid names like Tom and Nell and it's so fucking hot."

Olivia wrapped her arms around Ruby's shoulders.

"We're almost there," she whispered.

The first thing Olivia noticed when she woke up the next morning was that there was a cool breeze coming through her windows; the heat had broken.

Then she remembered that today was the day. Ruby's baby was due today. She thought of that doctor, spinning the little plastic wheel, lining up the months and dates and coming up with today. It had seemed so far off then. Some babies, the doctor had told them, were born right on schedule.

Olivia got out of bed, the cool floor a surprise under her feet after so many weeks of heat. She peeked inside Ruby's room, but the bed was empty, a messy tangle of sheets, a pillow thrown on the floor. Ruby had told her that it was impossible to find a comfortable position for sleep. That all night she tossed from side to side. The baby kicked and turned, her nose was stuffed up, it was too hot, and she got up and paced or added more pillows, fewer sheets, any combination that might work.

Olivia yawned and made her way downstairs. It was almost cool enough to need a light robe. Good weather for having a baby, she decided.

She didn't get nervous until she went into the kitchen, where the fan still sat whirring on the table. The parental consent forms had blown onto the floor. A loose screen flapped against the window frame. Otherwise, it was too quiet here.

"Ruby?" Olivia said, not expecting an answer.

Still, she looked in the living room and out in the yard, where Ruby's chaise longue sat empty. She looked because she had to go through the motions. But what Olivia knew was that Ruby had left her again.

Back in the kitchen, she tried to think of what to do, but she came up blank.

Then she saw the note on the counter by the sink, held in place under a glass.

"Olivia" was written on the front. Ruby's penmanship was the opposite of Ben's, the kind Olivia's mother would call "chicken scratch."

Olivia unfolded the note and read it. The message was simple and clear:

I am so sorry, but I just couldn't do it. Please don't hate me.

Love,

Ruby

P.S. I'm not in labor or anything, so don't worry about me like that.

When the phone rang and Olivia answered it, she heard Winnie's voice.

"Do we have a baby yet?" Winnie asked.

"No," Olivia said.

"Isn't this D-day?"

"She's gone," Olivia blurted. "She changed her mind and left."

"You mean she took the baby?"

"I mean she's keeping it," Olivia said.

Winnie tried to sort it out: "Where did she go? Should we call the police? Didn't she already sign those papers? Olivia? Olivia, are you okay? Maybe you should just come home."

But Olivia could only think of how much those nouns still hurt. She thought, Home. Baby. Ruby.

Olivia drove to Jake Maxwell's house. It looked different in the daylight. There was a splendid stained-glass window that, Olivia noticed as she climbed the stairs to the front door, caught the sunlight and sparkled, amber, blue, and gold. She rang the doorbell, clutching the papers with Ben's signature, even though she knew they were worthless.

When Jake answered the door and saw her there, he looked more suspicious than surprised.

"She's gone," Olivia told him.

Jake opened the door wider and motioned her inside.

"I don't suppose she ever signed those papers?" he said. Then he added, "Not that it matters now."

Olivia saw a woman standing in the doorway to the kitchen, wearing a man's robe. It was the woman from Amy's Fourth of July party, probably the same woman he'd tried to have a baby with. The on-again, off-again girlfriend, clearly on-again.

"Shit," Olivia said.

Jake followed her gaze over to Patricia and said, "We've got some business to discuss."

When Patricia didn't move, Jake did, taking Olivia by the elbow and leading her into one of the parlors. The walls were pink, like cotton candy.

"You know," Jake told her, "she might just be scared. Need some time to think things over. I've seen it happen. The birth mother changes her mind one way, then the other."

"And where does she end up?" Olivia asked.

Jake shrugged. "I've seen it go both ways."

"Shit," Olivia said again.

"I wish I could do something."

"Why?"

"The thing is," Jake said, "I like you. And I want—"

Olivia put her fingers against his lips to quiet him. "Don't," she said. "Don't want anything. I don't want anything."

That night, when the quiet of the house grew too loud, Olivia drove to the A&W.

She did that every night for three nights.

The teenagers were still there, in the far corner of the parking lot, stoned and pierced, frightening. But Ruby was not one of them.

When Olivia asked if they had seen her, waving twenty-dollar bills at them, they laughed. One of the boys, a tall, skinny one with a ponytail hanging out from under a captain's hat, grabbed at the money.

"Get the fuck away from me," Olivia told him.

"Whoa," someone said. "Tough lady."

After that, she stopped going.

On the fourth night without Ruby, Olivia called Jake Maxwell.

He wasn't there, so she left him a message.

"I lied," she said. "I want everything. I want it all."

. . .

"Dear Amanda," Olivia wrote over and over, starting a new letter each time. "Dear Amanda." But she could not for the life of her think of what to say to the girl. She just wrote "Dear Amanda" and stared at the blank paper until she gave up and threw it away.

In the middle of the night, when the phone rang, Olivia hoped it was Ruby. She hoped it was Jake. She hoped it was good news.

"Olivia?" Winnie said, her voice shrill and high. "It's a girl. My water broke and all of a sudden there was the worst fucking pain I've ever felt and the next thing I know, we're in a cab racing to Beth Israel and I'm screaming, 'Give me drugs!' But it was too late. The whole thing took under three hours and I've got a daughter! A baby girl! Aida, like the opera. What do you think?"

Although Olivia made all the right noises of excitement and asked all the right questions—"How much does she weigh? Does she have hair?"—what she really thought was that she wanted Ruby back even more.

On the fifth night, when there was a knock on the door, Olivia jumped to answer it. Ruby was back and Olivia was going to keep her. The thought took Olivia's breath away. Keep Ruby? She realized that it wasn't so much the baby she missed; it was Ruby herself. Somehow, the girl had become her family. Somehow, the girl had gotten her through these months.

But it was Jake Maxwell at the door.

"You called?" he said.

In the living room, he sat across from Olivia, at a safe distance.

Although they were facing each other, they managed not to look at each other.

They sat that way for some time, before Jake cleared his throat and said, "The wall? In the kitchen?"

"It helped," she said.

"Are those bugs on it?"

"Coffee," she said. "From Guatemala. It's a long story."

He nodded, as if that made perfect sense. "I can't wait to hear all of your long stories." He smiled. "Don't worry. I have a few myself."

The idea of that, of beginning again from nothing, made Olivia feel tired.

"Sometimes," Jake said, "I get to New York on business. Or to visit friends."

"Would this be you and Patricia?" Olivia asked him.

"This would be just me."

She waited.

"I could visit you in New York, one of those times. Maybe."

This is how you start, she thought. "Yes," Olivia said.

"I didn't mean to take advantage of you," he said.

Olivia laughed. "Whoa," she said. "I meant to take advantage of you. What I didn't mean to do was actually like you."

"Oh?" he said. "You like me?"

Olivia sighed. "I like you."

"That's good to hear."

When he left, Olivia leaned against the screen door and looked out into the darkness. But there were so many stars, the darkness was not even that dark.

Olivia decided that it was time to go. One week after Ruby left, Olivia started to pack up. She took all of the baby clothes, the blankets and toys, and the formula and diapers and put them in boxes. She would give them all to Winnie and Aida. Already, Winnie had Fed-Exed pictures of the baby, all bloody and new, then cleaned up and sleeping, then looking right at the camera, frightened. Olivia studied the photographs, searching the scrunched-up face for something she could not name, expecting to feel jealous or sad or defeated. But she felt nothing except amused at this child of Winnie's.

She sat at her kitchen table and stared at the wall, considering adding to it. But she had nothing to add, she realized.

She said to herself, "I am a widow. I am a woman on her way home. I am scared."

Olivia looked at her suitcases, at the boxes of baby things.

She tried to imagine herself with a newborn baby right now. But she couldn't. For a moment, Olivia thought Ruby had actually done her a favor by keeping this baby; she just did it all wrong. Olivia stretched out her arms and began an awkward dance, a solo jitterbug to a Van Morrison tune that she hummed in her head.

She did not know how long she did that, humming and dancing by herself, before someone spoke.

"I leave you for one week and you go completely bonkers," Ruby said.

Olivia stopped dancing, not really expecting to see Ruby standing there.

But she was. She was standing in the doorway, still pregnant.

"You hate me, huh?" Ruby said.

"I don't hate you," Olivia told her, and it was the truest thing she could say.

"I couldn't just leave like that. I had to come back. To explain. At first, I thought that Ben would just change his mind. I mean, all along he was the one talking about Bali, about us keeping the baby and raising it free on an island. So that morning, I hadn't slept at all, and I decided I had to see him. I mean, what is love if it isn't this?" She cradled her stomach. "Oh," she said, "I took a hundred dollars from your purse."

"You did?" Olivia said.

"I figured you wouldn't mind. I mean, you wouldn't want me pregnant and hitchhiking, right? I bought a train ticket, and it took forever to get up there, to that camp. How was I supposed to know it was the last weekend before the thing shut down? Everybody had gotten pretty cozy up there over the summer. So I come waddling in, and there's Ben in his tennis whites, sitting under a tree with Cindy, some skinny blonde who goes to Vassar or something. 'It just happened,' he said. 'I didn't mean to fall in love with her or anything.' She taught swimming. What a pair, huh?"

Olivia expected Ruby to cry, but the girl was past that; she was all cried out.

"I never trusted him," Olivia said.

"You were right. He's a total asshole. He's like 'Don't you think you'd better go back and have the baby?' He was scared shitless I'd have it right there in front of Cindy. That I'd embarrass him or something. At least my father had the balls to be there when I was born. I mean, he had his problems, but he was there. He saw me all covered with birth guck, and you know what he said? He said I was the most beautiful thing he'd ever seen." She took a deep breath. "But Ben, he wants nothing to do with me or the baby. He made that clear. In fact, his father is going to send me a big fat check to make sure we stay out of his life for good."

"Where does that leave everything?" Olivia asked.

She wondered if a part of her was still hoping for that baby? She paused, trying to find it. But no. Now that Ruby was back, Olivia realized that it was Ruby she had missed. She could see her own life before her: her apartment, the city in autumn, walking through the West Village, her local Chinese restaurant welcoming her home, the smell of the caffè latte she got each morning on Bleecker Street, her little shop on St. Mark's, her hats. Olivia could see it as if she were already there.

"I couldn't very well go home," Ruby said. "On the way back

here, I actually thought about it. About my room and stuff. It's just a crappy little room, but I painted it lavender. Real pale. And my mom made me these pillowcases out of yellow velvet and on one she stitched DREAM and on the other one she stitched DO." Ruby shook her head. "But she deserves a second chance, you know? We all deserve that, right?"

Dear Amanda, Olivia thought.

"And I kept thinking about you," Ruby said. "How I used to sort of hate you. And how we became a family. You know?"

Olivia nodded.

"But we can't stay that way. You've got your real life back in New York and everything. It felt good, though, to think we were one. My friend Betsy's like me. Kind of free-floating. I mean, she's got a mother who's always in rehab herself and these uncles who come and live with them for a little while, except we're old enough now to figure out they're not exactly uncles, if you know what I mean. And Betsy and me used to sit around and get high and make up lives for ourselves. Like the kind of house we'd have and the kind of husband. So I went and found Betsy. You remember my friend Betsy?"

"Yes."

"The funny thing is, she's pregnant, too."

"Not again," Olivia said.

"She's keeping this one, though," Ruby said. "And she got a place—in Providence. It's nothing special. But I figure I could stay with her, the baby and me. We'll be like Kate and Allie. Betsy's still in school. They have day care there, too, like in San Francisco. The thing is, I want to be something. I mean, like the way you are. So strong. And kindhearted. And sophisticated. That restaurant you took me to? I want to eat in places like that."

Olivia nodded again. But she was thinking how Ruby had said she was strong. No one had said that to her since David died. Yet here she was, a year later, on her way to her life again. Surely

Ruby was right; she saw the strength in Olivia when Olivia herself could not.

"The thing is," Ruby said, "I've got to keep my baby. I mean, it's right here inside me. I can't give it away. But the thing is, I've got to keep you, too."

Now Ruby was crying, and there was nothing more for Olivia to wait for. She rushed to the girl and took her into her arms.

"You're stuck with me," Olivia told her.

"We could visit you there, right?" Ruby said. "In New York? And you'll still come here sometimes? And we'll all go to the beach. Hey, you could even baby-sit."

"Yes," Olivia said. "Yes."

Oh, she saw it, her life opening up still more. She saw Ruby and this baby a part of it. It was not the life she ever imagined for herself, but it was the one she got. It was a good one.

Ruby reached into her big macramé bag.

"I got this for you," she said. "I couldn't come back to see you until I found it."

She held out something in the palm of her hand.

The cassette with David's voice on it.

Olivia took it from her, folded her fingers around it.

"Thank you," she said.

Ruby shrugged. "Yeah," she said. "Well." She looked around at all the boxes and suitcases. "It looks like you're going, huh?"

"I bought all these baby things for you. Lots of black."

"Cool," Ruby said. "I saw the doctor. He says I'm still not dilated. What a drag, huh? Betsy says she'll be my partner if I'll be hers. Are you like really insulted?"

"A little," Olivia said. "But I want to go home."

"And get on with things, right?"

"Right."

Ruby nodded. "But I'll call you as soon as something happens."

"You'd better," Olivia said.

"What were you doing?" Ruby asked her. "When I walked in?"

Olivia laughed. "The jitterbug."

"My mom taught me that," Ruby said. "There's an old song, 'Ruby, Ruby.' Not the one by the Rolling Stones."

"I know it," Olivia said. She sang " 'I knew a girl and Ruby was her name. . . .' "

"That's the one," Ruby said. "My mother actually told me my father wrote that. That he wrote it for me. What a dope I am, huh? I believed her."

Ruby took Olivia's hands in hers and led the dance. Even this pregnant, she could spin Olivia and twirl her across the floor.

Olivia closed her eyes. Dear Amanda, she thought, and only one word came to her mind. Dear Amanda: Live. She could smell autumn coming. She always loved autumn in the city. It was time for her to start her winter hats. The tape bounced in her pocket, safe. When she opened her eyes, the light shone around Ruby's head like a halo, showing off her freckles, the ring in her nose. She is lovely, Olivia thought.

The two women danced the jitterbug across the worn floor. They sang together slightly off-key. They danced like that until the room grew dark and the cool air from the ocean crept into the room, like a ghost stopping in to say good-bye.